Betting the Rainbow

Betting the Rainbow

JODI THOMAS

BERKLEY BOOKS, NEW YORK

THE BERKLEY PUBLISHING GROUP
Published by the Penguin Group
Penguin Group (USA) LLC
375 Hudson Street, New York, New York 10014

USA • Canada • UK • Ireland • Australia • New Zealand • India • South Africa • China

A Penguin Random House Company

BETTING THE RAINBOW

A Berkley Book / published by arrangement with the author

Copyright © 2014 by Jodi Koumalats.

For information, address: The Berkley Publishing Group,
a division of Penguin Group (USA) LLC,
375 Hudson Street, New York, New York 10014.

ISBN: 978-1-61129-228-2

PRINTED IN THE UNITED STATES OF AMERICA

Cover art by Jim Griffin.
Cover handlettering by Ron Zinn.
Cover design by George Long.
Interior text design by Kristin del Rosario.

Betting the Rainbow

Chapter 1

JUNE 2013
HARMONY, TEXAS
LANDING STRIP

RONNY LOGAN CLIMBED OUT OF THE TINY PLANE AND STEPPED onto dry, packed dirt. A dust devil danced in the plowed field bordering the airstrip. *A lonely welcome home,* she thought as she circled, taking in the flat plains of Texas. White linen trousers flapped against her legs. She swore she could feel a thin layer of dirt settling over her, claiming her to the land.

Home, she thought, *after over a year, I'm finally back.* She'd returned to face her past and the memory of losing her future along with her one true love. She'd thought she would be marrying Marty Winslow last summer, not burying him. Time had passed. She'd grown wiser, but the ache inside her remained.

"Thank you, Mr. Derwood." Ronny looked at the old hippie of a pilot. His shirt was so spotted with chewing tobacco she thought he might have been wearing camouflage. "When I left Harmony I thought this little plane was a wild ride, but after flying over the Amazon, it seemed like smooth sailing today. I salute your skill."

"You're welcome, Miss Logan. It was a real pleasure to transport a nice lady like you. You was a pretty girl when you left, but traveling made you downright beautiful. Ever' single man in the county will be knocking on your mother's door begging you for a date when word gets out you're home."

She nodded thanks, though she knew she wouldn't be staying with her mother, Dallas Logan. In fact, Dallas probably wouldn't answer the door to the daughter she'd disowned for running away from home at twenty-seven. "I'm not interested in going out with anyone, but thank you for the compliment. I plan to rest and spend some time alone."

Smoothing back her short, honey-brown hair, Ronny wondered if her mother would even recognize her thirty pounds lighter and what seemed like a hundred years older.

Derwood might be twice her age, but Ronny could have sworn she saw him blush, realizing he'd been staring. "I'm sorry to pry. I ain't used to talking to passengers. My last trip was two crates of prize chickens for the Delaney farm. They complained all the way. If the flight from Amarillo had lasted any longer, I'd have had to wring a few necks."

"I'm glad I missed seeing that," Ronny said as she looked around for her ride. All she saw were a strip of dirt someone had scrapped years ago and left to dry rock-hard and one hangar built in patchwork style from used lumber.

Derwood took the hint. "You got someone picking you up? I could get the truck out and take you the last mile into town."

A long black Lincoln pulled off the main road and headed toward them, answering his question. Her ride had arrived.

Ronny stood frozen in the hot sunshine as the car drew closer. She'd known all year that this day would come. She'd have to step back into her hometown, but not back into her life. Never back into being the shy only child of the town gossip. Never back into caring so much for the first man who loved her that she wished she could die beside him.

In the year she'd traveled alone around the world, she'd

grown and realized she could live a full life without love or even company. She'd developed skills and learned to communicate in several languages. Surely she could handle the small-town people of Harmony. She'd left a few friends here, but she had never been a part of the town and she wouldn't be now.

All Ronny Logan wanted was a solitary nest to land in for a while. She needed the peace and calm of this place, not the people or the memories. Her soul was tired. She wanted time to think. Not to dream or to remember, but to plan. It seemed that since the day she'd walked out of Dallas Logan's house three years ago, Ronny had been changing, growing, morphing into someone she never thought she'd be able to be.

A tall, thin man in his sixties stepped out of the car and smiled at her in his polite way. "Welcome back, Miss Logan. I'm glad you're home."

She took his offered arm and moved toward the Lincoln. "I expected the ladies at the bed-and-breakfast would have fattened you up by now, Mr. Carleon. A year with Martha Q and Mrs. Biggs and you haven't changed a bit."

"Oh, but I have. You won't believe the strange world I've stepped into since you've been gone. I've even taken up writing my memoirs. I'm thinking of calling it *Adventures in Service*."

Mr. Carleon took two bags from Derwood and put them in the back of his polished car as he continued, "I followed your e-mailed instructions to the letter. I've told no one about your return, but there are lots of people in this town badgering me for news of you. When you're ready to make an appearance in public, they'll be waiting to welcome you. Until then, you'll have your silence."

"I need time. For right now I don't think I'm ready to see anyone."

He nodded. He seemed to understand, although she half expected him to tell her that Marty Winslow would have wanted her to visit her friends. But Mr. Carleon would never be so presumptuous. The old man must be the last of a dying breed. The perfect butler, confidant, chauffeur, organizer.

She had no doubt he could run the White House or Winter's Inn Bed-and-Breakfast with polished skill.

"I thought that might be your wish." He grinned. "Even though I had the duplex you last lived in cleaned and made sure the best room at the bed-and-breakfast was available, I also leased a cabin out on Rainbow Lane. It faces a small lake and it's not easy to get to, so that should be the perfect spot. There are walking trails, probably made by animals coming in to water, a porch swing, and no one close enough to see your lights at night. I've stocked it with a few basics, but if you'll call me after you've settled in, I'll be happy to deliver whatever else you need."

"Sounds perfect." Ronny let out a breath she felt like she'd been holding for days. "You're still taking care of me, aren't you, Mr. Carleon?" It had taken her a month into her trip to stop being surprised at the depth of details Mr. Carleon had covered. The hotels knew she liked a morning-sun window; a shower, not a bath. Fruit was always delivered each evening along with maps and a suggested agenda for the next day. Mr. Carleon was doing what he did best: taking care of people. First Marty Winslow and now her. "Thank you for being so thoughtful."

"Marty would have wanted me to. He gave me enough stock in his company over the years that I'll never have to work. I consider keeping up with you as my hobby. I've kept every postcard you've sent me pinned to a map on one wall of an office I rented downtown." He smiled as if confessing a secret. "I needed to have somewhere to go every morning. Hanging around the B&B wasn't an option. It was either cut my own throat to keep from eating all the cinnamon rolls each morning or find somewhere to go. Setting up an office within walking distance seemed the least violent solution."

Ronny didn't have to ask why—she knew the owner of Winter's Inn and could guess.

He opened the passenger door for her. "Where to first?"

"I need to pay Derwood for the flight." She reached for the leather satchel she'd carried through a dozen countries.

Mr. Carleon lowered his voice. "Already drafted from your expense account, miss, and you gave him a very nice tip."

"Good." She curled into the car. "Do you think we could drive by the cemetery before you take me to the cabin? I'd like to tell Marty I'm back."

"Of course." Mr. Carleon started the car and turned on the same soothing music she had listened to when she'd been driven to visit Marty at the hospital. Those days seemed a million years ago.

Ronny closed her eyes and let memories filter into her thoughts along with the haunting symphony that always seemed to be playing in the back of her mind.

Scenes of her life drifted like photos floating on midnight water. The childhood as the only daughter of a mother who wished she'd never been born. The job in the back room of the post office she'd gotten at eighteen so she wouldn't have to talk to anyone. One broken man who finally saw the real person inside her when she was twenty-seven. He'd pushed his anger at life crippling him aside long enough to care about her. The memory of his loving touch, still so vivid in her mind that she could almost feel it now. The darkness of his disappearance just as they'd begun to fall in love. His return to Harmony after a year so he could spend his last few days alive with her.

When the car turned into the cemetery, Ronny straightened and shoved a tear off her cheek. She'd carried Marty in her thoughts for a year, and now it was time to say good-bye.

His love would always warm her, but today she'd turn off all emotion, all feelings. The wound of losing him might never heal, but she could wall in her heart and will herself never to love again. After today she planned to be alone through life.

Never would Ronny Logan let emotion rule her world again.

Chapter 2

HAWK HOUSE
ON THE LAKE OFF RAINBOW LANE

AUSTIN HAWK MAINTAINED HIS PACE THOUGH HIS MUSCLES ached. Every day he'd go one more round on the obstacle course he'd mapped. One more circle, ten more minutes, until he was back to the man he'd been six months ago before he fell into hell.

As he gulped in air and ignored the pain, the memories of the fire came back to him. Austin never tried to push them away. The knowledge of what he'd gone through was all that kept him alive some days. He'd survived the firestorm and now he'd survive the recovery.

He plowed across the grass and ran through the back door of his grandfather's house. Two flights up. Two flights down. A sprint to the dock and then back to the tire swing hidden among the willows.

"Made it!" he heaved as he hit the swing, sending it twirling, before he dropped on the grass laughing. If anyone ever saw him, they'd think he was crazy as a rat left to live in a maze.

Only no one saw him out here. This small lake wasn't big enough to attract fish, much less fishermen. Twisted Creek, several miles downstream, was a wonderful getaway with huge old trees and a sandy bank just made for vacationing. In the hundred years Harmony had been settled, only three people had ever bothered to build out this far on Rainbow Lane.

The Delaneys were the first. They lived directly across the water in the little two-story white house in need of painting. They'd made their living with pecan trees and chickens for as long as anyone could remember. The once-big family had dwindled down to two girls, in their twenties, left to run the place.

The only other structure was a green cabin, a few hundred yards from him but completely blocked from view by the trees. Austin had heard it had been built by some rich guy back in the forties. The millionaire wanted to live like Thoreau on a pond while he wrote. Only he never wrote a word as far as anyone knew. Some said it took the would-be writer a year to drink himself to death. His little cabin on the lake went into an estate that rented the cabin out now and then.

Austin had heard the locals called the place Walden Cabin. The third place on the lake was his. Austin rolled so he could stare at his grandfather's sky-blue three-story misfit. The structure was simply called Hawk House because three generations of Hawk men had owned it. The structure looked more like it should be on a coastline with sailboats drifting by, but his granddad hadn't cared. He said he'd built it to remind him of his home in Maine. He even added the widow's walk around the single third-story room.

Austin felt sure his grandfather's fishing house had the only widow's walk in the panhandle. Lying in the grass looking up at it, he could almost see a sailing captain's wife looking out over the prairie as if she could see the ocean a few thousand miles away. "Proves all Hawk men are crazy," he said. "No wonder I feel so at home here."

Austin swore. Now he was talking to himself. What next? All he needed was an imaginary friend and they'd lock him up in the same place they finally locked up his grandfather.

All the family said he was insane, but Austin had always suspected he simply got tired of explaining himself and decided to make up his own reality. When they finally took him to the home, he made them bring a van so there would be room for all his friends.

The old man claimed he loved to fish out on this lake alone, but no one in the family ever remembered eating a single meal of freshly caught fish.

Austin drove out here alone and after staying a week, he could understand why his grandfather came to the lake house. The place had a stillness about it. A hideout where a man could be happy in the company of his own thoughts. A place where he could think about what he wanted to do next without having to listen to others telling him what he *should* do.

The Delaneys were the only people around, and they only talked to him when they had to.

After Austin's grandfather went to the home, Austin's dad, the only child, used to open Hawk House in the summer. Most years he was lucky to get away more than once or twice, but Austin remembered those summers as heaven. He'd even played with the Delaney girls and a kid staying with his grandmother in town. The girls were younger than he was and wild as jackrabbits. He'd run the woods with them, exploring caves and looking for buried treasure, loving the freedom he'd never been given in the city.

The Delaneys were women now, and he was little more than a stranger to them. Austin wasn't even sure they remembered him from those summers years ago. Even if they did, Austin had long ago lost the ability to be friendly. He waved to them when he saw them watching him switch out his truck for his boat in the garage he rented from them. He paid his bill for storing his boat and truck on their property by dropping the check in their mailbox.

In truth, he couldn't even remember their names, and in the months he'd stayed this time, he hadn't felt any need for conversation.

He'd started coming out alone two years ago when he was

on leave from the army. Somehow, it just felt right. Then, after the fire, doctors wanted to put him in a rehab hospital. There would be someone there helping him, medicating his pain, watching each time he stumbled.

Austin had packed his duffel bag and walked out. He ran all the way to the old sky-blue Hawk House and decided he'd mend his broken body and mind here by the water. He'd had all he wanted of people and crowds of strangers. For a while he wanted to walk on the muddy beach and know that any footprints there were his.

Rising off the grass, he headed back into the house, stripping off clothes as he moved upstairs. It was almost sunset and he loved watching the last bit of daylight dance off the water. He always ran in full gear just as he'd been trained to do in the army. By the time he reached the widow's walk on the third floor, he'd stripped to his briefs. His body felt so light he thought he could almost float off the roof.

The evening sun was there to greet him. The colors of the twilight sky did more for him than any antidepressant ever could. He was alive. He'd made it back and, for a moment, that was all that mattered.

As shadows grew, he heard laughter from across the lake. He couldn't see them, but he knew the Delaney girls were sitting out by the water. He barely knew them, but he liked the way they laughed.

Austin wondered if he even remembered how.

Chapter 3

DELANEY FARM
ON THE LAKE OFF RAINBOW LANE

DUSTI DELANEY TUGGED OFF HER JEANS, FOLDED THEM ATOP the splintery deck boards, and sat down next to her older sister.

Abby didn't say a word. Her feet were already in the water and her head was back as if she were sunning in moonlight. Her long blond hair blew in the midnight breeze, mirroring the weeping willows waving from across the water.

"I love this time of night," Dusti whispered as her feet slipped into the cool lake.

"Me too," Abby answered. "I read once that some people are born with the sound of the ocean waves for a heartbeat. They're never happy unless they live close to the sea. Maybe you and I are like that about the lake?"

Dusti laughed. "We have the lap of water against mud and frogs croaking in our blood. Or maybe the distant sound of a fish jumping or a turtle sliding off the bank and plopping into the water. Not near as romantic as ocean waves for heartbeats."

Abby finally looked at her sister. "What do you know? You don't have a romantic bone in your body."

"Maybe not, but I'm not attached to a water supply. I just like to cool off with my feet wet." Dusti saw her sister as the dreamer, so she had to be the practical one. It had been that way all their lives. She made lists of what needed to be done while Abby dreamed of what they might do when the chores were over.

Only the chores were never finished. Not on their little spread. They couldn't afford to hire more than summer help. Abby had given up her dream of being a nurse and come home to help when their mother got sick. After their mother died, there was never enough money to allow her to return. One semester more of school and she'd have had another life. One semester. Only for three years, that one semester had seemed as far away from being completed as ever.

Dusti shrugged, wishing she'd been allowed to at least get started on her dream. Abby could daydream about going back someday and finishing her nursing degree, but Dusti had nothing to go back to. She had planned to study photography in New York City but stayed home after high school to slowly take over the family business.

During her teens, her walls were lined with the skyline of New York. Every birthday and Christmas present was camera equipment. Only first her father died, and then a little over three years ago, when Dusti was nineteen, her mother got sick and the expensive cameras were the first things sold when they needed money.

She would do it again to keep her mother more comfortable, but, unlike her sister, Dusti didn't lie to herself. With her mother needing constant care and keeping up the place, all funds had disappeared. Now both parents were gone and she and Abby were barely hanging on to the land. No one was living their dream, or ever would.

Abby splashed water in Dusti's direction. "If Mom glances down from heaven and sees you showing your panties, she'll be looking for a switch."

Dusti smiled, remembering her mother in better times.

Their mother used to hate it when her youngest daughter stripped down to her underwear and jumped in the lake. "Who's going to see me? With Mom gone, no one cares."

They both looked out across the moonlit lake. Not a light blinked back.

"Mr. Hawk has probably got his binoculars out." Abby lifted her fists to her eyes as if she were using an invisible pair of binoculars. "The guy turns off all his lights and searches, waiting for you to come out and show your panties."

Dusti pulled her shirt high. "I might as well give the loner a heart attack. It's the only excitement I can have around here."

They laughed as they used to do when they were both in their teens and all the world was fair.

Dreams, Dusti decided, were just one more thing she could no longer afford.

Chapter 4

WALDEN CABIN

RONNY LOGAN UNPACKED AS SHE HAD A HUNDRED TIMES in the past year. Her two suitcases didn't fill the six drawers in the cabin's bedroom. Over the months she'd replaced a few blouses and shoes, but when she did she tossed the old ones. Somehow her belongings had thinned down to two suitcases. The perfect amount. Everything she needed, she could carry.

She pulled on her one pair of shorts and walked around the cabin barefooted. If was obvious that all the bedding was new, along with all towels, tablecloths, and rugs. Mr. Carleon hadn't forgotten a single detail, right down to the kinds of soups she always kept in the kitchen. He said he'd left a little food, but from the look of the supplies, it was more like stores for winter.

She wondered how many trips the white-haired man had made on foot from the main road before he bought the little ATV. There wasn't enough road left for his Lincoln to make the last mile to the cabin. She'd laughed and held on to the roll bar for dear life when he'd bumped down the rocky trail road toward the cabin's single chimney peeking through the trees.

When she commented that she had no idea what to call the little cart, Mr. Carleon said the man who sold it to him just called it "the mule." It was great for hauling supplies over back trails but seemed built with odd parts. Ronny had no idea what color it had originally been.

Mr. Carleon told her he'd had to buy a shed big enough to store the little half motorcycle/half golf cart in the trees by Rainbow Lane. He had it built, delivered, and nestled in among elms while he stocked the cabin. All in the week between her call saying she was coming home and today.

The three-room cabin had no phone, but that wasn't important. No television, but the grand view of the lake made up for all shortcomings.

She had her cell and a laptop. That was all she'd need. Mr. Carleon had said the electricity was iffy during storms, so he'd bought flashlights and lanterns.

"I don't want to bother you," he'd said as he walked out after setting her luggage inside, "but if I don't hear from you every week and I can't reach you by phone, I'll be hiking in to make sure you're all right. The leasing agent said there are wild pigs in the woods, so take the walking stick and watch for them."

"What do I do if I see one?"

"Make some noise. If they're wild, they'll run."

Ronny shook her head. "I doubt I'll be too afraid of a pig."

"Promise me you'll be careful," he added as he started up the walking trail. "These aren't the cute little pink pigs at the fair."

She promised to call in and waved good-bye as he hiked back up to Rainbow Lane. He insisted that she keep the mule near the cabin in case she wanted to drive out. Ronny watched him disappear before turning toward what she already thought of as *her* cabin.

After finishing unpacking, Ronny walked out onto the porch and decided that she had a million-dollar view. All around her, evening shades of green welcomed summer, and the slow lap of the water against the shore made her almost believe that she was the only person around for a hundred miles. She doubted she'd go anywhere, even for a walk, for a while. The jet lag had finally caught up with her.

Curling into the padded swing, she pulled an old quilt over her as the porch swing rocked her to sleep. There were no more planes she had to catch, no more lectures or tours or dinners. Only the peace of Harmony surrounding her.

Night drifted into dawn and still she slept. There was no schedule she needed to follow. Here, next to a no-name lake, she could finally sleep.

The day aged, growing hot enough for her to kick off the covers, but her bones seemed made of jelly and all she could manage was a yawn as the wind rocked her gently.

Night, black and silent, closed in over her again. Once, she felt the cold and moaned. The swing rocked as she hugged herself a moment before the blanket floated back over her.

"Thanks, Marty," she mumbled in her sleep. The thought of her one love smiling, watching her sleep, warmed her even though his arms never would again.

Hours later she woke with the sun sparkling between the trees along the other side of the lake. Sitting up, she stretched, realizing she'd slept almost thirty hours.

Stumbling through the cabin, Ronny tried to remember where the bathroom was located. One look in the mirror frightened her fully awake. Her hair looked like squirrels must have started nesting in it. What makeup she wore seemed to have slipped to another part of her face, and the silk blouse she'd pulled from her suitcase was so wrinkled and twisted she feared it was ruined.

Twenty minutes later she stepped from the shower feeling better. Two cans of soup and an egg sandwich finished the recovery, but as the day drifted, one thing bothered her. No matter how many times she remembered the night, the feel of the blanket being floated over her cold body never changed.

Blankets don't float and ghosts aren't real. As she folded the blanket she knew she hadn't imagined it.

When Mr. Carleon called to see if she needed anything,

she asked if he'd visited her early that morning and was informed, in his polite formal way, that he would never come unannounced unless he thought she was in trouble.

Five days and nights passed. Ronny could feel her heart slowing down. Peace. She found she rose early and watched the sun rise every morning, then walked and read, and even tried to fish. In the afternoons she slept in the porch swing, loving the low sounds of the lake and the swishing noise of the trees around her. She saw birds, a few deer and squirrels, but no pigs.

And no people. After being in crowded museums, art galleries, airports, and cities, the silence was grand. For the first time in a long while Ronny took a few minutes to listen to her own breathing. She called Mr. Carleon every other day, but she didn't bother to turn on her laptop. Nothing in the world seemed more important than being here.

The sixth day dawned, smothered in rain. A slow mist seemed to hang in the air more than fall. By midafternoon she'd curled up in her blanket and was almost asleep when she heard the swishing sound of a rushed movement through the bushes to the right of the house.

Ronny sat up, trying to make sense of the new noise in her quiet world. Someone, or something, was plowing through the brush toward her.

Before she could fight her way out of panic and move, a voice shouted, "You Ronelle Logan?"

She reached her hand out like a blind man trying to see the person who belonged to the voice, but there was nothing but gray fog past the porch steps.

Her feet hit the worn boards hard as she stood. Whoever was out there wasn't friendly. In fact, he sounded furious.

"Yes," she managed to whisper into the rain. "I'm Ronny Logan. Who and where are you?" Her hand reached for the walking stick just as a man's form appeared at the side of the cabin porch.

She might have been more frightened, but thanks to the height of the porch, the man's head came level with the railing,

making him seem elfish in his dark rain slicker and broad
shoulders. His feet were planted wide apart.

"What do you want?" Ronny took a step backward, wondering if she could make it to the door of the cabin before he
could bound over the railing.

"Your mother named Dallas Logan?"

"Yes." If he'd come to kill her, he was starting out on a
strange note. Ronny wasn't sure, but she doubted a check of
family history was required before murder. During her childhood, Ronny's mother loved reporting every crime she heard
about. By the time Ronny was ten, she'd started staring at every
stranger wondering which kind of criminal they might be.

This one's face was almost completely hooded in the
slicker. All she could see was his nose and mouth. Not much
to go on if she was asked to identify him in a lineup. But then
if he had come to rob her, he was going to be disappointed.
She had little of value. If he had come to kill her, she wouldn't
have to worry about memorizing his features.

"What do you want?" she said again, holding the walking
stick in front of her. A little compass bobbled at the top, and
Ronny wished it were a knife instead.

The stranger must have noticed her shaking with cold and
fear. He backed away a foot and said in a normal voice, still
not friendly, "I want you to come out in the rain and get your
mother the hell off my property. She turned down the wrong
road and now she's stuck on my land."

Ronny frowned. Worse than robbery and death, her mother
had come to visit. "I don't want her. She's on your land. She's
yours."

She swore the stranger growled before he raised one finger and pointed it at her as if it were a weapon. "Look, lady,
I already got a mother and I don't want another one. Not one
like yours."

Ronny didn't argue. Dallas Logan was probably the most
hated woman in Harmony. She got into everyone's business,
then trampled on their nerves. She thought the world revolved
around her. She'd disowned Ronny a few years ago and told

everyone who would listen that her only child was dead. If Dallas Logan had been the first plague rained down on the Egyptians, there wouldn't have been any need for more.

"Where is she?" Ronny murmured as she reached inside the door for her raincoat. Whatever Dallas was didn't matter; she wasn't this stranger's problem. Ronny would at least go help get her back to the main road. Knowing her mother, she planned to continue the habit she had last year of driving by Ronny's house and not looking at her.

"She's stuck about halfway down my road in a boat of a car. I'm surprised you didn't hear her screaming. When I offered to help, she told me her trouble was all my fault for not keeping a passable road to the lake. When I said I didn't have or want visitors, she accused me of being the next generation of Unabomber and that she was going to call the FBI and have me arrested before I mailed off a wave of pipe bombs."

"They don't take her calls," Ronny said as she took one step off the porch and felt her sneakers disappear in mud. "Neither do the Texas Rangers, the IRS, the state troopers, the—"

"I get the picture." He offered his hand. "Look, if you'll help me get her back to the road, I'd appreciate it. I don't really care what's between the two of you, but I'm betting it's ninety-nine point nine percent her doing and I don't even know you. If we get her back to Rainbow Lane, she'll take one look at the mudslide that used to be your road and forget the visit."

"Not likely." She had gone back to whispering. She'd started to point out that he was assuming her mother might use logic when Ronny noticed him staring at her as if questioning her sanity. She said in a normal voice, "You're right, though. It's not your problem. I knew I'd have to face her sooner or later. It might as well be in the rain." She pointed to the mule. "Could this thing make it to her faster?"

"It might even pull her out," he said as he tugged Ronny toward the ATV.

When her feet refused to pull free of the mud, he circled her waist with his big hands and lifted her up. She was sitting barefoot in the mule before she recovered from his touch. He hadn't asked. He'd just lifted her like it was nothing personal. He had no idea how rarely she'd been touched in her life.

If she'd thought the ride was rough with Mr. Carleon driving down to the cabin, it was nothing compared to the way this stranger took off. He sprayed mud like a speedboat sprays water. Ronny held on, her knuckles white, her jaw clamped. She was afraid if she opened her mouth to scream, she'd be eating mud.

He drove along the uneven beach to a dock that he apparently used to put his boat in the water. An old rowboat was shoved into the trees near the water's edge. From there, he climbed back behind a huge house she hadn't even noticed among the willows north of her place.

Rain splattered around the little windshield and dripped from the canvas just above the roll bar. Ronny kept herself from becoming hysterical by counting the ways she would probably die at any moment. Thin branches from willows kept slapping her, making her lose count as they climbed up what once might have been a road.

"How do you get supplies down to your place?" she yelled, knowing he didn't use this path, for they were mowing down saplings as tall as the hood.

"I park my truck at the Delaney place and keep a boat over by their dock to row across to my place. Good way to discourage company."

"I'll remember that," she yelled back. "What is your name?"

"Why?"

"In case I fall out. I want to know who to yell at."

When he glanced at her, she saw his eyes. Green eyes, predator eyes, glaring at her as if he had no idea she might be kidding. "Austin Hawk," he finally answered.

"Like the city?"

"No, like the hero. The father of Texas. Everyone in my family is named after Texas fighters. It sounds like a roll call of the Alamo when we have reunions." His voice was cold and clipped, as if he were simply listing facts.

She couldn't believe he was giving her a history lesson as the mule rocked from side to side. The last thought she'd have when the ATV started rolling back downhill would be the battle cry, "Remember the Alamo."

She was torn between screaming and cussing, neither of which she ever did, but at the moment both seemed appropriate. Her mother was top on the list of people she never wanted to see again, and Austin Hawk was climbing straight toward her. Picking between a crazy neighbor and an angry mother wouldn't be easy.

Five minutes later the blurry image of her mother's old car washed from the rain. Dallas Logan was sitting inside, the engine running as if she were simply stopped at a light and not stuck hip-deep in mud.

Austin Hawk drove around her, rocking Ronny so hard she bumped against his shoulder before she could get a firm grip. He didn't seem to notice. For the second time they'd touched and it didn't affect him at all.

Hawk jumped out, untied a rope hanging beside a first-aid kit in the back, and began locking it onto the car's back bumper.

When he stood, mud covered his face, but green eyes stared straight at Ronny. "Can you drive to pull her out when I give the word?"

She forced herself to move without looking back at her mother. Crawling over to the driver's seat, she fastened her seat belt. "What's the word?" Ronny yelled back at the mud monster standing by her mother's car.

"What the hell does it matter? How about 'go'?"

"Stop yelling at me, Mr. Hawk." Ronny couldn't believe she was picking a fight with the only man who might help her. No one else was likely to come along in this rain, and if they couldn't get the car out of the mud, she'd have to take her mother back to the cabin.

Looking over her shoulder, she saw the stranger open her mother's car door. "If you'll get out and walk," he ordered, "we'll try to get you back to the main road, lady."

"I'm not getting out in the rain," Dallas shouted. "I don't

weigh that much. Push and pull with me in the car." She leaned her head out a few inches. "Is that my daughter in that funny little cart? Where'd she get something as dumb as that thing?"

"Nope," Austin answered. "It's not her. I heard your daughter is dead." His hand closed around her upper arm. "Let me give you a hand, Mrs. Logan."

"I'm not getting my hair—" She gave up talking as the rain hit her face.

Dallas squealed louder than any wild pig as Austin pulled her out and away from the car, but he never let go. Hawk obviously wasn't a man who gave folks much time to think about his orders.

"Stand back out of the way or you'll get covered in mud," he said to the dripping, chubby woman. "Just walk behind us once we start moving, and we'll be back to the road in no time. Stay in the car's ruts and don't wander off. If you get lost, I'll never find you in this rain and I'll be too tired to try."

"Well, I never," Dallas yelled back, but then she began to follow his directions.

Reaching into her car, he shifted to neutral and went to the front end, now planted bumper-deep in mud. "Go!" His shoulder shoved against the hood.

Ronny gunned the engine as the heavy tires chewed into the road. It was slow going, but with Austin's pushing and her pulling they made it to the road. He had the rope off and the door open to Dallas's car when she finally tromped up behind them.

"The rain's getting worse; you might want to head for home." Austin stood beside her car, blocking any view Dallas might want of Ronny.

For once Dallas didn't argue. She climbed into the mud-covered seat and drove away.

Austin walked over to the driver's side of the mule. He looked like a mud man from an old horror film.

"Do I look as bad as you?" Ronny asked as she moved over to the passenger side. "If I do, it's no wonder my mother didn't recognize me."

He pulled a mud-covered willow branch from her hair.

"You look just fine. Want to drive into town for dinner since we're already on the main road?"

"Not on your life, but thanks for the offer. I wouldn't feel right without my shoes." She glanced down Rainbow Lane as the taillights of her mother's car disappeared. A dread came over her. This wouldn't be the last time Dallas stormed the walls she'd built.

Ronny looked back at her neighbor and fought down a laugh at just how ridiculous they both looked. If they walked into the diner downtown, old Cass probably wouldn't even recognize her. "Thanks for helping me out, Mr. Hawk."

"Just Hawk, or Austin." His request sounded more like an order.

"All right. Thanks, Austin." She smiled, wondering if she should consider his progress.

He headed back down toward the lake at a slower pace than the one he'd climbed with. "What choice did I have? If I hadn't hiked through the trees to your place, I would have never gotten her back to the road and then she'd have had to stay with me." He patted the little metal mule. "This thing came in handy. I plan on getting one the next time I'm in town."

Ronny leaned back. "I just hope she doesn't come back."

He patted her knee, making her almost jump out of the seat. "Don't worry. I predict a few trees falling right now up by the entrance to what once was your road. She couldn't have made it down in that car anyway, but she might make it halfway before she figures that out. A couple of downed trees will make sure that doesn't happen."

"Thanks." She glanced over but still couldn't see his face. He'd pushed the hood back, showing hair the same color as the mud, but he was far too dirty for her to see anything but his mouth and green eyes.

Ronny stared at his strong muddy jaw and watched his lips twitch slightly into a smile. *Kissable lips*, she thought. If she had to ID him in a lineup, she'd say simply that he had kissable lips.

Chapter 5

HAWK HOUSE

A WET TWILIGHT MOVED ACROSS THE LAKE IN TIE-DYED SHADES of orange and red as Austin drove Ronny home. He tried to think of something to say, wanting to talk to her but realizing he was too out of practice.

Finally, when they rounded his place and hit the uneven banks of the lake, he asked, "Want to go for a swim and wash some of this mud off?"

"I would, but it's lightning. Isn't there some kind of rule about never going swimming during a storm?"

She watched the trees, never looking directly at him, and he guessed she faced few people directly. She was probably one of those mousy people who thought if she didn't look at anyone, then no one saw her.

"What if I said I know a place we'll be safe even in a storm?" His leg and shoulder were hurting. He needed the water. "I'll show you where it is, and then you can decide if you're up for a swim."

He drove around a bend where land jutted out, making a natural barrier between their two shorelines. Willows had grown huge in the sheltered spot, with ten-foot-long branches touching the water. "My grandfather used to claim this was the best fishing spot on the lake. Not that he'd know. I never remember eating fish while we visited the old guy."

Cutting the engine, he stepped out into ankle-deep water. Without looking at her, he pulled the low branches apart like a curtain. The hundred-year-old trees had created a chamber completely hidden, with lake water for a floor and solid green for walls and roof. Lightning flashed and blinked in reflection like diamonds spotting across still water.

"Welcome to my secret swimming hole."

Austin waded into the hidden spot, tossing his rain slicker and shirt toward the shore as he disappeared. The branches brushed back into place, offering one last glance of her still huddled in the ATV.

She'd come, or she'd drive the few hundred feet back to her cabin. Either way, he wouldn't have long to wait.

Ronny's laughter drifted through the branches separating them. "My mother would have a fit. Swimming with a stranger. She'd never live down the shame."

He walked toward the center, relaxing back, letting the water wash over his shoulders. "I could go get her if you like. Or, if you're brave enough, you could come in alone. I won't tell her if you don't."

To his surprise, he saw the branches open and she waded in. Her raincoat had vanished and the thin white shirt hid little in the twilight glow. Her body was slender, but rounded out in the right places.

He had to remind himself to breathe. She seemed far more vision than real. When she was five feet away from him, she lowered into the water, disappearing for a moment. When she broke the surface, her short hair was slicked back and her face glowed moonlight white.

She was the first woman he'd seen, really seen, in years. Ronny Logan left him speechless. Beautiful, stoic, like a marble statue coming alive. The strange thing was, he had a feeling the lady had no idea just how breathtaking she was.

"The fish will nibble on me," she whispered as she waved her hand across the top of the water as if playing a liquid piano.

"I don't think they much care for humans."

"Are you sure there are no snakes?"

"I've never seen any around here, but there are turtles. Whatever you do, don't wiggle your toes." Slowly he moved toward her, fearing with each step that she might vanish. "This is a magic place, Ronny. No one can see you here. No one can find you. You can let down your guard and relax."

"What makes you think I need to relax?"

Austin didn't answer. He didn't know how he knew, he just knew. Fellow loners recognize each other. They spot members of their tribe in airports and the back of almost-empty bars. They take the last seat. The dark corner. The back row. Something about the way they turn away from people, even as they talk, always let him know he'd encountered another like himself. Something would flash in their glance that said they never looked too deep inside people.

She moved now in the water, her eyes closed, embracing the gentle current. He was almost close enough to touch her. The last of the day's light had faded, and all he saw was her silhouette. She dipped her head again and shook her hair under the water. When she swung up, she arched her back and sent water and mud plopping all around her.

He did the same, scrubbing the last of the mud away.

When he came up, she was floating on the water, her creamy blouse and trousers drifting like a feather. He reached his hand out and gently cupped the back of her head. "Relax, Ronny, just relax. There is no past here or future to worry about. Just drift. I'll keep your head above water."

She spread her arms out and did as he'd suggested.

His free hand stretched wide along her back and moved her gently. Every afternoon since she'd arrived, he'd stood at the side of her porch and watched her sleep, wondering what had happened to this beautiful woman to make her need isolation as dearly as he did.

Cloud shadows crossed over them, painting the night into

shades of black. He knew when she opened her eyes she would panic in the total darkness.

"It's all right. I'm here. I know the way out." He slid his hand along her arm and took her hand.

She relaxed beside him. "I know that the world is invisible now, but it's strange, I feel like we are too. Like even if we walked through the willow branches, no one would see us."

"Sometimes I wish that were true." He pulled her closer in the water until their arms brushed.

"Me too," she answered.

He slowly led her toward the branches, closing all the world out. "If you were invisible, Ronny, what would you do?"

"Live," she answered. "All my life I've been afraid to do anything: dance, act silly, run wild. I've always been afraid someone would notice me if I did." She breathed in a long breath. "If I were invisible, I'd live life on my own terms. I'd run like a wild mustang and dance until I dropped. I'd gulp life in hungry bites so I could remember each moment I'd been totally awake for all the days I still breathe."

"Me too," he answered, thinking he'd been following orders for as long as he could remember. He might not be able to say things like she did, but he understood.

She laughed and swung her arm along the water. She was nervous even now, but her guard was melting away. "What would you do if no one would see? No one would judge. No one would know."

"I'd kiss you." The words were out before he thought. He couldn't take them back. He wasn't that good of a liar.

She stood still and silent for so long, he thought he must have frightened her. He had that effect on most folks. He'd given up trying to be friendly. No wonder every woman his buddies tried to set him up with ran. If he'd just turn green, he'd be the Hulk's twin brother.

"If you kissed me," she whispered so low he barely heard her, "and no one saw, then we could pretend it never happened. Once we cross out of this place we could both remember it as a thought in time like a dream or a fantasy."

He wanted to ask why a lady like her would let someone

she didn't know kiss her, even in the darkness. There was something so fragile about her. But he couldn't ask. He didn't know her well enough to pry.

He turned toward her, gently brushing her shoulder with his hand, knowing he could never kiss her as gently as she deserved to be kissed. He didn't even know how.

Slowly he moved closer until his lips touched her forehead. "When we leave here, this kiss never happened. You don't need to feel like you have to wave at me and you won't be angry about the kiss. We won't owe the other anything, not even an explanation or apology. Fair enough?"

"Fair enough." He felt her words brush against his throat. "Only one promise first."

"What?" He wanted to swear. If she asked for a soft virgin kiss, he wasn't sure he could hold back that much.

"Make me feel alive," she said as she turned her face up. "I've been dead a long time."

His arms lowered to her waist and he pulled her slowly against him while the water swirled around them as if pushing them together. Lowering his mouth, he tasted the cold skin of her cheek as the warmth of her entire body pressed against him.

When he brushed her lips, her mouth was open slightly, giving him all the invitation he needed. His mind told him to go slow, be gentle, but he couldn't. He kissed her completely, taking both their breaths away.

She swayed against him in the water as he held her so close he felt her heart pound against his own. The need for her rolled over all other thought. There was no before or after this time. There was only now, only her.

He dug his fingers into her wet hair and held her as if for this moment she was his. When she wrapped her arms around his neck, he knew there would be no battle between them, no games, no conquering or surrender.

There would also be no forgetting. Both would remember this instant of being totally alive for the rest of their lives. Even if they never spoke again, they'd shared this one perfect moment. The tie would bind them forever.

Slowly, the kiss turned tender as she moved her hand over his heart. He might be only a shadow, but she was silently telling him that she saw him, the real him, and all the toughness he'd spent years caking on like armor didn't frighten her.

He lifted her up and carried her to where the leaves brushed against them. If he didn't let her go now, he wasn't sure he'd be strong enough to ever turn away from her.

"Thank you," she whispered as she touched his throat with her lips, then stepped through the curtain.

As if she were no more than a branch brushing against him and then gone, she wasn't there. When he felt the chill from the water rushing around him and her no longer near, he took a step, wanting to run and catch her.

They didn't need a moment, a kiss. They needed a night together. A week. A month. A lifetime.

But when he stepped out of the shelter of the willows, she was gone.

Austin stood in the gentle rain trying to hear her movements in the darkness. He didn't know if he'd kept his promise. He didn't know if he'd made her feel alive.

But she'd done just that for him. She'd brought him back from feeling nothing for so long.

And now, with her gone, she'd also made him feel something new. Loneliness.

Chapter 6

Buffalo's Bar

Dusti Delaney leaned against the bar. She'd been playing with the same bottle of Coors for an hour and having the same argument with her sister for what seemed like years.

If the crop of pecans was good this year and if nothing broke down, maybe, just maybe, one of them could follow her dream. Abby couldn't go for a semester to college, but maybe they could afford one online class and she'd be one step closer to her goal of getting away from the little farm on Rainbow Lane.

But Abby always argued that "if the pecans are good and nothing breaks," Dusti should buy at least one good camera. She could check out books on photography. Maybe even enter a contest. She could make a start at what she always wanted to do.

Dusti took a long draw on the beer. Both knew their argument was a waste of time. Neither remembered a year when the crop was good and they had money left over for extras. And, as much as they complained about being stuck on the little farm by the lake, neither would ever sell the place. Generations of Delaneys had been on the little piece of land next to the lake, and even if they both hated it some days, the land would remain theirs.

Funny thing, Dusti thought, this argument never happened on Rainbow Lane. They always saved it for time away, as if somehow their dead parents might hear them fighting over who would someday have to take the land.

Once a month, if neither managed a date, the sisters allowed themselves a night out. They paid the ten-dollar cover charge at Buffalo's, ate the greasy food, and listened to Beau Yates play. The hometown boy was making it big in Nashville, but he still drove back to Harmony once a month to play three sets at the bar where he'd started.

Abby lost interest in the argument with her sister as they watched the two-man band set up. Beau Yates was as handsome as his band partner was ugly. Dusti wondered how many drunk fans flirted with Beau all evening but woke up with Border Biggs come morning. The only thing alike about them was their black hats. Beau probably wore his because he looked so darn good in it, and Border probably just wanted to cover his bald head.

"I heard someone say Beau was underage when he started here. Harley used to lock him in the cage." Abby put her elbows on the bar and leaned back. Her worn western shirt tugged across her breasts. Even in old clothes she looked like a model. Blond hair, big green eyes, and tall.

"Now Harley needs to lock the girls out," Dusti said, guessing if she didn't watch out, her sister would be among the girls flirting.

Abby shook her head. "Word is he never goes home with anyone. Not that I'd offer."

"I find that hard to believe." Dusti giggled.

Abby frowned. "Is it hard to believe that I'd go home with him or that he sleeps around?"

"I know you wouldn't bring him home." Dusti laughed. Abby might flirt, but she never had one-night stands. Dusti only wished she could say the same. She usually leaped in only to find that the guy she'd taken home was too shallow to even keep a conversation going.

Turning back to the singer, she said, "No one sings like he does who hasn't had his heart crushed a few times. Beau Yates was born to love women."

"He's got the looks and the voice, but as for love, I don't know." Abby shrugged. "One time I parked out behind a dance with a guy playing in a college band. Later I was real disappointed with myself for sticking my tongue in a brainless animal's mouth."

Both girls laughed. Since they'd first discovered boys, they'd shared everything. Even if *everything* was mostly Abby's fantasies and Dusti's mistakes.

A short cowboy wearing a hat that was two sizes too big stepped in front of the Delaney girls. His eyes darted from one to the other as if picking his favorite candy.

Both girls frowned.

Dusti figured she must have not looked mad or irritated enough because Chester O'Toole focused his shifty eyes on her and not Abby.

"How you doing, Double D? You feel like dancing tonight? I've been practicing." His eyebrows wiggled like hiccupping snakes.

"Don't call me Double D, and no, I don't want to dance. The music hasn't even started." Dusti swore if he looked down at her double Ds, she'd flatten him on the bar floor . . . again. The man had to be a masochist to keep asking her out.

His eyeballs seemed to shake with the effort, but he kept staring at her face. "Maybe when the music starts you'll change your mind?"

"I might if you go tell that cousin of yours I'd like to talk to him."

Chester frowned. "Why?"

"He was born in Scotland," Dusti answered. "That's interesting."

Chester hesitated. "I'm from Paducah. That's interesting." When she didn't answer, he added, "Besides, Kieran is afraid of you. He told me so."

Dusti looked over at the tall redheaded man talking to Austin Hawk. For a blink she wondered what the two of them would have to say to each other. Kieran had been spending summers in Harmony with his grandparents since he was a kid, but she'd never gotten to know him well. He'd been talking to Austin Hawk, another one who only appeared in summers, since he'd walked in and never even glanced her way.

She turned back to Chester. "Why would your cousin be afraid of me? He's a foot taller than me." At five feet five she didn't consider herself short, but Chester's cousin towered over most people.

Dusti watched as both Hawk and the Scot turned to greet Reagan Truman like she was kin. Apparently the Scot wasn't afraid of all women, and from the looks of it he knew Reagan well.

Chester didn't seem to notice that her attention had shifted. "Kieran says women like you and your sister are aces and eights to a man like him. Besides, he came down from his job in New York to play poker, not get mixed up with women."

Abby finally decided to join the conversation. "There's an illegal game in town? Don't tell the sheriff."

Chester smiled, loving having the attention of both women. "This one's legal. For twenty bucks you're in. They're holding it over at the Truman farm and half the men in the county are buying in. Tables will be set up under the trees unless it rains, then we'll move into the barn. Half the money goes to the library, but a thousand goes to one lucky winner for the buy-in to a real game in Vegas. She'll get her way paid with what's left over. The airfare, hotel, and even meals will be covered. Word is the pot at the big game could be a million. I hear if you make the top ten in Vegas, you win thousands."

Abby lost interest, but Dusti had to ask, "So, twenty could win a man or a woman thousands?"

"Yep. Kieran told the family he was coming down to see his grandmother, but he booked the flight the day I e-mailed him about the game. Word is he paid his way through college playing poker." Chester grinned at her. "If you're thinking about buying into the game, forget it. A woman wouldn't want to join in. Poker's a man's game."

She ignored his last comment and concentrated on the prize. "I'll dance with you," Dusti promised, "and so will my sister, if you'll get your cousin over here."

Chester's eyes were darting from one to the other as if he'd just doubled down on kings. "I'll be right back." He two-stepped his way across the bar, making several people laugh.

"Are you nuts?" Abby whispered. "I hate dancing with Chester. I swear he hunches down to bust level just so he can bump into me during every dance."

"You could dance a fast one with him." Dusti laughed. "I got a plan. We're going to enter that poker game and make enough money for you to finish school, and that handsome Scot is going to teach us how."

"Not me. I tried strip poker my freshman year and had to walk back to the dorm wearing nothing but a smile."

"All right, I'll do it. Dad and I used to play for pennies, and I always beat him. How hard could it be?" Dusti didn't want to think about the fact that her dad might have let her win. It would be worth twenty dollars to test her skills. If she lost, at least she'd tried. If she placed in the top ten, there might finally be a chance for her sister to finish school.

She looked at her sister, but Abby was too busy watching the good-looking redhead across the bar.

"It's impossible to believe those two are related." Abby frowned as Chester and his cousin started toward them. "All the good genes must have gone over the pond to Scotland."

"Just one dance is all I need," Dusti begged.

"All right, I'll dance with Chester while you talk, but if you go with this crazy scheme and win any money, Dusti, you follow your dream. I'll stay and run the farm while you're gone."

Dusti shook her head. "We'll argue about it when I'm in

the top ten, and we see how much money I've won. Every brain-dead cowhand thinks he can play poker, so I should be able to learn in a few hours."

Abby's frown grew. "All right, but don't trade anything but eggs or pecans for lessons." She stared at the handsome man coming toward them. "And I'm going to be right by your side as chaperone. After all, it's my duty. The last guy you flirted with asked me to marry him after you turned him down, just so he could be close to you."

Dusti wasn't really listening. She was plotting. She'd do whatever it took to win and give Abby her dream, even if it meant practicing day and night until she was a pro.

Chapter 7

Buffalo's Bar

RONNY LOGAN HADN'T PLANNED ON MAKING HER HOME-coming so public for a while, but two reasons drove her to Buffalo's Bar on Saturday night. One, her former neighbors and good friends were playing.

Despite Border Biggs frightening her when she'd met him, she loved the tattooed kid dearly. He reminded her of an alley cat. Once she fed him, he was loyal for life. In the early days when she'd first left home and moved in next door to Border and Beau, she'd fallen asleep every night listening to Beau Yates play. His music seemed to float in the night for a long while even after he'd turned in. Border might not have the great talent Beau had, but he made up for it by being a solid friend to Beau.

The second reason she came tonight was the hope that in the crowd no one would notice her. Except for a dozen people, most folks in Harmony didn't know her well enough to rush up and ask questions. Her best friend, Summer, was home with her baby and planning to marry her handsome fireman. Mr. Wright, the funeral director, would never hang out in a bar, and Cord McDowell had texted her a few weeks ago to tell her he and his wife would be traveling most weekends this summer with her prized horses.

So, as the lights dimmed and the show began, Ronny slipped into the back of the bar to hear Beau Yates play his guitar and sing.

Tears were rolling down her cheeks ten minutes later. If possible, he'd gotten better in the year she'd missed hearing him. He and Border were still kids to her even though they were bound to be twenty-one or twenty-two by now. The boys who'd lived in the other half of the duplex might not have had much in the way of family, but they'd had each other as friends.

Within days they were like family to her also. Then, a year later when her first love came back to Harmony to die, they'd been there for her. She'd traveled the world in the dozen months since the funeral, but she'd never stopped missing them.

"He's good, isn't he?" A low voice came from behind her.

"Better than good." She smiled up at Brandon Biggs, Border's older brother. "How are you, Big?" If people came in small, medium, and large, Big was made in extra large, and as near as she could tell, his heart matched his size.

Smiling proudly, he nodded. "All I can say is that from where they started, they didn't have anywhere to go but up. I used to order pizza and feed them during practice sessions just to give my ears a break."

Memories flooded back as she watched the tattooed biker playing backup. He'd found her hurt on the road one rainy night and gently taken her home so Marty could doctor her up. The Biggs boys were gentle giants.

Last year when she brought Marty home from the hospital, his body had already started shutting down, but somehow she believed that if she loved him enough he'd get better. He'd stay alive for her. Border, Beau, and Big had helped all they could, and then they'd carried Marty's body to the grave.

Without a word Big leaned down and lifted her in his huge bear hug. "I'm glad you're home, Ronny. We've all missed you."

When he set her down, he asked her to join him and his

friends, but Ronny backed away, promising she would next time.

She listened until the boys stopped for a break and then walked out of the bar. They were stars now. Fans crowded around them.

She climbed into the black Lincoln waiting for her.

"Where to next?" Mr. Carleon asked. His white hair shone silver in the dashboard lights.

"Take me back to Rainbow Lane, please." She glanced at the sun setting over the town she'd lived in all her life. "I want to make it home before dark."

Mr. Carleon nodded. "You having any trouble with the mule?"

"No, but I practiced handling her before heading up the old road to where you parked to pick me up. She handles like the Jeep I drove in Brazil."

"Do you need anything, miss?" He always asked, as if he could provide "anything."

"Do you think you could get me a little boat with a motor? I think I might like to take it around the lake. I could even cross the water and you could pick me up at the Delaney farm. Their house is close to Rainbow Lane."

"I'll find you a boat by the first of next week." He hesitated, then added, "Did you enjoy the first set the boys played?"

"I did, but it's too soon to step out from the shadows. I think I just want to stay at the cabin another week, maybe two. No one noticed me in the back tonight except Big."

Mr. Carleon laughed. "Big Biggs. He still comes to see his grandmother at the bed-and-breakfast every Sunday evening. You wouldn't believe the food she cooks. I've eaten at Golden Corrals that didn't put out as much food."

Ronny leaned forward. "Mr. Carleon, when you stop at the light, can I sit in the front with you?"

"Of course. Mr. Winslow used to do that even when he was a boy."

As she slid into the front seat, she realized how deeply this man must miss his employer. "You all right, Mr. Carleon?"

The butler smiled. "I am, miss. I'm lucky he left me enough to retire comfortably. I can live at Winter's Inn and don't even have to make my own bed or breakfast." He looked in her direction. "And best of all, I have you to keep up with. When you're ready we'll go over your options, but take your time. I'll be watching over you for as long as you need me."

When they pulled to the shoulder of Rainbow Lane, Mr. Carleon got out to shine a flashlight while she stepped over two recently fallen trees and walked the few feet to where she'd stored her ATV. It was almost dark, but the trees lined the old road down to the cabin, throwing it into shadows.

"You sure you'll be all right?"

"I'll be fine. I'll be in the cabin before full dark." As always, she wanted to hug the dear guardian angel who'd been watching over her for so long, but she didn't. He wouldn't have thought it was proper.

The need to be alone seemed to push her to drive the mule faster. The memory of all the people at the bar, their voices, their smells pressed down on her. She wanted her swing and her blanket. She wanted the night so she could relax alone.

She was almost to the cabin when darkness settled in around her. The headlights blinked from one tree to another, reminding her of the opening to a horror film.

Ronny forced herself to slow down. Leaning forward, she gripped the wheel and mentally figured out how many minutes before she'd be home. Five at this speed. Maybe six before she rounded the cabin. The trail from Rainbow Lane had been built to wind around trees, not cut straight through to the lake.

A flash in the night, like a snapshot blast, blinked something big and black in the middle of the road. It was almost the height of a deer but three or four times wider. Teeth and tusks reflected milky white in the headlights.

Ronny veered off the road, fighting her way past saplings as tall as the ATV but only an inch thick.

She heard the animal's snort, half growl, half squeal, but she didn't turn to look. Anything that frightening at first glance had to be dangerous, maybe deadly.

A few heartbeats later she saw a huge tree blocking her path ten feet ahead. She had to turn toward the animal or crash.

Ronny gripped the wheel, turning right as the lights flashed back to the trail in time to see the short-legged beast vanish on the far side. He left broken bushes and branches in his wake.

Gunning the engine, she held on tight as she bumped down the road as fast as she could go. She had to get to the cabin fast before he decided to turn around.

Gulping for air, she fought frantically to concentrate on driving until the ATV's lights flashed on the cabin. She saw her porch swing. Her quiet place by the water. Austin Hawk sitting calmly on the steps. All looked peaceful.

It took a moment for her to react. She hit the brakes and managed to stop with the left front tire bumping the porch steps.

Austin swore, jumping out of the way as if he feared she might be planning to mow him down. He was dressed in khaki pants and khaki shirt with a rifle strapped over one shoulder as casually as if it were a satchel.

Ronny climbed from the seat, shaking so badly she wasn't sure she could stand. "I . . . I . . . saw a pig."

Austin lowered his rifle to the porch and moved swiftly toward her. His arms circled around her as he laughed. "Run into porky, did you? I saw him once at dawn, but I didn't think he'd come too close."

"He's so ugly." She forced a slow breath, feeling suddenly safe. "And his teeth. You can't imagine his teeth!"

"Yes, I can. I know. I was close enough to shake hands with him before I noticed him sleeping in the weeds." He brushed his big hand over her short hair and smiled as it curled back into place. "I dropped by to tell you to watch out for him." Austin's words were casual, but his touch seemed gentle along her back, almost caring.

Ronny stepped away. Marty had been too much with her tonight to allow her to take even comfort from another. "Thank you for your concern. I'll be fine. You needn't have worried." Her back straightened, pulling her emotions in check.

Looking up, she expected to see hurt in his forest-green

eyes, but she saw no feelings at all. He could have been a ticket taker at one of the hundred trains she'd ridden in the past year. She was just someone passing through. Men saw her as no one worth even the time to smile at her.

Austin Hawk shoved his hands into his pockets and walked away without looking back.

That night, in her dreams, Ronny looked for him. The background of her dream was a county fair like the ones that pull up in a vacant lot and stay for a week. Electric lights kept blinking on and off at odd intervals, and faceless people walked among the trees decorated with carnival prizes. She was darting among worn-out rides and small groups huddled together laughing, unaware that she was looking for Austin.

When she woke the dream hung in her mind, almost a memory. Standing, she stared out the window and thought she could barely make out his big house on the other side of the willows. She couldn't shake the feeling that he'd been the one lost in her dream, not her.

A little after nine, Ronny called Mr. Carleon and asked him to buy her a gun.

He hesitated for a moment, then said he would.

If Ronny left the safety of her cabin again, she planned to be armed.

Chapter 8

Buffalo's Bar

HALFWAY THROUGH THE SECOND SET AT BUFFALO'S BAR, Dusti finally got a few minutes to talk to shy Kieran alone.

They walked out on the long patio Harley had added to the front of his establishment. The bar owner claimed it classed up the place, but no one believed that staring at the muddy parking lot added anything to the ambience. Harley had even offered half-price hot wings in the fresh air, but apparently everyone wanted bar air.

Kieran navigated around scattered lawn furniture to the farthest empty table and pulled her chair out for her.

"Thanks," Dusti said, falling into the plastic with more swiftness than grace. "You're a good dancer. Where'd you learn to two-step in Scotland?"

He took the seat across from her. "I haven't lived in Scotland since I left for college. For the past few years I've been based in New York and, believe it or not, they do have country-western bars in New York City."

"I'm not surprised. They have everything there. I'd love to go someday just to see so many people crowded together."

"It is fun. New York reminds me of London."

She'd noticed his accent came and went. Sometimes she swore she heard the Highlander in his voice, and then he'd speed up and the New Yorker would come out.

Dusti couldn't help wondering what accent he used when he made love. Maybe he used different languages depending on what he was doing. Maybe he just stayed silent.

She mentally slammed a club against her head. That was her problem: From the first time she talked to a man she started visualizing him in bed. A few times the scene was so horrible she stayed on the straight and narrow, but more often in her late teens and early twenties, she "went to sin city," like her mother used to say. Luckily, her mother only knew of a few of her trips.

When Abby left for college, the family didn't have enough money for Dusti to go away to school, so she went wild for a few years. Then her father died of a sudden heart attack. Dusti took on the extra load. Within a year, her mother got sick and Dusti took on all the load. Partying on Saturday nights now and then was her only release. She thought of them as midnight breaks; after all, college kids got spring break. When she went crazy, Dusti didn't much care who she was with.

"You're a good dancer too, lass." Kieran broke into her thoughts. "I like a girl who's not afraid to lead now and then."

Dusti realized she hadn't been following the conversation. "Thanks," she managed to say as she leaned closer. "I didn't just want to dance, Kieran. I wanted to talk to you."

The clipped New Yorker replaced the Highlander. "Shoot."

"I heard about a poker game and I plan to enter."

"So do I," he said, making everything plain from the first.

"Only I have one problem and I thought you might help. Would you consider teaching me to play? I know the rules. I know how it works, but I'd like to know how to win."

His big body shrugged in the shadow. "Even if I teach you, I'll still win, so wouldn't it be a waste of time?"

"I just need to make it to the money at the end. You can take home the top pot next time."

"Why should I teach you to play?" His grin gave no hint of whether he was kidding. "I don't see any advantage in it for me other than having one more person to beat."

"I can pay you in eggs and pecans. A year's supply."

"I'd have trouble getting eggs home and I don't eat nuts. In fact, just sitting next to someone eating them on the plane makes me swell up and have trouble breathing."

Dusti crossed her arms over her chest. "Teach me to play and you can name your prize. Anything."

She studied her hands. Abby was right, this was a crazy gamble and without the help of someone like Kieran, she didn't have a chance. It was also the only hope of a way out that she'd thought of in three years.

He stared at her. "You, Dusti." His voice was low in the midnight breeze. "I want you. I've wanted you since I saw you that summer when you were about twelve and I was maybe fourteen. You were wilder, running the land, swimming the lake, than Austin and I could ever be. That black braid of yours dancing down your back when you ran and your laughter stuck in my brain long after I left that summer."

There went her mind again, back to tangled sheets. She got out the mental club and slammed the idea out of her brain. "What exactly are you asking?" Treat it like any other negotiation.

He was silent for a few minutes, then bumped his knee against her leg. "Come on, what have you got to lose? We could swim in the moonlight again, only this time we wouldn't be kids."

She forced herself not to jump. She'd hear him out. If the price was too high, she'd walk away, but she wanted this dream for Abby. Her sister was the good one, the Florence Nightingale. She was a year away from her goal of being a nurse. If Dusti couldn't follow her dream, at least Abby would get a chance to follow hers.

Dusti tried not to think about what she'd pay for lessons. Kieran was good looking, but who knew what he was into? After all, he'd been to New York City and London.

"If I teach you to play—"

"And I make it into the money in the finals," she added.

"And you make it into the money," he repeated, "then you pay the price. You go out with me on a real date, anywhere I say, anytime I say. I'm based in New York, but I travel several times a year. I can't remember the last time I spent an evening with a beautiful woman."

"Would dancing be involved?" She thought about asking if sex was expected, but she didn't want to give him any ideas.

"Dancing, dinner, drinks. I'll even toss in a drive in the moonlight. We dress up and go out on the town."

She grinned. If he picked Harmony, that would be dinner at the diner, then walking across to Buffalo's. Or they could drive to Amarillo and have a few dozen great places to eat, then take in a movie. The moonlight drive would take two hours each way. "All right. When do we start the lessons?"

"I'll drop by for breakfast tomorrow morning. If I'm going to teach you, we only have a very short window for you to learn, and I promised my grandmother I'd build her more bookshelves before I leave. She naps most of the morning these days. Says some parts of her body don't wake up till after lunch and the soaps are over."

"All right. I still have a farm to run, so no more than three hours of lessons a day."

He offered his hand. "Fair enough."

When she took his hand, she added one point. "You know, Kieran, you could have just asked me out. I would have gone."

He didn't turn her hand loose. "I did, Dusti, the last three times I came home. You were always too busy."

She thought about what he said. She barely remembered talking to him during the times he'd visited. Once her mother had been ill, and she and Abby were giving up every other night of sleep to sit with her. The next Christmas she'd seen him, even talked to him a minute at the post office, but her mother had just died. Then, maybe she'd turned him down last fall when all hands were needed to harvest the pecans. During those weeks she and Abby didn't have time to put on makeup, much less go out.

The realization that it had been two years since she'd had a real date or kissed a man shocked her. Wild Dusti Delaney had been living the life of a nun.

When Abby came home from school they'd been so busy. They'd talked about going out, even sized up every eligible man in the county, but there had been no time. At this rate they'd become the two old sisters living in the retirement home wondering where their lives went.

She stood. "Kieran, would you mind if we sealed this bargain with a kiss? I'm not much on handshakes."

He looked surprised, so she guessed she might as well go for total shock.

Dusti crawled onto his lap, wrapped her arms around his neck, and pressed her lips against his.

For a college graduate, he didn't seem too bright. From the way he kissed, sleeping with the man would be a real snooze. She'd get more action kissing the Blarney Stone.

Raising her head, she stared at him.

He didn't move. His arms were still at his sides, making her feel like she might as well have been a pigeon perched on his knee.

She climbed off the man, wondering if he was shy or gay or both. Maybe he was broke. That might explain why he didn't date.

"I wasn't ready," he said calmly.

"That's all right." She must have been real dumb to think he was making her a hot proposition. Obviously the man only wanted a date. Now, after she'd just scared him to death, he probably didn't even want that. "I guess the deal is off?"

He stood, towering over her. "The deal's still on. I'll teach you to play and we'll have the perfect evening after you win money." When she didn't comment, he added, "And, Dusti, I'll let you know when I'm ready for that kiss."

Chapter 9

IN FLIGHT

REAGAN TRUMAN BUCKLED INTO HER SEAT ON A SOUTHWEST flight heading out of Dallas toward Las Vegas. Since the night she'd talked to Dusti Delaney at Buffalo's, she'd known what she had to do. If the Delaneys could fight for their dream chasing a wild poker game, she could fight for hers.

As the flight attendant blared safety information, Reagan smiled. Her uncle Jeremiah used to tell her that if a dream wasn't worth fighting for, it wasn't worth having. He always said something like, "Whether you make it or not, kid, how are you going to feel on your deathbed if you didn't try? Seems to me, even if you don't make it, you'll die knowing you gave it your best shot."

She'd loved the old man from the moment he took her in and claimed her as kin. She'd gone from being a runaway foster kid to the niece of the last of the Truman family.

Before he died, he'd given her everything she'd ever dreamed of: a home, roots a hundred years deep, and his last name. Only now, after she turned his farm into one of the most successful businesses around, she wanted one dream more. Noah McAllen. Maybe she'd always wanted him, even that first day they'd met in high school. He'd grown up in Harmony and knew everyone. She knew no one. But he'd walked up to her with his friendly smile and told her they were going to be friends. She'd done her best to push him away, but he kept coming back. She couldn't help but love him.

Only Noah McAllen loved the rodeo. At first it was the thrill, the excitement of the crowd, the need to break his father's records, but now it was the money. With all the endorsements and personal appearances he might make a million this year. How could he turn that down?

Noah loved her too. She knew he did. When he won big, she was the first call he made. When he was hurt, he'd always have her come. Every time he came home he told her he loved her, and she swore she could see the truth of it in his eyes.

He was wild and reckless and she was grounded and shy, but somehow they matched. When they were together, the whole world seemed in balance.

As the plane rose into the clouds, Reagan counted the weeks since he'd been home. The small ranch his father had given him when he turned eighteen only had herds of tumbleweeds rolling across it now, and the house he'd told her would be their start was crumbling. Just like their plans to be together.

Noah always said they were young. Twenty-three is too soon to marry. They had plenty of time. The rest of their lives.

Only he hadn't called in over a month. Something was wrong. As much as Reagan hated traveling and crowds, she had to go to Noah. Deep down she knew he was slipping away, out of her life.

She might not have heard from him, but she knew where he'd be. This week every cowboy riding the circuit would be in Vegas at the rodeo. Only two nights were left. She'd find him tonight and watch him ride tomorrow before she went back to her quiet farm. Two days of crowds would be worth it if she could be with Noah.

Closing her eyes, she flipped through memories. The night he'd first kissed her. The days she'd spent watching over him after a bull had stomped on his chest. The first time they'd made love and she'd made him do it again just to make sure it had really been so good. Dozens of long hello kisses and tearful good-bye hugs at airports. It seemed like her whole life in Harmony had been measured in the heartbeats of Noah.

Dreams mixed with truth as the plane rocked her to sleep. He was waiting there, always in her dreams. Holding her. "I'll be your family," he'd whispered after her uncle died. "I'll always be your family, Rea, and you'll always be my anchor."

The sun was low over Vegas when the plane taxied in as she awoke. If she hurried, she might be able to make it to the rodeo grounds before he rode. He'd look up and see her and she'd see that wide lovable smile. Then she'd know everything was all right.

The rent-a-car place was crowded. The parking lot at the arena was full. By the time she walked to the entrance, her curly red hair was wet with sweat from the 105-degree heat that had baked into the asphalt that day. She'd worn her boots and jeans. Not the right attire for Las Vegas in summer.

By the time she spent half her cash on a ticket and walked to where the contestants had parked their trailers and pickups, Reagan wished she'd just found a hotel and called Noah. She lived in a world where personal space was measured in feet and everyone around here seemed to think an inch was plenty.

Finally she reached the guard to the contestants' gate. He was dressed in a red western shirt with an official circle logo on his pocket. Over forty and bored, she thought, with ex–bull rider written all over him.

"I'm with Noah McAllen," she yelled over the voices behind her. "I'm his friend."

"Sure you are, miss." The guard's voice had a chain smoker's rattle about it. "You don't even look like you're out of high school."

Reagan fought down an oath. She'd always looked younger than she was. At five feet three with no makeup, she probably did look seventeen. With her luck, she'd probably be carded until she was forty. "Can you get a message to Noah? He'll want to know I'm here."

"For twenty bucks I'll try."

Reagan backed into a corner and scribbled a note to Noah on the sleeve that had held her plane ticket. He hadn't answered the dozen messages she'd left. Probably lost his phone again, she reasoned as she folded a twenty around the envelope.

The guard took it without a word, just winked at her as if they now shared a secret, and shoved the note, along with the twenty, in his back pocket.

Reagan waited, moving back in the crowd far enough to breathe, but so she could still see the passageway. If Noah got the note, he might have time to come find her before he rode.

No one paid any attention to her. In the ocean of people wanting through the gate, only a trickle made it. Several other women around her were dressed in fancy western wear. They were hanging around laughing and waving as a few of the cowboys rode past. Some were made up to look younger; a few were trying to look older. All fought to look available. All the cowboys competing were professionals. The money was good and the rides were wild, in and out of the arena.

Reagan smiled. When she found Noah, they'd laugh about how some of these outfits would scare cows. She'd tell him some of the things the girls said about the riders.

An hour passed and the rodeo started, but she didn't move. Anyone riding tonight would have to pass by here. Noah might not be close enough to hear her yell, but if he glanced her way she knew he'd see her. He used to laugh that he could pick her out of any crowd. All he had to do was look for her hair. He swore no woman ever born had hair the color of sunset across open plains.

Guards changed at the gate. She watched the winker head back to where horse trailers were lined up. He reached in his back pocket and pulled out the airline envelope she'd given him with her note written on it. Finally her message would be delivered. Her long day, her long trip, would be over.

The guard shoved the twenty in his front pocket and tossed the envelope in a trash can as he passed.

Reagan fought back tears, thinking that coming here had been the dumbest idea she'd ever had. Noah knew she never liked to watch him ride, not since the early days when she'd felt like a part of her died each time she saw him fighting to get out from under a thousand pounds of angry bull.

Even if she went to the stands, he'd never see her. Not among thousands. Not as high up as her seat was. People began to move away toward the show, but Reagan stood with a dozen others waiting. She had no idea where he was staying. He might be sleeping in his newest trailer. He'd said something about wanting one, but she hadn't paid enough attention to remember if he'd bought it or just added it to a wish list. He'd told her it had living quarters bigger than some hotels he'd stayed in during his early days of rodeo.

Her only chance was to stay right where she was and hope that eventually he'd pass by. Or, she realized, be sensible and go back to Harmony. Eventually he'd come back, he always did. The first few days back he played the star, but finally the rodeo champion would melt away and her Noah was there again, saying he didn't want to leave her, telling her what their life would someday be like, loving her.

One of the glitter cowgirls noticed Reagan. She shook her overstyled, oversprayed, overcolored curls. "You all right, honey? You look like you might faint. This your first rodeo?"

"I'm fine. I'm just waiting for someone."

"One of the riders?"

Reagan nodded. She really didn't want to talk to anyone, but she couldn't be rude. "Noah McAllen. I've been watching him ride since we were in high school."

The Dolly Parton lookalike smiled. "I hate to tell you, honey, but McAllen won't be interested in seeing you. He's all business. Never picks a girl up. He stays alone and, win or lose, drinks alone."

"You know him?"

"I've seen him. Heard about him mostly from a few of the other riders. They say he's a loner who does his job and steps

away from the lights as soon as he's finished. He's not in it
for the fun. I know most of the girls who follow the circuit,
and not one of them has gone more than a few rounds on the
dance floor with him."

Reagan was glad to hear that he didn't sleep around, but
if he was burned out, why hadn't he come home? Why stay?
He'd made enough money. Every ride was a roll of the dice
that he might get hurt again, and one time he might not walk
out of the hospital. He might never walk again.

"How do I get to him, or at least get a message? I really
do know him."

The blonde shrugged. "You probably do. No woman would
wear that outfit and come here hoping to get picked up." She
lowered her voice as if passing a secret. "My Johnny says he
sometimes goes downtown to a little bar near the Golden
Nugget. It's so dark in there no one would recognize their
own mother. You might try there. I think it's called the Lucky
Sevens."

"Thanks." Reagan watched several riders pass by. All
were tall and lean and wore their hats low.

For a minute none looked familiar but, in a blink, one turned
toward the gate and stared directly at her. Tired brown eyes
took in all the crowd, the bright lights making the night bright
as high noon.

"Noah!" she yelled, shoving her way to the front of the
crowd. "Noah."

A few other cowboys glanced in her direction, but Noah
turned away. He hadn't seen her.

She'd become invisible in his world.

Chapter 10

HAWK HOUSE

AUSTIN HAD JUST FINISHED HIS MORNING RUN AND COLLAPSED in the shade-covered grass beside his house when he heard movement in the willows.

Slowly he stood, shedding his pack and lifting his rifle. Wild hogs could weigh hundreds of pounds, but they had poor sight. If the hog was in the brush there was a good chance he hadn't spotted a human yet.

Scanning the trees to the lake's edge, Austin made out Ronny Logan walking toward him. Her slender body seemed to sway with the branches, blinking in and out of sunshine. Like a kid, she tapped the trees and brush with a stick as she walked, one arm swinging free and the other holding the strings of a bag over one shoulder.

He rolled his shoulder as if shucking off the alert, then lowered his rifle atop his pack before she looked up. As always, she didn't smile, but watched him as if somehow thinking she could understand him just by sight.

Forcing a grin, he stepped into the sun. "You scaring off pigs for me with that stick?"

Pushing down the urge to yell at her and tell her to go back to her side of the trees, he forced an easy manner. If she knew how damaged he was, she'd probably run. Maybe he should warn her. Some days he felt more machine than human. He'd kept everyone at a distance for so long he didn't know how to talk to normal people. Ronny Logan was shy to start with, and if he growled at her, it would probably frighten her more than the pig had.

But damn if she didn't look adorable and totally out of place in her tailored linen trousers and silk sleeveless blouse. The woman was a jigsaw puzzle with half the pieces missing. She'd be polite and cold one minute and vulnerable the next.

He didn't want to even think about how he felt when they'd kissed. That side of Ronny was sexy as hell and was still keeping him awake half the night.

The lady didn't look at him even now but turned to study Hawk House as if she'd never noticed it before.

"That house doesn't seem to belong out here on a little lake. It looks like something I saw in Maine. It should be staring out at the Atlantic."

"Yeah, tell that to my grandfather. I inherited it from my dad, who spent every summer pretending like he didn't hate having to stay out here away from work for a week."

"What about your mom? She must have loved it."

He shrugged. "She split when I was five. I have no idea what she loves. To me, Mom is a Christmas card once a year. But at least I get that. She didn't even bother to send a card when my dad died."

Better change the subject before I start blabbering on about being a motherless child, he thought. "But I loved it out here as a kid. My dad usually got bored by the end of the first week and left me alone with the housekeeper. We had a great agreement for the rest of the summer. I'd leave her alone until dark and she'd feed me supper. I made a few friends and this place was our playground."

"Is that when you met Kieran?" She walked toward the house, still more interested in it than him.

"You know Kieran O'Toole?"

She shook her head. "My first job was sorting mail in Harmony. I knew his grandmother. She didn't trust mailboxes, so I'd hold her mail until she walked two blocks to pick it up. Kieran's grandmother was always talking about him."

Austin thought he saw her blush, so he waited for more.

Without facing him, she added, "I used to read the postcards he sent her. Folks around here call him the Scot, but he's lived all over the world. Now and then, he'd asked about you in his notes. Things like, 'Tell my old friend Hawk hello.'"

Austin stood perfectly still. This was more than Ronny Logan had ever talked to him, and he didn't want to do anything to screw it up. He figured he had a pretty tight window of opportunity here. Somewhere between shoving her down and making love to her on the grass and asking her in for tea. If he guessed wrong, the only woman he'd found interesting in years would disappear.

"We keep in touch now and then on the Internet." She didn't look like she cared, but he had to say something.

He'd never been good with boundaries and he had no idea why she was here this morning, so he'd better be careful. She'd made it plain that she didn't want him talking to her or touching her the other night when he'd told her about the pig. Maybe she'd just been afraid, or maybe she'd been mad that she came home to find him sitting on her porch.

She kept standing in front of him now, so he guessed she wasn't ready to leave. He couldn't think of anything that made sense to say. All ideas for action were R-rated, and he didn't think she'd be interested.

"You want something?" He finally managed to come up with a question that had sounded better in his head than it did in the air between them.

Now she looked down. But she didn't run. He considered that progress.

"I want to ask you a favor." A breeze caught her short hair and brushed it across her forehead, shading her eyes.

Austin relaxed. He could handle that. A favor. Start her

car? Drive her to town? Fix her stopped-up sink? "Name it. It's done," he answered.

"Aren't you even going to ask what it is?"

Oh yeah, he should have done that. "Ronny, if I can, I'll help you out. It's not complicated. You must think it's possible or you won't have walked over here to ask me."

Finally, she looked at him and he saw indecision in her eyes. "Will you teach me to shoot?"

Holding out a leather case, Ronny looked like she didn't even know how to open it. The minute he took the small bag, she stepped back as if she didn't want to stand too close.

He pulled out an old but well-cared-for Colt .45 and turned it over in his grip. "Pretty powerful piece."

"A friend bought it for me."

"Mind telling me why you want this?" If she said she needed it to protect herself from her crazy neighbor, Austin swore he'd move.

"Because of the pig. I think I'd better have protection with me or leave. And I don't want to leave."

He checked the weapon to make sure it was unloaded and offered it back to her. She didn't reach for it. "You got any bullets?"

She shook her head. "I forgot to ask for them."

Austin folded the Colt back into its pouch. "How about we have a cup of coffee on my porch that you think doesn't belong here and talk about this favor you're asking for?"

She had that look of a wild animal about to run, but finally she nodded. He walked ahead of her to the porch and held the front door open until she walked in.

The place was all in order, just as he'd found it, with the same layer of dust covering everything. To be honest, he hadn't noticed until today. The third-floor bedroom, the bathroom, and the kitchen were the only three rooms he used.

"The kitchen's clean," he said as she followed him down the hallway.

They silently agreed to suspend conversation while he made coffee. He didn't miss that she looked around, always returning to the leather gun case on the counter as if it were a rattler in the room.

She held the tray as he stacked mugs, a glass coffeepot, and paper towels. As an afterthought he added a tin of short-bread cookies he'd picked up at the last airport layover before he made it here. "Nearest I have to coffee cake," he said, trying to act like he had a plan.

"Looks nice," she lied back.

He held the door again as they moved outside. Huge old wicker chairs sat in one corner. Both looked like they were ready to be tossed, but he'd tried them out and knew they'd hold.

She took a seat carefully and he poured her coffee into a stained mug.

"Thank you," she said, as if he were handing her fine china.

Austin took his seat and poured his coffee. Neither touched the tin of cookies.

This time it was her turn to break the silence. Austin waited her out.

Finally, she said in a whisper, "What did you and Kieran do out here in the summers?"

Austin relaxed. Safe territory. "One year we built a fort in the trees. I usually go out to make sure it's still there, hidden away, but this time I think I'll wait until I know the hogs aren't out."

She lifted her cup to her lips, but he couldn't tell if she drank any coffee or just pretended.

"When we were just into our teens, we spent a few summers swimming with the Delaney girls, but then one summer they wouldn't speak to us. Might have had something to do with us giving up bathing that year. Or, maybe it was because they developed breasts and realized we weren't like them.

"I remember every hot summer day Kieran would ride his bike out, and we'd run wild till almost dark like we were the lost boys. His grandmother must have had the same rule as my housekeeper did . . . be home by dark. Only she usually packed him a huge lunch. I'd sneak into the house and steal drinks. Once in a while I'd take a couple of the housekeeper's beers. She drank so many I don't think she noticed. Kieran and I would sit in the fort and feel all grown up."

"It sounds like fun. My mother would never let me play with the other kids in the neighborhood. I spent my childhood staying right beside her. Wherever she went, I went. Summers were usually endless soap operas and trips to the grocery store."

"You never went wild?"

Ronny smiled. "Sometimes I'd sneak out at night and walk the creek bed behind our house."

"I'm guessing your mother would like to have you back under her thumb since she came all the way out here the other night." He could almost see the shy little girl inside the woman before him.

"No. She disowned me when I left home at twenty-seven. I lived on my own for a time, and then my boyfriend moved in for a while. I've been traveling since he left. Dallas probably only dropped by to remind me she's still not speaking to me."

"You all right with that?"

"With her not speaking to me, yes. With her dropping by, no."

Austin leaned forward. He'd spent enough time with small talk. "Ronny, want to tell me what you're afraid of? If you got a gun, I'm guessing it's more than the pig."

She stood, walked to the porch railing, and turned her back to him. Her warm brown eyes seemed to hold an ocean of secrets. She crossed her arms as if the morning had suddenly grown cold.

He'd started down this road, he might as well continue. "You don't want a gun, Ronny. Hell, I'm betting you're more afraid of it than the pig. Not much chance I can teach you to shoot when you won't even hold the thing."

She couldn't have been more still if she'd been made of glass. He placed his untouched coffee beside her cup and moved beside her.

"I'll take care of the pig. Don't worry about him. The

Delaneys told me they've already called in the game warden. Pigs can do a lot of damage to the land. He could root up several of their pecan trees in one night. Wild pigs eat everything in sight, including pets and small livestock. I promise, before you could learn to load a Colt, the pig will no longer be a threat."

He brushed his hands from her shoulders to her elbows. Her skin was warm but she didn't respond; she only turned to stare out into the water.

"You're not in danger here, Ronny." He wanted to pull her against him, but she seemed rooted in one spot. "Hogs usually run if they see humans."

Finally, he rested his hands at her waist, waiting for her to relax or walk away. She felt so good to touch. Almost as if he'd crossed the ropes at an art gallery and was touching a masterpiece.

To his surprise, she swayed slightly toward him as his hand moved slightly. "You're in no peril here, lady," he whispered again.

"Yes, I am," she said when she finally turned toward him. "I'm in danger of feeling, and I don't want to feel anything, not for anyone and not for you." Her words were no more than a lingering whisper between them. "If I had a gun I wouldn't have to run to you if I saw a pig. I could survive alone, without feelings, without caring for anyone."

What she said almost took him down like a blow to the back of the knees. The honesty frightened him, and he reacted with frustration and anger. "You don't have to worry, lady, I'm incapable of feeling. I gave it up years ago when I walked out of a fire and left my friends to die."

Ronny finally stared at him. "You think you should have saved them?"

"No." For the first time he said the words he'd always thought. "I think I should have died with them."

He had to get away. He couldn't answer any more questions. In one fluid movement he jumped from the porch and ran. Maybe away from her. Maybe away from his own reality. He'd just admitted the one reason he couldn't recover, no matter how hard he worked.

Deep down he knew he should have died.

One shy stranger had drawn out of him what no doctor had been able to do.

The truth.

Chapter 11

HAWK HOUSE

RONNY TOOK THE TRAY OF DIRTY COFFEE CUPS INTO THE house after Austin Hawk simply ran off his own porch and left her there.

She was numb inside, as if she'd frozen from the core out. She had spent a year feeling sorry for herself because her one true love had died, even thought she was somehow a coward for not dying with him, and now Ronny had met a man who mirrored her pain. Only he'd lost all his friends.

His depth of grief made her feel shallow. She'd known Marty Winslow was dying when he moved in with her. She had known, but she'd ignored the truth. Marty had given her time to know that he loved her, a long good-bye, but all she saw was that in the end, he'd left her. He'd left behind money for her to travel the world and Mr. Carleon's promise to watch over her. In a way, even after a year, he was still loving her, but all she'd seen was the grief.

For the first time since the funeral, she realized what a gift he'd given her and not what he'd taken away.

After she washed the dishes and put them in an orderly

cabinet, Ronny went back to her cabin. She wasn't sure if the day had become cloudy or if it was only her mood, but she pulled on a dark blue rain jacket and walked down to where she'd tied the boat Mr. Carleon had brought her when he'd arrived with the gun.

For once, she didn't want to be alone, and going back to Hawk House didn't seem an option.

The old boat was the best Mr. Carleon said he could find on short notice. A blue flat-bottom with a little engine on the back that looked new. Full speed was probably less than ten miles an hour, and it would take a tsunami to flip it over. Mr. Carleon's one lesson in operating the craft had only taken the few minutes when she'd driven him back across the water to the Delaney dock where he'd left his car.

The rickety dock in front of her cabin was small, made more for jumping in the water than for mooring boats. Ronny stepped around broken planks and climbed into her boat. With little skill, she started the engine. While the sun blinked between clouds, she puttered slowly back across the lake. At this rate she'd know the Delaneys well, coming to call twice in one day.

A few minutes later when she docked, she saw Kieran O'Toole walking out of the Delaney barn.

He knew her just well enough to call her by name. "Would you look at yourself, Ronny Logan. You're driving a boat, you are."

His open smile had always been friendly, even when he was a kid. He used to come into the post office when she was eighteen and had just started working. Whoever was on the front desk would send him back to collect his grandmother's mail. Though younger, he'd already been taller than Ronny and most grown men in town.

She'd been so shy she wouldn't even look at him. He wasn't much better, but as the weeks of his stay lingered into summer, they'd manage to say a few more words each time.

She'd been eighteen and he must have been sixteen, because he got his license that summer. Like shy people do, they talked quietly. She'd discovered his keen sense of humor.

Over the years that she worked in the back of the post office, she often thought some of what he wrote on the postcards to his grandmother was meant for her.

Apparently, Kieran remembered her also. He rushed to help her tie up. "Maybe I could drive your boat sometime, Ronny. After all, there's no right or left side of the road to worry about."

She laughed, remembering his near-death tales of learning to drive when every fool in town was on the wrong side of the road. "I'm guessing, Mr. O'Toole, that you've solved that problem, since you're still alive."

He winked. "That's why I took up flying. No roads."

"So you're still a pilot?"

"Five years professionally. I do mostly international flights out of New York. In truth, crossing the ocean isn't near as hard as learning to drive that summer. Granny had just acquired her bifocals and she thought a bug on the windshield was an oncoming car. Luckily, we were on a back road, but my ears hurt for days from both our screaming."

"I've nothing so exciting to report about boating." Ronny shrugged. "I just learned my way around this little lake an hour ago."

Ronny almost said she was proud of him for following his dream. For a kid dragged all over the world, it made sense that he'd be at home no matter where he went. His grandmother used to claim her daughter and the crazy Scot she married were like migrant birds born without a sense of direction.

"While you're here, you want to see some little chicks?" Kieran pointed to the barn. "The Delaneys got dozens delivered yesterday. Cutest balls of fuzz you've ever seen."

Ronny nodded but didn't take his hand when he offered to help her from the boat.

Ten minutes later she laughed as she sat surrounded by baby chicks. Dusti Delaney came in and welcomed her as if Ronny were a friend and not just someone she'd seen a few times. The good and bad thing about living in a small town is everyone knows pretty much everyone on sight even if they never talk. Dusti might be a few years younger, but Ronny was sure she'd heard of Dallas Logan. Ronny's mother was at every town hall meeting, usually causing trouble.

Thankfully Dusti didn't mention Dallas or the fact that she'd once cornered the Delaney girls in a store and demanded to know why their eggs weren't all white.

Dusti's one kindness now marked the young farmer as a possible friend, so Ronny offered a true smile to the dark-haired beauty.

"Kieran came over to teach me to play poker if I'll feed him breakfast first." Dusti grinned back. "Want to join us? We're having omelets, of course, and we've got plenty."

Ronny was shaking her head as Kieran said, "Of course she will. She's probably starving." He winked at Ronny. "Maybe you can stall Dusti a few minutes while I try to remember how to play. It's been so long since I've sat down to a game. I may have forgotten a rule or two."

"He's already bluffing, Ronny. Don't let his shy ways fool you, the man can charm or lie in several languages."

"Maybe it's lucky I came along to referee you two." She remembered the terrible coffee she'd tried to drink at Austin's place. It hadn't gone down well. Breakfast sounded wonderful. "I'll referee for the price of an omelet." She didn't want to go back across the lake. Not now.

Within the hour Ronny had become the dealer while Dusti and Kieran played Texas Hold'em. Dusti's sister circled past now and then but didn't seem interested. She obviously didn't believe in Dusti's crazy plan to learn to play poker well enough to win a tournament where two hundred people had signed up.

"Half of the entry fee money will go into the library fund," Dusti explained. "But one lucky player will win the thousand-dollar buy-in to the big-time in Las Vegas, with another thousand going to pay plane tickets and expenses. I'm going to be the one from Harmony."

"Sure you are, lass." Kieran laughed.

Dusti stuck her tongue out at him, and the big Scot just grinned as if she'd kissed him on the cheek.

Slowly, Ronny felt the tension of the morning leave her. Dusti assured her the wild hog would be taken care of by a game warden or one of the farmers around them. Kieran even offered to help Austin track the animal.

The cloudy morning passed in easy laughter. Storm clouds were moving in as Kieran walked her back to her blue boat. Ronny had promised to come again to act as dealer for the pair, and they'd all exchanged cell numbers.

In an odd way, they all fit together. The easygoing Scot, the outspoken Dusti, and her, the shadow of a person afraid of the world.

"You going to be all right on the water?" Kieran asked.

She nodded. "You can watch me cross, and if I flip, you can watch me swim back here or home. Whichever's closer."

"Right. Say hello to Hawk for me if you see him. In my mind we were Tom Sawyer and Huck Finn those wild summers. I've tried to keep up with him but haven't heard much for six months. I thought the army was probably keeping him busy fighting fires or training. Had no idea he was here relaxing."

"You two have been friends a long time?"

"We were summer friends as kids. Two strangers sent to spend the summer in a small town where everyone else already had their full serving of friends. We were close but lost track when he joined the army. Now we touch base on Facebook now and then. I heard he specialized in oil rig fires set by troublemakers all over the world. He told me once, when we were both home a few years ago, that sometimes his team goes in to fight a fire with bullets flying. He said half the time they're in some country he couldn't even spell."

"What's happened to him lately?"

Kieran shook his head. "He didn't say when I saw him at Buffalo's, but he was thinner than when I saw him before. Said he was living here for a while. I guess he got out." Kieran untied the rope. "When we practice poker again, invite him to come if you like."

"I don't know him that well," she said.

By the time she crossed the lake, the howling wind was

making Ronny nervous. She tied the boat up to one of the dock boards and ran for the house.

Dusti called her a few hours later to tell her a group of hunters was going after the hogs as soon as the rain stopped, but Ronny's nerves still hadn't settled. Rain pounded the cabin, making it seem more like evening than afternoon.

She hadn't slept well the night before. Even her nap on the porch wouldn't work today. She felt a restlessness in her body that she could never remember feeling.

A little after nightfall, the lights flickered and died, blanketing the cabin in deep shadows. It took her several minutes to locate the lanterns she'd tucked away thinking she'd never need them. Flipping one on, she thanked Mr. Carleon for remembering to put batteries in it.

The light made her cabin glow in an eerie light, not enough to read by, too much to sleep with.

Finally, feeling trapped, she decided to step out on the porch and see if the lights were out at the Delaney place also. Every night the glow of their barn light was like a setting moon across the lake. It offered her comfort but no company.

She wrapped herself in the blanket that covered the back of the cabin's old couch and opened the door.

Two steps out, her feet sloshed in water. If she didn't know better she'd swear it was raining sideways, coming straight off the lake.

The rain was too hard for her to see her shoreline, much less across the lake. She stood, letting the cold water brush over her toes while she decided this was what lonely really felt like. Maybe if she hadn't spent the afternoon laughing? Maybe if she had something to keep her busy? Maybe if she'd stop running and start living, then she'd care about something or someone again?

Her heart seemed colder than her feet. Blinking, she couldn't tell if her face was wet with rain or if she was crying.

Staring into the night, she tried to will the Delaney barn light to shine.

As she turned to go back inside, she saw the silhouette of a man leaning against the cabin at the far corner of the porch. He was sheltered from a direct downpour, but wind rattled his thin coat.

Gulping down a yelp, she squeaked out, "Austin?"

He straightened, his raincoat hood pulled low like it had been that first time she'd seen him.

"I didn't mean to frighten you." His words were caught in the wind and seemed to circle around her. "I just came over to see if you were here and all right."

She glanced out at the storm. "Where else would I be?" This didn't seem like a good time for a walk.

"I don't know," he shouted, angry as usual. "I saw you motoring off this morning like you thought you knew what you were doing. I didn't see you come back. About an hour ago, I noticed the storm had washed that blue flatbed boat up on my shore. Hell, if you weren't here I'd already decided I'd have to go get help to dredge the lake."

She tried to see him in the shadows. "You thought I drowned?" She was surprised how much it meant to her that he cared.

He didn't answer. He just stood there like a tall lamppost with the light shot out.

She took another step toward him. "You were worried about me?"

No answer.

Ronny moved closer. "You thought I needed help?" The man was not only bad tempered and moody, now he was going deaf. "You really thought I might have drowned in the lake?"

He swore. "Of course I thought you drowned. What else would I think? It never occurred to me that you'd not be smart enough to pull the boat to shore and tie it to a tree. Hell, that dock of yours is little better than driftwood. I'm surprised you don't fall through one of those broken boards and dunk yourself every time you walk out on that platform."

She was a foot away and could see his irate features. Calm, she thought of him as handsome. Mad, he was downright frightening.

One step closer for a better look. She'd expected to see anger in his eyes. It shocked her to see fear. He'd been truly worried about her, afraid for her!

"I know people die, Austin, but you don't have to worry about me." Ronny wasn't sure why she yelled those words at him. Maybe it was the storm, or maybe it was because she was being yelled at. She lowered her voice. "But I'm still alive—and I'm not going to bother you again, so you don't have to run away when you see me. You keep to your side of the willows and I'll keep to mine. From now on just consider me your out-of-sight neighbor and *don't* bother waving when you happen to *not* see me."

"I wasn't running from you before." He had lowered his voice too. "I was running from me. But that never works."

Ronny lifted her hand to cup his unshaven face. She knew him so well, this man she didn't know at all. She understood him. Somehow, as different as they were, they'd walked the same path.

His gaze bore into her. "I didn't want anything to happen to you, Ronny. It may not sound like it, but I like having you here."

She was so close she could feel his words on her cold, damp face.

"Do me a favor, Ronny." His request sounded more like an order. "Don't go out in that damn blue boat when a storm's coming in."

"All right, but you have to promise to stop yelling at me."

"I'll try"—the hint of a smile lifted his lips—"but I was born yelling and never bothered to stop. In my line of work it was a necessary skill."

He took a step toward her. "And before you go on about it, I'm glad you didn't drown in the lake. I don't think I would have been happy about that."

"Are you ever happy, Austin?" She somehow doubted it.

"Stop asking questions."

An order again, she thought, but he was now so near she had other things on her mind besides asking questions.

She wasn't sure which one of them closed the distance

between them, but in a heartbeat she was being crushed against the hard, wet wall of his chest.

For a moment he just held her as if needing to know she was solid. Real. Alive. Then his mouth lowered to hers.

His kiss was wild, nothing like the long slow one they'd shared in the water. She was lost to all else. A tidal wave of feelings surrounded her. There was no time to think, only to react. She tugged his raincoat open, wanting to feel the warmth of this cold man against her heart.

He dug his hands into her hair and kissed her as if it were the last kiss he was allowed for this lifetime.

She melted into him, loving that someone, if only for a moment, might need her so dearly. Maybe it was the storm, or the night, but she didn't want to let go.

Without breaking the kiss, he lifted her up and moved inside, bumping the lantern she still carried hard against the side of the cabin door as he stepped out of the rain and into the shadows of her place.

When he set her feet down she backed away, afraid more of the way she felt than of him. Her cabin seemed so much smaller with him standing in the middle of it.

"I'll get you a towel," she whispered, already running into the bathroom.

When she returned, he'd tugged off his raincoat and soaked shirt. Both seemed to have lost the power of speech. What they'd shared seemed foreign to each. No words would explain it away.

He nodded his thanks as he took the towel.

She hung up his shirt and coat. He lit a fire in the old fireplace tucked in the corner of the room that served as living room, study, and kitchen. The furnishings were old overstuffed leather pieces that appeared almost boulderlike in the shadows.

When he stood, she watched the firelight dance across the scars on his shoulders and arms. The muscles beneath looked powerful, but the skin was twisted and discolored in spots. Burns, she thought, deep burns.

"Do the scars bother you?" His voice seemed as rough as

the damaged skin. "I've had them long enough now that I don't notice them."

"No," she lied. It bothered her greatly that he must have been through a great deal of pain, but she knew by his tone that he didn't want to talk about it. He was a man foreign to comfort or pity, and he allowed none now.

"I'll leave as soon as the rain lets up a little. When I saw you were all right, I decided to wait out the downpour on your porch. I wasn't expecting you to come out and find me."

She wasn't sure whether his words left her disappointed or relieved. Maybe both. "Want some coffee?"

He wrapped the towel around his neck, absently covering most of the scars. "It's bound to be better than the coffee I made this morning."

"I hope so," she said, then smiled as if she'd let the words slip. "I've heard tell of cowhands who made their coffee with an old sock, but I'd never tasted it before."

Her teasing broke the tension and they both relaxed a little.

He looked around her cabin, claiming he'd never been in the place, while she made them coffee. "Kieran and I probably would have explored in here when we were kids, but the locks were too strong to pick."

When she set the tray down by the fire, a real coffee cake that she'd made from a boxed mix rested beside two matching mugs. He folded the throw she'd wrapped in back on the couch and offered her it as a seat, then sat beside her on the floor.

He sipped the hot coffee and ate half the loaf before he spoke. "If the rain keeps up, any chance you got something for supper? I don't remember eating today."

"Sure, soup, sandwiches, cookies, fruit salad. I could warm up a pasta casserole or a potpie if you like. I'm well stocked thanks to a friend in town."

He took another piece of cake. "That sounds great."

"Which one?"

"All the above. I've been living on power bars for a week. Last time I was at Buffalo's Bar for a meal, I ate three baskets of wings while listening to the music. Would have ordered another, but folks were starting to stare at me as if waiting for me to explode."

Ronny studied him, trying to figure out if he was kidding or not. It was hard to tell.

She remembered the Biggs boys back a year ago when she cooked for them. If it didn't crawl off the table fast, they ate it. "I'll warm it all up."

"I'll help," he offered, sounding more like he thought it was something he was supposed to say than that he was willing to actually be helpful.

She nodded, unable to lie and tell him to stay where he was. With Austin, ten feet away seemed far too close.

As she'd expected, in the small kitchen area he was mostly in the way, bumping into her every time he turned around, but she told herself she didn't mind. It was nice to have company for a change. The first few brushes surprised her, but she soon grew used to his nearness, as he did hers.

At least when he was around, she could feel like she was alive, and that seemed a step up from how she'd felt all day.

They cooked and ate in comfortable conversation. Nothing personal. The weather. The rain. The lake. The weather. At one point she wondered if either of them was really listening to the other. But they had to continue or the silence would be too great between them.

He even pulled his shirt on as they sat down at the table, claiming it was dry enough to wear. They both knew it wasn't.

Slowly, like muscles unknotting in warm water, they began to relax and really talk to each other. To her surprise, they had the world in common. He'd been most of the places she'd traveled. He explained that most of the time, when he got leave, he traveled instead of coming home. Only she had the feeling he'd seen the bars and military posts and she'd seen the museums and cathedrals.

When he helped her with the dishes, she felt comfortable enough to say, "We probably need to talk about that kiss earlier."

"What about it?" His words seemed suddenly guarded.

She turned away from him. "It was nice, real nice, but I don't think it should happen again. You see, I'm not ready. I'd appreciate it if you didn't grab me again, or hold me like you did, or kiss me like that. If we're to be friends, I'll have to draw a few lines. I'm not the kind of woman who's usually kissed like that."

"What was wrong? The grabbing, the holding, or the kissing?" He looked like he was having trouble defining words. He was an organized man who couldn't seem to make the feelings he had for her fit into his life.

"I'm not sure." Maybe she shouldn't have brought it up. The kiss was just something that happened. They'd reacted to the moment. The storm, or the fear that she'd drown, or the need to be alive. But she wasn't going to mention any of that or he might give her another multiple-choice question.

"Maybe we should do it again so you could make up your mind."

"Probably not a good idea." An accidental kiss and a planned one would be two different things, yet she couldn't bring herself to say no.

He moved behind her and placed his hands lightly on her shoulders. "Whatever you want, Ronny. If friendship's what you want, then that's what we'll have. I'm not much good at it. Only have one friend, and that's Kieran. We talk every six months or so whether we need to or not." He bumped his chin against her hair. "If being friends is the only offer on the table, I'll try my best."

She smiled, relieved that they'd dropped the whole kissing talk.

As he turned her to face him, he asked, "Only I need to know what it is you're not ready for. You seem a woman fully grown and able to know her own mind."

He leaned closer.

Curiosity kept her from stepping away. They'd talked about no grabbing, or holding, or kissing, so she had no idea what he planned.

She felt his breath first, warm against her throat.

"Ronny," he whispered as she closed her eyes, breathing

in the fresh smell of him. Rain. The fireplace. Him. "What do you want, Ronny? What do you really want?"

His mouth slid along her throat to her ear. "You're a liar, pretty lady, if you say we shouldn't be this close. You are a woman who should be kissed like I kissed you. Just like that or harder, and more often."

Before she answered, he brushed her mouth lightly with his and whispered again, "You, Ronny, should always be kissed with a passion that takes your breath away and almost knocks us both down. You may not be sure what you want, but you are hungry to find out. How about we explore just what it is you want?"

His words against her slightly bruised lips almost buckled her knees.

She opened her mouth to protest and his kiss captured her. Without another word he took control, kissing her like no one had ever kissed her before. With a fire that warmed her to her toes. With passion sweeping over them both. With a hunger that surprised her. His words might have been playful, but there was no playing in the depth of need he showed.

She felt light-headed and her insides ached with a need she couldn't explain. She wasn't sure she even liked this moody man with his angry outbursts and his broken life. Only this wasn't about like, or love. What he offered her was about need.

And need was all she felt firing off in her veins like dynamite. When her body shook with the force of the blast, he pulled her closer as if he felt it also and the only way either would survive would be if they stayed together, close together.

When he finally broke the kiss she realized he wasn't holding her. His arms were at his sides and her fingers had knotted into his shirt. She'd been the one holding tightly to him. He hadn't stolen a kiss, she'd demanded it.

For a few breaths they stood so near, their bodies melted into each other. The world around them seemed to settle back into place.

He kissed her nose. "We'll have this discussion again anytime you like." He pried her fingers off his shirt. "It's been really nice talking to you, but I have to go." His laughter was deep and loving as he teased. "It's stopped raining and the game warden will be waiting for me."

While she stood by the fire trying to piece together what had happened, Austin put on his raincoat and opened the door. "Thanks for supper." He hesitated, his back to her. "I'm real glad you didn't drown."

Then he was gone, vanishing into the blackness outside her little cabin.

She walked to the door and looked for him, wondering how he could be so calm after what had just happened between them. When his gaze had met hers after his last kiss, she knew the truth. He wasn't calm. He was fighting to keep it together the same as she was.

She didn't know when, but he'd come for her, and when he did she wouldn't turn away.

After closing the door, she walked into her bedroom and collapsed on the bed without bothering to take off her clothes.

Only one fact made any sense.

She wanted him. All the reasons for why she shouldn't or couldn't didn't matter. Ronny Logan, who'd been afraid to ever want anything in her whole life, wanted her crazy neighbor.

What was totally embarrassing was that he knew it.

Chapter 12

TRUMAN FARM

REAGAN ROSE AT DAWN. BY THE TIME SHE MADE IT DOWN-stairs, the coffee was ready. She poured a mug and walked across to what she still called "the barn" even though it was far more. Her business, Truman Orchard, shipped apples to a dozen states and jellies to forty independent grocers.

Walking past machinery and loading docks, she flipped on lights as she stepped into her office.

She'd been back for four days and hadn't stopped work-ing. On a farm there was always something to do to make it better, but there was nothing she could do about Noah. He'd have to find his way back. Until then, she'd work and wait.

At this rate she'd keel over from exhaustion before she turned twenty-four.

As they had every day since she'd been home from Las Vegas, the memories flooded back as she worked alone on the books.

The night Noah had looked in her direction and not seen her waiting at the gate had almost broken her heart. She'd stayed the entire rodeo, fighting down tears, but he'd never walked past the gate again.

The overly made-up blonde, Candy Lee, had invited Reagan to join her and her Johnny for a drink. He hadn't won his event, but he'd made a good ride, so Johnny seemed in good spirits.

Candy Lee said she felt like slow dancing and suggested the Lucky Sevens bar downtown. Johnny went along with the idea. In fact, if Candy Lee unbuttoned one more button, he'd probably go along with robbing the first bank they passed.

Reagan remembered that she'd ridden in the front of the cab and talked to the driver while the couple got friendly in the backseat. When they reached the lights of the Strip, Reagan paid the cabdriver and helped pull the couple apart.

The bar proved to be round two for them, plus liquor. They didn't bother to talk to her, their mouths were too busy. But Reagan was glad to have someone to be with, even if they were pretty much ignoring her. She watched every tall man who came through the door, looking for Noah.

By midnight, Johnny was drunk and Candy Lee giggled even when he burped. Reagan said good-bye, lifted her backpack over one shoulder, and walked down to the Golden Nugget. She figured she looked more like a runaway than a businesswoman. Not even the panhandlers asked her for money.

One good thing about Las Vegas, it never closed. She played penny slots for a while, then ate breakfast and watched the people. After living in a town where she knew almost everyone, it seemed strange to watch hundreds of people go by and not see a face she knew.

About four the crowd changed. Gone were the sightseers and the partiers. In the hours before dawn, all that were left were the hard-core gamblers, the druggies and drunks, and the hookers. Reagan felt like she'd flipped the brightly colored beast over and was looking at the scarred, dirty underbelly. If a gambler or drunk wasn't depressed yet, he would be by this time of morning.

At five, she strapped her backpack back on again and caught a cab to the airport. She decided she'd rather wait outside the airport than see anymore. By dawn, she was heading home.

She slept until Dallas, then got a large coffee to wait out the two hours for a flight to Amarillo. The romantic weekend had been a total bust. She'd seen Noah, but he hadn't seen her. She'd thought they'd laugh and make love, then order pizza delivered to the hotel and talk until dawn. He'd ask about everyone back home and she'd want to know the details of every rodeo. But that didn't happen.

She'd called every hotel he'd ever mentioned staying at and a few he hadn't mentioned.

No Noah.

He'd told her once that he always stayed in good hotels where desk clerks didn't give out room numbers because he liked using his own name.

She'd tried everything to get into the contestants' parking, but short of breaking in at gunpoint, she saw no way. He hadn't been at the bar where Candy Lee thought he would be, so wherever Noah went after the rodeo, he was probably sleeping late and not even aware she'd searched for him.

The only good thing she knew for a fact was that he hadn't been hurt. He'd had the best time on his ride, pushing him up in the rankings. She only wished she'd been there to celebrate with him. He hadn't even looked at the crowd when he'd walked out after his ride. His head had been down as if he'd lost, and half the crowd wasn't on their feet cheering. The wide grin and one hand reaching for the heavens were gone; Noah seemed to be only doing a job.

Reagan closed her eyes and smiled, remembering how they used to celebrate with a warm root beer and a bag of Oreos. He'd be talking and driving through the night toward home and she'd have her feet on the dashboard tapping with the song on the radio. Once they'd stopped for a malt and almost gotten in a fight with the locals. Big Biggs was just a thug then and joined their side of the fight just for the hell of it.

As she waited in the crowded DFW airport, Reagan forced herself to stay awake. If she fell asleep at the gate, no one would wake her up until closing time, and she'd miss her flight.

Checking her phone, she found two missed calls since she'd turned it off at six. She didn't recognize the number, but since she'd agreed to host the poker game for charity, people were always calling.

Another reason she'd wanted to get away from home for a few days. Hosting a game was turning into a part-time job.

Reagan called the number and someone who sounded more asleep than awake growled a hello.

"This is Reagan Truman. You call—"

"Just a minute. I'll get him." The voice still didn't sound friendly.

A moment later Noah's voice came through loud and clear. "Rea. Is this you? I'm sorry I'm calling so early but I wanted you to know I won last night."

She almost yelled that she knew. "That's great."

"Yeah, I lost my phone again so I borrowed a friend's who crashed here last night. This win could mean big money, Rea."

"Where are you, Noah?"

"I'm at the Hampton in Vegas, as always. It's quieter than any of the hotels with casinos." He lowered his voice. "You don't sound so good, Rea. Did I wake you? Are you sick or something?"

"No." She managed to keep from saying that she knew he was lying. "I just didn't get much sleep last night." She'd called the Hampton twice last night and asked to be put through to Noah McAllen's room. She'd gotten the same answer both times. No one under that name was staying with them.

"Not me." He laughed. "I must be getting old or something. I was in bed by midnight. A horse danced on my hat last night, so I thought I'd go shopping this morning. Wish you were here."

"Me too." She couldn't stop the tears from rolling down her face.

"You sure you're all right, Rea?"

"Just missing you," she whispered.

"Me too," he said. "I love you, you know that, don't you?"

"I know."

"While I'm out shopping, I'll buy a phone and text you my new number."

"All right."

"I have to go. I promise I'll be home soon as I can. One of these days I'll climb off this merry-go-round and hang around long enough for you to get sick of me."

"Someday," she whispered.

She hung up without remembering if either of them said the final good-bye.

Reagan wasn't sure how long she stared at the phone. Finally the last call for her flight shook her enough to make her jump. She tossed her coffee and ran to board. All she wanted to do was go home.

When she slid into her seat next to the window, she pulled her jacket over her and closed her eyes, wanting to dream about the days when she and Noah were best friends. When he'd teased her and made her laugh and never lied to her. When she believed that he really loved her.

An hour later when the plane landed, Big Biggs was there waiting for her. He picked her up in his strong arms and gave her the hug she needed. In truth, she barely remembered calling him just before she'd silenced her phone. He was her one friend who never asked questions before standing on her side of any fight.

Reagan tried to smile, but he saw right through her pretend bravery. "What did that bum of a cowboy do to you this time? I swear I'll knock that oatmeal he's got for brains right out of his head this time."

Now Reagan smiled. "He didn't do anything, but thanks for the offer. I might remind you of your plan one day."

"It's been a standing offer for years, Reagan. In fact, you're probably the only reason he's alive today. Course, you're the reason I want to kill him too. He's never known what a treasure he's had in you."

She stood on her toes and kissed Big's cheek. "I love you, Big."

"I know. I'm downright adorable. My Ester tells me I should be the first human cloned; then there would be more me's to go around."

They walked toward his truck. "Where is Ester?"

"She pulled an all-night shift in the emergency room last night. I had some vacation coming so I'd already planned to take off today and cuddle in with her. When you called, she told me to come on over and get you so she could get a few hours' sleep. I promised to wake her when I get home."

"Got time to buy me breakfast before we head back?" she asked, knowing the answer.

"Sure. I'm starving. Only you're buying. I'm saving my money for the game. My grandmother says every room in town is booked with poker players coming in. The ones staying at the bed-and-breakfast are already playing every night to practice. If Ester works another night shift, I might go over and get a little practice in too. Martha Q makes them play for toothpicks 'cause she swears she won't allow nothing illegal to happen at Winter's Inn."

Reagan raised an eyebrow. She'd never thought of Martha Q as the "by the letter" type.

Big blushed. "The crazy owner told me she was too old to get arrested and have to use a toilet in front of jail guards."

Reagan fought to get the image out of her mind. "I didn't know you were a poker player, Big."

"I'm not, but I plan to stay around eating barbecue and drinking beer while I watch all the fools I work with lose. A twenty-dollar buy-in will be worth the price. Half the men on my road crew think they're born to gamble."

Reagan climbed into his pickup and they stopped to eat at the first truck stop out of Amarillo. She told him about the trip and how it was all her fault. Big, as usual, didn't believe a word she said and swore it was all Noah's problem.

She didn't tell Big about Noah saying he'd been at the Hampton when she'd checked and he hadn't been registered.

When they started home, Big pulled an old blanket from

behind his seat and she curled up against the window and went to sleep. The rocking of the truck, the warmth of the day, and the comfort of knowing she was safe let her relax into dreamless slumber.

The next morning Truman Orchard business took all her energy. Planning a fund-raiser is no easy job, but having a successful one was almost unheard of in the history of Harmony, and Reagan had to do it on top of all her normal workload.

A dozen people had offered to help, and all wanted to be kept informed on every detail. Around it all she had a business to run, and they'd be moving into their busy season soon.

Since the day she'd made it home, Reagan had tried not to think. Logic told her not to dwell on Noah's deliberate lie. She just worked.

Chapter 13

DELANEY FARM

DUSTI STRETCHED OUT IN THE KITCHEN'S BAY WINDOW AND alternated between watching her sister bake pies and staring out the window down Rainbow Lane.

Her great-grandfather had walked up on this land a hundred years ago and seen a rainbow over the lake. The house might be falling down around their ears now and the barn needed major patching, but this little spot had been her home all her life.

She dreamed of traveling and living other places, but she couldn't sell the land for her dream any more than Abby could sell it to reach hers. They had to find another way, and this one poker game just might be that way.

It was an hour past time for her poker lesson, and Kieran hadn't shown up yet. She wasn't sure whether she missed him or was simply angry that he'd skipped a lesson he'd promised to teach her this morning.

"What's the matter with you?" Abby tossed a cracked egg at her.

Dusti made no effort to catch it. She just stared at the spot on her knee where the yolk exploded. "Nothing," she said, answering the same question for the third time.

Abby lifted another fresh egg and took aim.

"Just the cracked ones," Dusti yelled from five feet away. "Remember what Mom said."

Both girls laughed, obviously sharing the memory of an argument they'd had one morning when they'd been small. Neither could recall what had started the disagreement, but four dozen eggs lay splattered around them like deformed sunflowers in the dirt when their mother had stopped the fight.

"We were still in grade school. We didn't know eggs meant money." Abby smiled. "I swear I started gathering eggs the day after I learned to walk."

Dusti nodded. "You told Mom they were all cracked the day of the great egg fight. She made you clean the coops for a week for lying and another for fighting."

Abby went back to her baking. "She grounded you from swimming for starting the fight."

"I never thought that was fair." Dusti wiped off her jeans. "Why'd she think I started it?"

"Because you always start the fights, Dusti." Abby reached for the small pitcher full of wooden spoons, obviously picking out another weapon to keep handy if the ingredients ran out. "I remember the twenty-six months of my life before you came along. I was an only child, not knowing how great the title was until I lost it. No one yelled at me. No groundings. No fights. The world was a peaceful place before you were born."

"You think you had it bad. Imagine being me and finding out my parents had already tried having a kid and failed at the job. I can just see Pop looking at Mom and saying, 'Surely we can do better the second time. I'm afraid, dear, we'll have to sleep together again.' Then, I come out and you take on the job of bossing me around."

The argument they'd loved for as long as either could remember was on. Pie ingredients and insults flew back and forth in rapid fire along with wooden spoons, eggs, and tin pans.

Dusti didn't notice the back door had opened until it was too late to stop a pie pan in flight.

Kieran took the blow to his forehead without ducking. He just stood like a statue watching two grown women covered in eggs and flour. Calmly, he looked around as white dust settled. "I guess I must be too late for breakfast."

Abby and Dusti both tried to act as if they weren't covered in ingredients, but it was hopeless. Both doubled over laughing.

When Dusti finally got control enough to look at the big Scot, she saw blood dripping from the pie pan wound. "You're hurt? Oh, Abby, you hurt him."

"I hurt him? You threw the pan."

"But you started the fight."

He touched the blood on his forehead, brushing it into his hair of almost the same color. "I'm sorry," he said simply. "This is my first encounter with insane country cooking. We must not get that channel back East."

The New Yorker in him was in full control as he added, "It's probably on the same cable as mud fishing and distance barfing."

Another pie pan sailed through the air. Kieran had the sense to duck this time.

Dusti stared at Abby, who, of course, looked innocent. "Don't aim for the head. You've got to leave him with enough brains to teach me to play poker."

Abby curtsied. "So sorry. Want me to patch you up, Mr. O'Toole?"

"No, he's my teacher, I'll put the Band-Aid on him." Dusti took his hand and tugged him into the downstairs bathroom. The little powder room was barely big enough for them both to stand.

Pushing him down on the stool covered to match the rose-colored shag carpet, Dusti stood between his legs and opened the door to the medicine cabinet behind his head. "When we were growing up, we called this the hospital. If one of us got hurt, this was where we came. Scrapes were so common, Mom didn't want to waste time or get blood on the stairs so she kept everything needed for doctoring here."

Kieran didn't say a word. In fact, he didn't move while she cleaned the small cut and doctored it with antiseptic. When she leaned to turn the water off in the sink, her leg brushed the inside of his thigh and she felt the muscles tighten. As she set the first-aid kit back above him, the side of her breast brushed his cheek. Again, he froze.

"Are you all right?" He looked strong as a linebacker, but maybe he was one of those people who fainted at the sight of his own blood. "The cut wasn't deep. In fact, it's stopped bleeding. I don't think you really need the Band-Aid."

"I'm not worried about the cut." The hint of the Highlander was in his voice. "I'm just not used to being so close to the nurses."

Leaning back, she looked down at him. "Does my being so close to you bother you, Kieran?"

"No," he answered, staring at her face. "But I'll admit *you* bother me, Dusti. You always have."

She didn't lean away. "That why you told your creepy cousin that you were afraid of me?"

"I *am* afraid of you." Before she could react, his hand brushed upward along her leg. "Even covered in this mess, you bother me, lass."

He brushed flour off the side of her shirt, then rested his hand in the spot he'd cleaned. She could feel his warm palm moving along her ribs to the side of her breast. "When you're near I forget which way is north. It took me a year to ask you out and you turned me down in five seconds."

"My mother was ill," she said.

His hand kept moving over her shirt, almost touching, as he continued to torture her. "And the second and third time?"

Dusti closed her eyes. "I can't think with you doing that."

The urge to kiss him almost buckled her knees, but she remembered he'd said he'd let her know when he wanted to kiss her.

Slowly, he straightened to his full height, suddenly making the room seem very, very small. He moved his hands up her body as he stood so close she could feel the heat of him even through both their clothes. He bent, picking up the towel she'd used to wash the cut, and began blotting flour and egg from her face.

Keeping her eyes closed tight, she let the feeling of being cared for, cared about, pass over her for the first time in a very long time.

He picked bits of eggshell from her hair and soaked the towel in warm water before moving slowly over her face and down the V of her shirt. His touch was gentle, like he was treasuring her, like she was priceless.

When she lifted her gaze, she saw the passion in his gray eyes. The room must be running out of air. They'd pass out at any moment, like miners trapped in a cave. He didn't seem to notice. His hand, wrapped in the corner of a towel, moved feather light down over her shirt, making her ache for a more intimate touch.

"You going to kiss me now?" she whispered.

He dropped the towel as his hands circled her waist. With one tug she was against him from chest to knee, and it felt so good.

It had been so long since she'd been so on fire for a man. They'd have to do it standing up, but if he wanted her, the tiny room would have to work. She wasn't sure she could wait until they ran up a flight of stairs to her room in the attic.

She leaned closer, opening her mouth, dying for the feel of his lips on hers.

But Kieran pulled away.

Patience was never a high card in her deck. "Aren't you going to kiss me?" She had other things in mind, but she'd start with one long "turn to jelly" kiss.

"No. I was just cleaning you up so we can play poker. I wouldn't want the deck getting dirty." His hand slid below her waist to her hip and he gently patted her as if hurrying her along.

The man patted her bottom!

If she'd had another pie pan he'd need more than a Band-Aid to cover his next injury.

In one glance she realized he had no trouble reading her thoughts.

"First lesson," he said as he moved to the door of the bathroom. "Never show your emotions. Never let another player see you upset. If you do, he's just found the way to control you and the game."

Dusti turned her violent nature inward. If she had a pie pan she'd beat it on her own head. In fact, she'd become a one-woman band. All her wild Saturday nights, all her "going to sin city" in the back of some guy's car hadn't prepared her for Kieran O'Toole.

If he played another trick like that one, she'd go out of her mind. How was she going to sit across from him and play cards?

Right now she didn't care about poker. She wanted revenge. Apparently she'd asked the Loch Ness Monster to teach her to play. He might want her showing no emotion while he turned her on and walked away, but Dusti wasn't built that way.

Who knew, maybe he was simply torturing her to death for turning him down for a date three times in a row.

Dusti smiled. Two could play the torture game, and this time she had skills. This time he'd be the first to fold.

She might not know poker, but she knew flirting. She considered herself world class even if she hadn't played in a while.

Chapter 14

DELANEY FARM

WHEN DUSTI FINALLY FOUND ENOUGH CONTROL TO LEAVE the bathroom, she was surprised to see Austin Hawk standing in the open front doorway. He was dressed like he'd just made a cameo appearance on *Wilderness Journey*. His hair needed cutting and his beard looked to be three or four days old. For an unfriendly type, he still looked sexy.

She must be so sex-starved even the local recluse looked appealing.

Two good-looking men in her house at the same time was definitely overdosing. Only Austin wasn't shy, he fell more into unsociable territory. He'd been back at Hawk House for weeks this time and barely did more than wave at them when he walked across their front yard to the garage where he stored his Jeep or boat, depending on which one he wasn't using.

They'd charged him double the usual rate to use one of the storage barns. Abby thought he looked like the kind of man who kept bodies pickled in his basement, but Dusti was willing to give him the benefit of the doubt since he had been a nice kid a dozen years back. Only nice had vanished along with his pimples.

"May I help you, Austin?" She fought the urge to pick up the rifle kept stored on the hallway bookshelf. Austin was big like Kieran, but Austin was dark, moody, haunting. Whereas the Scot looked fit, Austin Hawk looked hard. Like sometime between the days that he'd been a boy running about the lake and now, he seemed to have had parts replaced and was more machine than human.

"I'm here to see Kieran," he said, as if she were no more than a voice box near the doorbell. "He texted me to come over."

"Oh, sure." She relaxed a fraction. "Come on in. I think he's in the kitchen." Dusti was glad to pass the guy along. Let the Scot, who'd probably never get around to kissing her, handle Hawk.

Austin followed her past the powder room to the kitchen. She just stood silent at the door and let him step around her and stare at the chaos before him. No explanation for the mess came to mind for flour, sugar, and eggs to be everywhere.

He finally looked at her. "Smells good," he said, as if stating a fact and not paying a compliment.

"Thanks. We're baking pies for the livestock auction lunch tomorrow. They always order twenty buttermilk."

He nodded as if the world made sense.

Dusti decided she liked Austin Hawk. After all, he wasn't feeling her up and refusing to kiss her. On today's scorecard that made him the winner.

A moment later, Ronny came through the back door with Abby. They were laughing about the chickens.

For just a flicker, Dusti caught something in Hawk's eyes. One look that vanished as quickly as it had sparked, but it told her something.

Austin Hawk had eyes for no one but Ronny Logan, and Dusti doubted the woman even knew it.

While she scratched Hawk off the list of eligible men in the world, her Scot stepped into the room. Suddenly, the kitchen seemed way too small for them all. Dusti swore she could feel Kieran's hands on her even though he was five feet away.

Kieran moved, not toward her, but next to Austin, and the men shook hands.

"Thanks for coming. Ronny said you'd act as dealer this morning so she could help with the pies." Kieran moved the couple toward the dining room table. "Sorry we're getting off to a late start. My grandmother had a guest this morning." He smiled and looked at Ronny. "Your mother came by to pay a call."

Ronny took her seat without looking up at anyone. "I'm glad you stayed with your grandmother. My mother tends to eat the weak."

No one laughed. They'd all been around Harmony long enough to know Ronny's words were true.

Then, as if a bell had sounded, everyone except Ronny began talking at once. All wanted to change the subject.

Austin asked if anyone had seen the wild hogs.

Kieran picked up the deck of cards and said as he removed the jokers, "I found the deck. We're all here finally," as if they'd been lost. "Maybe we should get started."

Dusti offered everyone coffee and promised the first pie out of the oven as a snack during break time, as if poker games always had snack time halfway through the game.

Ronny finally raised her head and smiled gratefully at all of them.

The lesson began with Austin dealing and Ronny circling by to watch now and then. Kieran explained all the rules again as if this were the first lesson, Dusti took it all in, nodding to let him know when she remembered a rule.

By the time Abby brought in slices of warm pie, Dusti had decided she could learn this game . . . along with whatever other ones the Scot wanted to play.

In the end, he'd be the one begging for a kiss and, who knows, for once in her life, she might be the one walking away.

Chapter 15

TRUMAN FARM

ONE OF THE MEN LAYING PIPE FOR IRRIGATION IN A NEW section of the orchard stopped by Reagan's office to tell her he'd seen an old Chevy drive onto her land and park at the house.

Reagan stood. Trucks, tractors, and mail cars weren't unusual, but none of the hands drove an old Chevy. Every man who worked for her knew she didn't like company. She always took the news with a frown.

"Have any idea who it was, Joe?"

"A woman. Not from around here."

Reagan was already moving to the open barn door. "How'd you know?"

"Drove right up to the front door."

Reagan waved good-bye to the volunteers running off rules for the Texas Hold'em tournament. Everyone knew her office was in the barn, and she'd be there or roaming around the orchard from dawn till dusk, so whoever had come to call in the Chevy must be lost or selling something.

As she walked across the yard, Reagan remembered how

run-down the old place had once seemed. She'd been a runaway looking for someplace that would let her work. Old Jeremiah had taken her in and paid her wages along with room and board, but he'd made her go to school. He'd treated her like she was worth something long before she even believed she was. She'd lied about being his niece, and he'd taken the lie and made it true.

The last Truman. That was what folks called her. If her dream of being with Noah didn't work out, she'd stay on this farm and be the last Truman until the day she died. Like the apple trees, her roots dug deep into this earth.

As Reagan passed the beat-up Chevy, she saw the dents and bald tires. Mud was caked across the back and front so thick she couldn't even see a license plate. Whoever owned the car wasn't taking care of it and didn't care what kind of shape it was in.

Looking up, she saw a woman only a year or two older than she was, twenty-five at most, sitting on the porch. She looked the kind of tired that settles into people who run double time through life like it's a race. Her hair needed fresh color. Her western clothes were wrinkled and stained.

"May I help you?" Reagan asked.

"You Reagan Truman?" The woman stood, looking unsure of herself.

"I am," Reagan said as the smell of cigarette smoke reached her. She must have been smoking as she drove, because the odor seemed baked into her clothes.

"I heard tell you know Noah McAllen. That right?"

Dread settled into the pit of her stomach. Whoever this woman was, whatever she wanted, it couldn't be good. "We've been friends since high school. How can I help you?"

"I don't need no help, miss, I just stopped to drop off something that belongs to Noah." She straightened, apparently relieved to have reached the end of her journey.

Reagan let out a breath. Maybe he left his bag or a rope somewhere. "Whatever it is, I'll see he gets it when he comes back to town."

"You do that, honey. You keep it for him 'cause I sure as

hell ain't taking it home with me. My husband would throw a fit."

Reagan waited as the woman walked to her car. Somehow the blonde didn't seem the Good Samaritan type. She reminded Reagan of the women she'd stood with at the gate in Las Vegas. A party-hard woman looking for a one-night stand with a rodeo cowboy.

It took the woman a few tries to get the back door of the Chevy open, and then she leaned in and pulled out a box.

Reagan recognized the logo on the side. Truman Orchard.

"Noah don't know about this, but I listed him on the paperwork. It's his even if he was probably too drunk to remember what we did."

As she swung around, Reagan saw the blue blankets and knew what was inside one of her custom-built apple boxes.

A baby.

Announcing his arrival, the baby cried out.

The mother didn't seem to notice. She simply set the box on the porch and faced Reagan. "I don't want to ever see it again. I got three others of my own to raise. The last thing I need is a bastard to feed. You see Noah gets the baby and tell him never to contact me. It'd only mean trouble."

"But . . ." A hundred questions logpiled in Reagan's mind. "You can't leave a baby with me."

The blonde frowned. "Look, lady, I've traveled three days looking for someone who knew Noah. Some rodeo clown told me he grew up in Harmony. Every person I ran into when I hit town and asked if they knew him clammed up like they was protecting a god. Finally I said I was really looking for Noah's Reagan, and they pointed me this way. Truman Orchard, just like the boxes say that I noticed Noah packs his gear in." She frowned at Reagan as if preparing for a fight. "You said you knew him. Well, you gotta keep what's his. I told you. I ain't taking that kid home."

Reagan wasn't buying her story. This could be a trick or someone's idea of a sick joke. "How'd you know my name?"

The woman's grin was wicked. "Easy, honey, that's the

name he called me when we was together. Never even asked
if I had a name."

The woman took a step toward her car.

Reagan blocked her way. "You can't just leave your baby.
You'll be sorry. You'll regret it. He's yours too, just as much
as your other kids. He's got a right to know who you are."

"No, I won't miss him, honey, and he ain't got no rights.
That kid ain't mine as far as anyone knows. I hid the preg-
nancy as long as I could, then I told my husband my sister was
sick. I birthed him in an overcrowded hospital using a
made-up name my sister thought sounded like a rodeo queen's
name."

She let out a long breath that smelled of cigarettes and
coffee. "I don't want nothing tying me to this kid. He ain't
mine. You get that? He was just a mistake I made one night,
and I don't plan on paying for it the rest of my life."

"But Noah will know who you are. He'll find you." Reagan felt like she was holding the pieces of her heart together.
She couldn't deal with what she was learning about Noah.
Not now. Not here in front of this woman. Reagan refused to
worry about herself while she dealt with this crazy woman.
One of them had to think of the baby. The baby had a right
to know who his mother was.

The blonde shook her head. "I'm betting he don't remember the night, much less me. I was just out collecting a bull
rider as a trophy, thinking I deserved a night out to forget
everything but having fun. I didn't even tell him my first
name or where I was from, and he didn't bother asking." For
a blink the woman seemed to see Reagan, really see her.
"You know him. You said you did. Give him the kid, and
then, if I was you, honey, I'd get as far away from him as you
can. He's a man riding for hell and he'll take you with him."

"But . . ."

"No *but*s, just deliver the box. Tell Noah I named the kid
Utah. Maybe he'll know why. Maybe he won't."

Reagan shook her head. None of this could be true. Noah
had promised her he would never cheat on her. She knew he

drank, but he always went home alone. He always said he loved her, only her.

Maybe someone wanted to hurt Noah, taint his reputation. Maybe this wasn't the last she'd see of the woman in the Chevy. She'd come back wanting money or her fifteen minutes of fame.

Her belief in Noah fought the doubts she couldn't shake. Reagan didn't know this Noah. The man who walked away from a great ride without raising his hand to the crowd. The man who lied.

The car flew down the drive toward Lone Oak Road, sending dust flying.

The woman didn't look back. She wasn't coming back. Reagan knew it all the way to her bones.

Reagan had to get control of her emotions. She had to deal with what was real. The baby was real. Whether he was Noah's or a plot to get money, she didn't know.

Reagan watched the Chevy disappear along with all her dreams of what might have been. Two lies, she thought. Noah had lied to her twice. How many more were there that she didn't know about?

He was the first boy she'd trusted. The first man she'd loved. The only lover she'd ever had.

Only he hadn't loved her, at least not enough to stay true. She wanted to run to the orchard and curl up among the roots. She wanted to cry so hard she had no feeling at all left inside her.

Only, a baby in a box was already doing that.

Reagan forced her body to move. She picked up the box and walked into the house. She knew she'd have to call the sheriff but hesitated. Alex Matheson was Noah's sister. Everyone in the county would know about the baby.

The town's hero would tumble to the dirt before anyone even knew if the story of the woman in the Chevy was true. If others knew what had just happened here, right or wrong, Noah would never live down the gossip, and neither would the child. Little Utah would walk with the scar all his life.

Reagan picked up the tiny bundle and the crying stopped.

Two letters lined the box. One was a birth certificate listing the mother as Marilyn Stardust, twenty-four, homeless, and the father as Noah McAllen of Harmony, Texas.

Reagan let tears roll down her eyes as she saw the birthday. Utah was exactly twenty-one days old. The same age she'd been when her mother abandoned her.

Chapter 16

HAWK HOUSE

For the second night in a row Austin Hawk dressed in black and joined an organized hunt for wild hogs. At first he'd thought there was only one big boar roaming the area near the lake, but a farmer on the other side of Rainbow Lane said he'd seen three, maybe four plus piglets. They'd also found half-eaten remains of a half-grown pig.

Wild hogs have been known to eat their young or any other animal weak from sickness or injury. They were on the move and hungry.

As he walked among the trees behind his house, Austin listened. The game warden had told everyone who'd met yesterday to join the hunt that he'd been down in south Texas a few years ago when wild hogs charged a hunting party.

One man hesitated to run or shoot and was gouged in the leg. All he got out was, "I've been hit," before he passed out. He was dead before anyone could get a tourniquet on his leg.

Against the warden's advice, Austin decided to hunt alone. All his years on the army's special oil fire units, he'd worked as part of a team. Now he didn't want to trust anyone with his life. Or maybe, he decided, it was more that he didn't want anyone else to trust him.

The memory of being the only one to survive ate away at him. Had he missed something? Could he have done more? They were all highly trained professionals going in to fight the fire. They went in together. They came out together. They lived and died together.

Only one time, the last time, that hadn't happened.

Austin pulled his mind from the dark place he'd had to fight to keep from living in since he woke up in the hospital badly burned, but alive . . . the only one alive.

As he stepped from the trees walking toward Rainbow Lane, he thought of the night he and Ronny had pulled Dallas Logan out of the mud. The knowledge that Ronny had grown up with such a dominant mother bothered him. Ronny was one of those gentle souls. Hell, she probably shooed spiders out of the house. He didn't like to think of her in the same county as the bossy woman he'd met that night in the rain.

He'd heard of people like Ronny, but he couldn't ever remember meeting one. As a kid he'd had bossy housekeepers who were usually fired by his father long before Austin ever got attached to them. Once he was in the army, girls like Ronny didn't hang around the bars near the forts. The only women he'd known since he'd joined up were one-night stands. The kind who were just passing time, not falling in love.

Hell, half of them didn't bother to say good-bye at dawn.

The rustle of leaves pulled Austin to full alert. He raised his rifle and looked through the scope.

A squirrel jumped from one branch to another.

Austin forced tight muscles to relax. He should have slept in this morning and not gone with Ronny over to the Delaney place. Two sleepless nights in a row couldn't be smart. Only he hadn't said no to the gentle lady; he wasn't sure he ever could. Even when he snapped at her accidentally, she saw right through him. If he thought about it much, he'd probably decide that he was far more afraid of her than she'd probably ever be of him.

He might have been in the army, but she'd grown up in a combat zone.

But this morning Austin told himself he really had no choice but to go along with Ronny. When she asked him if he wanted to deal cards, it was either go with her or worry about her crossing the lake alone. Plus, sitting next to her had been pure pleasure. Though he was polite, almost formal during the practice session, his thoughts were definitely R-rated about what he had planned as soon as they got back to the other side of the lake.

The few kisses they'd shared still cluttered his thoughts. He might have been the one who kissed her at first, but she'd taken it to a new level. He knew she must have been thinking about him also, and wondered if she wanted more as much as he did.

She wasn't some girl just out of high school. She was full grown, maybe a few years older than he was. When they'd talked she'd said something about living with a guy who left her. If she wanted a little action, he had no objection. It might even be good for him, but still he hesitated. Ronny wouldn't be easy to walk away from.

He could feel a habit coming on and he wasn't a man who carried habits in his luggage.

Maybe it was the innocence in her eyes, or the way she stared at him as if afraid to trust. He had a feeling, no matter how much he thought about it, he wouldn't be making the next move. She would.

Still, as he'd dealt cards in the Delaney dining room, he thought of later when he'd have Ronny alone. Several times she'd accidentally brushed against him, stirring up his brain like a cement mixer. He was lucky he had enough sense left to deal. All he could think about was later.

Only there was no later after the game. She'd let the Delaneys talk her into helping them make pies. They'd promised to watch her cross safely before dark.

Since they hadn't invited him to join them, he'd hiked along the border of the lake to his place looking for any sign of hogs. All he found was the game warden waiting at his door.

Before dark Austin joined the hunt again and tried to forget about what might have happened if he and Ronny had come back together. He might not be spending his second night plowing through brush and mud looking for pigs.

A sound pulled him to full alert.

In the quarter moon he saw two more hunters walking the fence line across the road. They were lanky and thin, with rifles carried carelessly over their shoulders like baseball bats. The two sons of the farmer. Austin had complained that they were too young to be on the hunt, but the farmer said they could go as long as they promised to stay on his land.

Austin swore. They were making so much noise they weren't likely to come across any animal in the night except roadkill. At least the farmer had been smart enough to make them walk. Maybe they'd get tired and quit.

He melted back into the shadows, not wanting the boys to see him and decide to tag along with him. The plan was that they'd stay on their side of the road and he'd patrol the land between Rainbow Lane and the lake.

As the boys' footfalls faded, the night came alive with sounds. Most he recognized. Carefully, Austin stepped to the edge of the shadows and focused on a clearing. Something was rummaging through roots near where Ronny's old road used to be. It could be a raccoon, or an armadillo. It could be wild hogs heading in his direction.

Austin stood his ground and raised his rifle. They'd have to move out into the clearing in order to keep moving. If it was hogs, he'd take his best shot then.

He knew he could get off two, maybe three shots before they could turn and run back, or reach him if they charged. If they didn't see him, he could swing up in the oak behind him and fire from there. He was a good enough shot to get them all.

As they drew closer, there was no doubt there were hogs coming toward him. They were ripping through everything in their path, snorting and eating as they came closer to the clearing.

Austin waited until he had a clean shot at all three. A huge reddish-brown boar was in the front, with two sows that had to weigh three hundred pounds each behind him. They'd been living off this land for a year, maybe more. If so, there were more pigs than three, he'd bet on it.

Just as he lowered his rifle and raised his hand to grab the nearest branch to swing up, the boar saw him and grunted as if sounding the alarm. The hog probably smelled him more than saw him, but Austin wasn't taking any chances.

He swung up, holding tight to his rifle. As his feet left the ground he heard shots, and for a second he thought the hogs were somehow firing at him.

Fire plowed through his leg halfway between his knee and hip.

The pain skimmed across his nerve endings and he lost his hold on the branch. He tumbled back into the muddy grass, fighting to keep from screaming.

The hogs didn't have guns. Someone, somewhere had fired and hit him by mistake. But the hogs were heading toward him now at full speed, as if they smelled fresh blood and wanted the main course. He had no time to think of the pain in his leg or where the bullet came from. If he wanted to stay alive, he had to act fast.

Austin rolled to his stomach, raised his rifle, and fired. One. Two. Three. The earth stopped rumbling as the last wild hog fell.

Rolling over, flat in the grass, he listened to the farmer's sons shouting as they ran toward him.

"I got one! I know I got one!" a boy's voice not low enough to be a man's shouted.

Austin tried to control his breathing, hoping it might slow the blood pumping out of his leg.

He heard horses traveling fast toward him. The warden and Kieran would reach him soon.

They'd know what to do, he kept saying in his mind.

They'd stop the bleeding. The last thing he wanted was the boy who shot him to try first aid.

Voices coming from several directions filled the night. He waited. Trying to stay calm. Trying to picture Ronny beside him. He should have kissed her one more time. He should have told her how she made him feel. He should have . . .

For a few minutes the air stilled and he was barely aware of the men around him. Kieran's big shadow. The warden shouting orders.

One tied his leg. Told him to hang on. Another called 911.

"Hold tight, Hawk," the warden kept shouting. "We'll get you to the hospital."

He tried to nod, but it seemed too much effort. Just before he passed out, he reached for Ronny's hand, but she wasn't there. She'd vanished into the blackness closing in on him.

Austin welcomed the silence. He'd been here before, far beyond where he could hear the world.

Chapter 17

TRUMAN FARM

REAGAN SAT IN THE PARLOR OF THE OLD FARMHOUSE HOLDING a sleeping baby in her arms. Joe, one of the first employees she'd hired when she started her business, might not speak much English, but he came running when he heard the baby crying.

He didn't ask questions, just called his wife. They knew babies. They had six of their own. Maria came with bottles, formula, diapers, and simple little gowns. She showed Reagan what to do, laughing and talking so fast Reagan only caught every third word.

Maria called the baby "Hoot-ah."

For the first time since Uncle Jeremiah's death, Reagan forgot about work. There was far too much to do. She caught herself looking down the road for the old Chevy to return. Surely the woman would think it over and come back.

No Chevy came.

At dusk, Reagan carried baby Utah to the chairs facing west and watched the dying sun. "Maybe your momma will come back tomorrow, Utah. She loves you, I'm sure she does. She'll come back and get you, you'll see."

Tears rolled down Reagan's cheeks as she realized she was passing on a story she'd told herself all her life.

She held the baby closer. "I'll keep you here with me till she comes. I'll watch over you and see that nothing bad happens to you."

Blue eyes looked up at her. His tiny finger wrapped around the tip of hers, holding on tightly.

"We'll shake on it. All right, Utah?" She stared out at her land. Tomorrow she'd take him in to the doctor. She'd tell everyone she was just keeping him until his mom got back. It was a lie she almost believed.

When Reagan finally took the sleeping baby upstairs, she put him back in the apple box. "If your mother doesn't come back tomorrow, I'll ask Maria if I can borrow a baby bed and more clothes," she promised as she kissed him good night. "Your momma will come back tomorrow. Once she sleeps on it, she'll know she needs you, and we'll see that Chevy coming right back up the road flying this direction."

Only tomorrow came without a Chevy driving onto Truman land.

By the third day Reagan was a pro at taking care of Utah. She carried him in front of her as he slept and she got ready for the biggest fund-raiser to come along in years. They walked in the orchard and Reagan found herself talking to Utah as if he could understand her words.

Everyone asked about the baby, and she simply said a friend had dropped him off while she had surgery.

Another lie, Reagan thought. She was getting as good as Noah.

Somehow, her anger at Noah settled into loss. Maybe because she didn't have time to think about it or maybe because of Utah. No matter how bad it hurt to think of Noah sleeping with another woman, Reagan couldn't bring herself to wish Utah didn't exist.

Reagan wanted to believe that the birth certificate with

Noah's name, the woman knowing her name was Reagan, and the apple box were no proof that the baby was Noah's. She could have made it all up just to find her baby what she thought would be a rich father. Maybe when her tricks didn't work with Noah, she'd driven to his hometown to try to find a relative to play the scheme on. Her plan might have been to try to milk money out of relatives. When that didn't work, all she wanted was to drop the baby off, and Reagan's farm sounded like a likely place.

But tiny brown eyes looking up at Reagan seemed to whisper that she was a fool. The woman hadn't tried to get money. In fact, she'd gone to some trouble to hide her name. Reagan hadn't even seen the car's tags to see what state she'd driven from.

Tiny brown eyes, she whispered. Just like Noah's.

On the fourth night of having Utah with her, Reagan finally got the nerve to open the letter tucked beside the birth certificate. It was addressed simply to *Utah* with a line below that read, *When you're old enough to read this—open it.*

The envelope hadn't been sealed. Reagan pulled out the note. It had been written on the back of a plain white paper napkin.

I'm doing what I think is best for both you and me. On a good day I'm not much of a mother, and on a bad day you'd be better off taking pot luck than getting stuck with me.

Don't try to find me. I won't claim you.

Have a good life, kid. Who knows, someday I'll see a cowboy named Utah riding bulls and know it's you. I gave you life, that's all I can do for you.

Reagan slowly folded the napkin. At least Utah would have this. She'd keep it for him.

Her cell rang and she picked it up without looking at the caller.

"Hello."

"Rea, you still up?" Noah's voice sounded loud and clear.

"I didn't ride tonight so thought I'd call just to talk. What's new?"

She couldn't tell him about the baby over the phone. "We're getting ready for the poker game this weekend. Two hundred signed up to buy in. I've borrowed every folding table in the county and we may have to use boxes for chairs."

Noah laughed, saying what she was doing sounded like fun.

"I wish you were here to deal. Finding dealers isn't easy." She knew she was rambling, but she was afraid if she gave talking too much thought she'd start telling him about Utah. "The Red Hat group asked if they could all wear their hats. I got Phil Gentry teaching them because he was the only one I could find who knew how to play but wasn't buying into the game." She kept it light. She wouldn't tell him about the baby over the phone. Over the phone, she wouldn't be able to look into his eyes and know whether he was lying or not. She could deal with anything but a lie. One more lie might just break her in half.

Noah's voice broke into her thoughts. "Why isn't Phil playing? My sister told me he used to run a game in his garage every week before she deputized him."

"The sheriff's office is working the party. They're hoping the three-beer rule will keep the fights down. Everything, including the beer, has been donated. Big says he's coming just for the food. Ribs, hamburgers, fried chicken, and baked ham. My whole loading dock will be set up as a buffet with cakes on one end and salads on the other."

Noah's voice hardened slightly. "You seeing a lot of Big?"

Reagan smiled. She'd figured out a long time ago that Noah wasn't worried about Big Biggs stealing his girl, but both men seemed to like keeping the rivalry going. "I'm seeing him," she admitted. "Went over to Ester's and his place last week for dinner, but I'm not kissing him anymore."

"Good. I wouldn't want my girl stepping out on me."

Noah's words sounded just like they always had—loving, teasing, caring—only they no longer made her feel loved.

She fought not to ask him why he'd lied to her. If the woman in the Chevy had been telling the truth, Noah had slept with her one night. Reagan had the proof sleeping in a bassinet beside her bed.

"When are you coming home?" Reagan needed to talk to him. She'd know the truth when she was face-to-face with him. Until then, she wouldn't mention the baby. She had to see Noah first. Had to see his eyes when he learned about the baby.

"Soon, Rea, I promise. I miss you so much. It's not like it used to be when I was with friends traveling around sharing food and gear. This is all business. I swear it's more like a job every day. Sometimes I feel stuck in a place like in the movie about the guy who has to live Groundhog Day over and over again. Half the time I barely know what town I'm in. I'm just eating, sleeping, and riding."

Reagan rested her finger lightly on the baby's hand. By instinct, Utah reached and circled the tip of her finger.

"We'll be waiting," she said.

Chapter 18

WALDEN CABIN

RONNY WAS ALMOST ASLEEP WHEN SHE THOUGHT SHE HEARD shots. For a moment, she curled up deeper into the covers, then climbed out of bed, frustrated that the shots had pulled her fully awake. She dressed in sweats and moved to the porch without turning on a light. If there had been shots, something must be going on near her cabin. Maybe the hog problem was over? Her fears would be too.

The night seemed cooler than usual and the slice of moon offered little light. Crawling onto the porch swing, she wondered if this might be the place she would settle, this little cabin near where she grew up but still away from everyone. It fit her more than an apartment in New York. Harmony was her home. Maybe it was time for her to step back into life. Marty would have wanted that.

Smiling, she remembered how during his last days, when his body was slowly shutting down, he'd talk of all his adventures as if she'd been there with him. "Remember the time we . . ." he'd start as he held her hand, taking her with him to a mountaintop or a jungle river or a dig in South

America. He'd been a man of the world who lived at full throttle and she'd been a mouse who'd never left home, but somehow they fit together.

A skiing accident had crushed his back and put him in a wheelchair. Yet he said the only thing in his life he would change was that he wished he'd found her earlier when he was whole and could have made love to her. He'd known the risks he was taking, but he hadn't known that she would be in his future. He hadn't realized his wild lifestyle would somehow cheat them both.

She remembered how his hands moved over her, sometimes in a gentle caress, but never in need.

Ronny smiled, recalling that she'd said kisses were enough, and they were. Every time he touched her, she felt loved. As he'd thinned and seemed to grow older by the day, she'd claimed she'd been with him for a lifetime.

Only it had been his lifetime, not hers.

In the black of the night, the memory of his hand gripping hers was no longer there. She'd felt him near after the funeral. All she'd had to do was close her eyes and she swore she could feel Marty beside her. He was there as she traveled, silently encouraging her to look for the wonder in the world at every stop. Whenever she was afraid or lonely, she'd feel his fingers lace with hers.

But now, the feel of his hand on hers was gone, and she couldn't even remember the last time it had been there. Somehow, he'd finally moved on and left her here. Left her with only memories, and memories weren't enough.

Tears bubbled over as she closed her eyes and reached for him, as if he would come back and watch over her.

Nothing. Not even wishing with all her heart could make it be real for one more night.

Like a hundred times before, the pain of his leaving tightened her heart. She might have shopped in Paris and had her hair cut by New York's best, but inside she was still the lonely child whose own mother hadn't loved her. The girl no one noticed. The woman whose life consisted of online accounting courses and crossword puzzles.

Marty had changed that forever, and now that she was back in Harmony, Ronny felt she didn't quite fit in her own skin.

A light flickered across the water, pulling her from her grief.

Ronny wiped away her tears and stood. The only person she could think of who might be coming to this side of the lake would be Austin. When he'd left the Delaneys' farm with Kieran, they'd been talking about wild hogs but she didn't know where he and Kieran had gone. Her little blue boat had still been docked, waiting for her, when she was ready to return home. She just assumed that he'd walked around the lake to his place or Kieran had driven him to the other side.

If it was Austin crossing the lake now, she'd go back inside. She couldn't see him tonight. Not when she'd been crying for Marty.

As she waited, she heard the *chug-chug* of the Delaneys' old engine. They'd come over once before after a storm to make sure her electricity was still on.

By the time they docked, Ronny had pulled on her tennis shoes and walked down to the water's edge.

Ronny barely noticed the water lapping over her shoes, soaking them with muddy water. She watched Dusti and Abby climb out of the boat. There must be trouble or they wouldn't be here.

"We wanted to come tell you," Dusti began. "Austin and a few others were out tonight hunting for hogs. Austin was behind his house almost to where Rainbow Lane turns in to your land. Kieran said he was on horseback traveling with the warden a quarter mile away when they heard the shots."

Dusti stared at her feet and Ronny stopped breathing.

"I don't know many facts, but Kieran called to say somehow Austin was hurt. They're taking him to the hospital now. He called from the ambulance headed into Harmony. Said there was a lot of blood, but Austin is breathing."

Ronny just stared.

They stood silent as the boat bumped against the weathered dock, making the ticking noise of an old clock in need of winding.

Finally, Abby broke the silence. "You want to go with us to the hospital? We won't be of any help there, but Dusti and I don't want to hang around here waiting for a call. Since Austin doesn't have any family that we know of, maybe they'd let us see him."

Ronny nodded and climbed into their boat.

No one talked as they moved over the lake. The normally calm water rocked the boat tonight and the willows blew in the wind, giving the place a haunted feeling as if trouble traveled with the moon.

The Delaneys' old border collie sat waiting, and greeted them with two barks when they pulled up.

Abby bent and patted his head. "Guard the house, Tippie, we'll be back soon."

They walked to a pickup with a faded logo of a rainbow on the driver's-side door. Ronny noticed every detail. The pickup door, the way the yard light creaked in the breeze, her mismatched sweats. Anything to keep from thinking about Austin bleeding.

As Abby drove through the night, Ronny thought of the way Austin's shoulders had felt all scarred from a burn. He hadn't hidden them from her or talked about them. They were simply a part of him. Now there would be other scars.

If he lived.

She fought down a scream. He'd live! He had to. There had to be a limit on the number of people one person can lose in a lifetime. She'd lost her father before she was grown. Marty before they married. And now maybe Austin, who'd made her feel alive for the first time in a year. It wasn't fair, but she didn't know where to mail the complaint.

Maybe she was the problem. She could go into business renting herself out as a girlfriend to anyone who wanted to commit suicide. One or two dates and you're sure to die. Kissing extra if you want to speed up the process.

She wrapped her arms around her body tightly. This was not the time to start cracking up. Maybe Austin needed her.

Ronny saw the lights of Harmony before she realized she hadn't brought along her purse or cell phone. But she had friends. The Delaney sisters were bookending her now.

The hospital parking lot was almost empty, as was the emergency room. A nurse told them that Austin Hawk was in surgery and they could wait in the family waiting area where it was quiet.

Abby was telling Ronny that the nurse shouldn't have given out any information to people who weren't family when they stepped into the little waiting area.

Kieran, a game warden, and two half-grown kids were all lined up on the back row of chairs, not saying a word.

The Scot stood and put his arm lightly around Dusti in almost a hug. Then he did the same to Abby and Ronny.

Dusti got to the point. "What happened?"

Kieran glanced at the two boys. "A stray bullet must have hit Austin. He was in front of the hogs. The shot came from behind them." He forced out the details. "Austin's got a few scrapes from hitting the ground hard. Even down, he fired off three shots and hit all three hogs coming toward him. The game warden said he didn't know if they were charging or just running away from the shot they heard. Pigs don't see well enough to know where the danger's coming from, they just hear or smell trouble and start running."

"A stray shot? That makes no sense," Dusti challenged. "I've lived on the lake all my life and never heard anyone shooting."

"The boys thought they were firing at a tree-climbing hog." Kieran lowered his voice as a middle-aged farmer entered the room. He looked like a man overloaded with worry as he marched to his sons.

Kieran nodded toward him and continued, "Jones was just talking to the sheriff about what happened."

The farmer stood as if blocking his boys from a lynch mob. "It was just an accident. My sons were shooting at the hogs. They didn't know Austin was behind the herd. It was too dark and he was dressed in black. It was just an accident."

"Sounder," Ronny said. "The word for a group of hogs is a sounder."

Everyone looked at her as if knowing the right word were far stranger than accidentally mistaking a man for a pig.

Ronny did not bother to tell them that she'd been working crosswords since she was ten. It might just add fuel to her nutcase file. Instead she asked, "Any word on Austin? Is he going to make it?"

All the men nodded, but none looked convinced.

"He's been in surgery almost an hour," Kieran said. "We should know something soon. The bullet went in deep, but the doc said it didn't look like it hit bone."

Ronny sat down on a chair covered in vinyl. She looked down at her sweatpants and realized she'd seen homeless people dressed better.

When Abby offered to go get everyone coffee, Ronny jumped up, wanting to help. Maybe on the way they'd pass a ladies' room and she could at least wash her hands and shoes. Walking around in wet tennis shoes was better than in muddy ones.

Three doors to the left they found a room with machines lining the walls. Abby dug in her purse until she found enough change.

At the break room door a cluster of gray-haired volunteers passed Ronny. She thought she recognized one as a woman her mother served on the church bereavement committee with years ago.

When Ronny and Abby returned to the waiting room, Dr. Addison Turner had joined them.

The doctor gave Ronny a warm hug before repeating what she'd just told everyone. Austin had lost a lot of blood, but the bullet passed almost through his leg to the back side, so they retrieved it there and didn't have to dig through already torn flesh.

"He's going to be fine," the doctor reassured them. "I plan to keep him only one night unless there are complications. He'll be all right. You all can go home and get some rest."

Ronny had known the young doctor before Addison

married Tinch Turner. She'd cared for Marty along with doctors who had been brought in from Oklahoma City. They'd been professional and kind to her, but Addison had become more, she'd become a friend.

"Thanks." Ronny managed a smile for her now.

Addison touched her shoulder. "We're all glad you're back, Ronny. We've all missed you. Mr. Donavan put up your postcards in the post office so everyone in town kept up with your travels. You've been places most of the people in Harmony will never see."

Ronny didn't want to visit. She needed to get to Austin. "Can we see Austin? His house is next to mine at the lake." Too much detail, Ronny thought.

"Of course, a short visit. Ladies first." Her gaze turned to the two boys looking like they were waiting for their own hanging. "The sheriff wants to talk to everyone else in the room about what happened. She says if any of you try to leave before she gets in here, I'm to shoot you." Addison showed no hint of kidding when she added, "I'd hate to have to dig another bullet out tonight."

Not one man moved.

Ronny ran out of the waiting room. The Delaney sisters were right behind her.

When they reached the door to recovery, Dusti held her sister back. "Why don't you go in first, Ronny? He's probably had enough excitement tonight. All of us might be too much company."

Abby stared at her sister for a moment, then stuttered, "Right, go in, Ronny. We'll wait out here for you. Dusti's right. He's been through a real shock. Too much company wouldn't be good for him."

When Ronny slipped into the room and rounded the curtain, she was surprised to see Austin sitting up in bed. He was bare to the waist with a sheet and light blanket covering his bottom half. There was a scrape along his forehead, but for a man just shot, he looked great.

He smiled at her, a smile that looked as if he were a little drunk. "Hi." His eyes drifted closed.

"Hi," she answered, noticing the IV in his hand. "You all right?"

"Fine," he said, obviously feeling no pain. "And you?"

She moved closer. "I'm a mess. Dressed in the dark and got mud all over my shoes. They'll probably kick me out of this place any minute."

"Me too." He grinned. "Nurse has gone to get help. Says I have to wear one of them gowns. Never wore a gown in my life and don't plan on starting now."

"What are you wearing?"

"Nothing but a bandage. Hog shot me in the leg."

Ronny couldn't resist brushing his hair back from his forehead. He really was a handsome man when he wasn't frowning at her. He felt warm and very much alive. "You sleeping here tonight?"

"Yeah, Doc's orders." He shook his head slightly, as if fighting sleep. "You want to sleep with me? I wouldn't mind, you know. There's enough room."

"Not tonight." She laughed. "Just rest. I'll see you tomorrow." She touched his arm, needing to know he was all right.

"Okay," he said, already half asleep. "Don't let that nurse put one of those gowns on me while I'm asleep, would you?"

"Sure," she said, but he was already out.

Ronny walked the Delaney sisters to the emergency room door and told them she was staying to watch over Austin.

Neither sister looked surprised. Abby fished in her purse and handed Ronny all the change she had left for coffee and snacks. Dusti gave her the work jacket from their pickup. It was patched and old, but clean.

As Ronny waved them good-bye, she thought she saw a car slow on the road just beyond the streetlights.

Without waiting, she turned and went back into the hospital. She'd spent the night in LaGuardia when a flight was late leaving New York. She'd waited in 100-degree heat on an old bus in the mountains of Colombia. She'd been locked out of her hotel in a dark side street in Amsterdam. She could spend the night in Harmony's hospital.

She had survival skills.

Chapter 19

DELANEY FARM

AS ABBY PULLED UP TO THE BARN, DUSTI'S CELL CHIMED. "Hello," she said as she checked the time. Eleven fifteen P.M. Far too late for a call.

"Dusti, lass," came through with a hint of a Scottish accent. "Since I know you haven't had time to be in bed yet, would you do me a favor?"

"What do you need, Kieran?" She could think of a few suggestions. A home-cooked meal? A date? Her body?

"I need a ride," he said, without knowing he was shattering the beginning to a great fantasy. "I could call my grandmother, but it would probably frighten her to death. I rode in with the ambulance. My rental car is parked across Rainbow Lane where we saddled up just before dark."

"I'll come get you, but you have to buy me a beer at Buffalo's." Since he'd destroyed one dream, she might as well work on another. "It's been a long day and I want you to explain a few more poker terms."

"One beer for taxi service, lass. And I'll explain anything you want me to explain to you."

His deep voice set off another moonlight dream. Dusti couldn't help but sigh. He was getting to her. She didn't know how much of this "playing hard to get" she could take from a man who stared at her now and then like he wanted her more than air.

Abby rolled her eyes and climbed out of the pickup. "I know you want me to go along to keep your pants on, but I think I'll call it a night. I have to get up with the chickens."

Dusti never laughed at her sister's old joke. "I won't be late and I've no intention of taking my pants off. The guy won't even kiss me, so I doubt I'll get into any trouble."

"Too bad." Abby headed to the house. "One of us should be having some fun."

As Dusti turned the truck toward town, she glanced back at her sister. Abby had been quiet since they'd left the hospital, and Dusti knew why. The visit reminded Abby what she should be doing with her life. Not raising chickens, not running a tiny farm. She should have been the nurse who met them at the hospital door, but instead, she was still one semester away. From the looks of things, she always would be.

Dusti fought down tears. The night air blew strands of her midnight hair free from her ponytail, but she barely noticed. Somehow she had to learn to play poker. She had to win the buy-in to the Vegas tournament, and from there she had to stay in long enough to show in the money. Even tenth place would be enough for Abby to go back to school.

And to do that, she reasoned, she had to stay clear of Kieran.

Dusti told herself she could wait for her sister to finish school; she'd waited before. If she ran the ranch and took care of her mother, she could run it alone while Abby went back to college. Then, maybe in a few years with the salary Abby would make as a nurse, Dusti would have her shot. She'd buy a good camera and go to a fancy school for six months. Then, who knows, she might open a shop in Harmony and do weddings.

Reality threatened to crush her dreams. Who would run the farm if Abby worked and Dusti went to school? How would they pay for a shop in town?

She'd worry about that later. Right now she had to concentrate on step one.

By the time she reached the hospital, she decided she'd do whatever she had to do to learn, and her only chance was the Scot. He was odds down the player picked to win. All she had to do was find his weak spot. Be able to read him, or better yet fool him into thinking he could read her.

She saw his big frame shove away from the side wall near the emergency room and walk toward her. For the first time, he seemed tired, bone tired. Maybe a drink wasn't a good idea, or maybe it would be the perfect time to ask questions until he let a secret slip.

A tiny bit of her said she wasn't playing fair. She was using him, but it couldn't be helped.

"Thanks for picking me up," he said as he slid into the passenger seat. "I could have ridden home with the farmer, but I have a feeling he'll be lecturing his sons for another decade or so."

"Is the sheriff filing charges?"

Kieran shook his head. "They were on their land. It was night. Everyone knew the shooting was just an accident. Unless Austin wants to press charges, there'll be no more said about it."

Dusti didn't know what to say. If someone shot her, she'd want to press charges.

Kieran continued, "When we rode up, the boys had found Austin and were both terrified. I'll be surprised if either one ever picks up a rifle again. The game warden made them help carry him out. Both got blood on them."

Dusti drove the pickup toward the bar. "Austin has to take some of the blame. He was wearing black."

Kieran stretched his legs, pushing against the floorboard as if he could extend it a few inches. "There's enough blame to spread around. One of us should have been with the boys, or with Austin. They shouldn't have been alone. I've hunted game before. I knew the rules."

"But the good news is he'll be fine."

"Yeah, and the bad news is the warden said from the size

of the sows they had to be three, maybe four years old. They've had a hundred or more piglets by now, and he thinks they're somewhere back behind the lake where no one has ever cut a road, much less settled."

"Who owns the land?" Dusti knew exactly where Delaney land stopped.

"No one seems to know. Jones said it's been sold several times over the years. He thinks an investment company out of Dallas might have bought it, planning to look for oil. Corporations bought up a lot of land in the seventies."

They bumped their way into the potholed parking lot of Buffalo's Bar and Grill.

"One drink is all we'll have time for." She switched off the engine. "Harley closes at midnight on weeknights."

As they stepped into the empty bar, Kieran whispered, "I can see why." Their footsteps echoed off the paneled walls.

Harley was washing up as he watched the news on a little TV by the cash register. He didn't look too happy to see them, but then he never looked happy to see anyone.

"Two beers." Kieran ordered with a smile.

Harley slid the drinks across the bar and took the money without saying a word or offering change.

They moved to one of the booths and Harley went back to his work.

"Friendly, isn't he?"

"I'm used to him." Dusti leaned back in the booth. "Tell me the secrets of how to win at poker. We don't have much time left." She couldn't resist bumping her knee against his.

"Pay attention," Kieran said. "Don't drink. Don't talk more than you have to. Watch how the others play. One way or another they all tell you what they're holding."

"Not me. Good hand or bad, when we practice, I keep a straight face."

He grinned. "You lift one eyebrow slightly when you have a good hand and you lick your lips when you're bluffing."

She shook her head. "It couldn't be that easy."

"Funny thing, 'tis. Every time you had a good hand, you played with your chips before it was your turn to check or raise. In a real game every person at the table would have known you weren't going to fold."

"And you? What are your tells?"

He winked. "I have none. At least none you'll have time enough to learn, but if you watch, you'll see players take a drink when they're excited, or move up in their chairs slightly, or blink more, or rub their hands, or a hundred other things. People are creatures of habit. They're predictable. You're not just playing cards. You're playing the other players when you play Texas Hold'em."

They talked until Harley blinked the lights. Kieran told her she should play only good starting cards, and they went through all the sets of two that would be considered good.

"An ace and a king might look great, but remember all it takes is a pair of twos to beat them."

Dusti stored away every point he made, picturing the hands he described in her mind as if she were taking pictures.

Kieran was explaining the river card when Harley blinked the lights again. The Scot took her hand and walked her to the door. Though she tried to concentrate on everything he'd told her, she had to admit that she liked the feel of her hand in his and the way he moved.

Every light in the place went out as the door closed, even the three outside lights of the parking lot.

"I guess we overstayed our welcome," she said, feeling her way along the railing.

When he stopped at the bottom of the stairs, she bumped into him. Standing one step higher than he was, she was almost the same height, but it was so dark she felt him near more than saw him.

"You can't see me now," she whispered. "You won't know if I'm bluffing or telling the truth."

Kieran slid his hand slowly along her arm until his fingers rested on her throat. "My dad used to tell me, after his divorce from my mother, that a man can always tell when a pretty lass is lying. He said her lips will be moving."

"Your mom must have hurt him really bad."

"She did. Almost killed him when she left him. After

twelve years of traveling everywhere with him, she up and left him for a Frenchman who owned a little winery they'd stopped at once. They'd only stayed a day, but Mom must have decided she liked the farmer more than she did Dad.

"I think the part about it being a Frenchman bothered Dad more than the leaving. For months he went around claiming he hated farmers, wine, and Frenchmen, not necessarily in that order."

"What happened after she left? Who'd you go with?"

They fought it out in the courts and she got me for the summers. I don't know if she was the one who won or lost that battle. Anyway, it didn't matter; her Frenchman didn't want me around, so I was always shipped here to my grandmother's as soon as I finished boarding school every spring. Which was fine. I loved my mom, but it wasn't worth staying with her and putting up with her new husband. He used to make fun of everything I said. I spent a week once with them over Christmas break and didn't say a single word. I'm not sure anyone noticed."

"So where did you feel like you grew up?"

"Dad never seemed to completely unpack anywhere. He'd be based in London one year and New York the next. By the time I was fourteen I was in boarding schools. When I went to college I decided to unpack in New York, so I guess if I had to pick a place to call home, 'twould be there." He moved a little closer to her and she felt his words against her cheek. "Funny thing is, when people in Manhattan ask me where I'm from, I often say Harmony, Texas. My roots are as much here as in Scotland. I've always thought of home as a person, not so much a place."

Dusti knew she should step away. Her eyes had adjusted enough that she could make out the outline of her pickup now, but she liked the nearness of this man. She liked the way Kieran talked, flavoring words until you felt you were traveling around the world in his conversations.

Shifting, she pressed her side against his chest. He was a man who liked women and was comfortable with them close, even if he did seem shy. He'd talked to her more in the darkness than he'd ever talked.

He was so close she could feel his words moving the air, but he didn't lean in to kiss her. She'd done everything but put up a neon sign inviting him in for a taste, but he didn't seem to notice.

She asked him more about poker just to keep him talking, but she wasn't paying near as much attention to his advice as she was the movement of his hand along her side. He was touching her in a very friendly way; maybe there was hope yet.

When his fingers brushed the side of her breast, it occurred to her that maybe this man wasn't so much shy as quiet.

In the shadows, with town only fifty yards away, she felt like she wasn't truly in the world. The man who had little to say could talk about poker easily, only they both knew he was making love to her not with his words, but with the way he said them.

They might not have kissed, but they'd begun the game all lovers play, only this time for her the stakes might be too high. With all the boys in the backseats of cars and the one-night stands, she'd never risked her heart. This time might be different.

She was falling hard for a man who wouldn't be in town long enough to carry out all the promises he was making with his touch.

Dusti had never played hard to get. In fact, she had no problem being the first to make a move, but this time she hesitated. She needed him and if she let things move too far, too fast, she might lose him. The smart thing to do was play along until the poker game was played, and then they'd finish the other game they both wanted to play.

Only not kissing him was pure torture when every bone in her body wanted to jump on top of him.

Finally, when a sheriff's office patrol car circled through the parking lot, they knew it was time to go.

She drove him back to where he'd parked his car, and he climbed out without touching her again.

"Tomorrow?" she said before he closed the door.

"I'll check on Austin and then be over."

"Good."

Neither said good night. As she drove away, Dusti tried to concentrate on the rules he'd told her, but his hand sliding along her side was all that she could remember clearly.

At this rate she wouldn't be able to play Crazy Eights by next Friday night.

Then, as she pulled the pickup beside the house, she realized something. Maybe he was already playing her. Maybe his plan was to turn her on to the point where she couldn't concentrate.

With a frustrated sigh, she realized he was succeeding. In fact, she was helping him along. If she didn't watch it, she'd be Play-Doh by Friday night.

Chapter 20

DAWN PAINTED THE EASTERN HORIZON OUTSIDE HIS WINdow when Austin finally managed to open his eyes. He felt like someone had super-glued his eyelids together. He had a headache that pounded so hard he feared it might fracture his skull, and his left leg throbbed with each heartbeat.

Wild guess, but this wasn't going to be a good day.

The night had been rough; he woke up a few times and remembered talking to Kieran once and the doctor for a while. He'd even thought that Ronny had washed the blood off his hands.

At some point he'd stayed alert long enough to piece together everything that had happened. The pigs heading straight toward him, the shot that hit his leg, the operation to remove lead. He remembered the doctor telling him he'd been lucky. If the bullet had been an inch over, he'd have bled out before help got there.

Somehow he didn't feel very lucky. If the bullet had been four inches to the left it would have hit the tree. Now that sounded lucky.

Each time he'd lost the struggle with pain, they'd give him more medicine, and the darkness pulled him back to his dreams as the world slipped away. Horrible nightmares he had to fight his way out of again and again. He'd gone back and forth so many times, at one point he couldn't remember which was real and which was nightmare.

Finally, it was morning and the dull pain told him he'd landed in reality.

He turned slightly and saw Ronny sleeping in the chair by his bed. She had on sweatpants with dried dirt stuck in several spots. Her top was a different color green than her pants and her shoes must have washed up on some shore before she put them on.

"Hey," he said, just loud enough to wake her. "Which one of us was hit by a truck last night?"

She stretched and smiled at him.

Austin forgot about his headache. "Dear God, I love waking up and seeing you first thing. Even dressed like you swam over, you're downright adorable, Ronny. I've never met a woman who settles my world like you do."

He reached for her and felt the straps around his arms and feet. Nothing new. He'd felt them before when he'd come to in hospitals. Restrained for his own good. So he wouldn't fall out of bed or tear his IV out. So he wouldn't fight his way out of one of his nightmares.

Austin kept his voice calm as he asked, "Any chance you could untie me and we could take a shower together?"

She scrubbed her head, making her hair fly in every direction before settling back into curls around her face. "The nurse tied you down last night when you kept thrashing around." She hesitated, then added, "I don't know if they'll untie you, but I could ask."

He saw a bruise just below her eye. "Did I do that?"

Ronny touched her cheek as if she could brush the proof away. "You didn't mean to. You were just having a nightmare."

He didn't bother to ask about what. His nightmares were all the same. He was trapped. Fire surrounded him. He could smell his own flesh burning. He needed to get out, but he couldn't find his team.

"I'm sorry," he whispered, realizing just how much he meant it.

She stood. "It doesn't matter. I'm glad I was here last night. I'm not sure the nurse could have handled you alone."

Austin closed his eyes, not wanting to think about what he'd done. They'd tied him down at night when he'd been burned. That was one reason he'd walked away from rehab. He didn't want to be tied down like an animal again.

"Tell the nurse to unbuckle me, would you?" He wouldn't have blamed her if she refused. "It's all right. I'm wide awake now."

Ronny nodded and left.

A few minutes later a nurse followed her back into the room. Cautiously, he released the leather first around Austin's hands and then his feet. "The doc will be in soon. You're scheduled to go home today, Mr. Hawk. Do you need a pain pill for the trip home?"

"No," Austin said, rubbing his wrists as if the binding had been handcuffs and not soft restraints. "I'll take any antibiotics I need to, but I don't want painkillers."

The nurse looked over at Ronny for confirmation.

When she nodded, he left.

Austin laughed. "Looks like you're responsible for me. That's what happens when you spend the night with a nut job—you have to take him home and care for him."

"You're not a nut job."

"I have nightmares that would send people running from the theater if they made them into a movie. I apparently beat up beautiful ladies in my sleep. That bruise proves it." He looked away, not wanting to see her feeling sorry for him. Hell, he'd had all the "feeling sorry" that he could handle in this lifetime.

Ronny moved closer and put her cool hands on either side of his face. "Look at me," she said.

He did what she said, not because it was an order, but

because he wanted to study her one last time before she said good-bye.

"What happened to me," she started, without turning his head loose, "was an accident. Nothing more. You didn't hit me. I just got in the way of your nightmare."

"I have them every night," he admitted, even though he'd lied to the doctors at the fort and said they were rare.

"Then I'm not sleeping anywhere near you." Without hesitation she lowered her mouth to his and kissed him hard and quick. "Does that settle the point?"

When she pulled away, he smiled, trying to figure out this woman before him. "So I guess this means you're not taking me home with you?"

"No. If they let you out today, I'll call Kieran. He said he'd help you get back to your place, and the Delaneys said they'd check on you twice a day till the doc says you're fine. Abby says she can change your bandage and check to make sure the wound is healing properly. I offered to deliver meals until you're getting around."

"You guys think you've got it all figured out." He lifted his hand to cup her face and ran his thumb lightly over the bruise. Part of him wanted to say he was sorry one more time, but he knew she'd have none of it.

"It's either put up with us or you move in with the Joneses. The farmer and his wife offered to house you until you're well."

"No way." His thumb brushed across her lips. "The last thing I want to do is see those boys again." Her lips were still moist. "Did you just kiss me, or was that just something I wanted you to do so badly I thought it happened?"

She smiled. "I kissed you. I've been thinking about it all night. Your body's solid as a rock all over, but you have the most kissable lips I've ever seen."

"So, you did spend the night with me? And apparently felt my body . . . all over."

She nodded. "I told the nurse that I was family. They even let me stay when they checked the wound on your leg. I guess you could say I've seen quite a lot of you lately."

"Wouldn't want to return the viewing, would you? Take off that sweatshirt and I think it might help with my healing. Better than any therapy." Even drugged up and hurting, he wanted her.

A noise from the hallway drew their attention. The nurse's tone sounded frustrated. "I told you, ma'am, you cannot come into this wing. Visitors are limited to family only."

"I don't want to see any patient, you idiot!" the woman yelled. "I'm here to see my daughter. Far as she's fallen into no telling what kind of sin, it's still my duty to help her."

Austin thought he recognized the voice. Dark rainy night. Bossy lady who was stuck in the mud. Dallas Logan had to be in the hallway and heading this way.

He turned to confirm his suspicions with Ronny, but Ronny had disappeared. The space between his bed and the window was empty.

"You can't come in here," the nurse ordered.

"Who's going to stop me? You?"

The door bumped open and an angry ball of a woman barreled through.

"I'm sorry, sir," the nurse shouted over her head. "I'll go get my supervisor." He looked like he thought a five-foot tumbleweed would be easier to corral than Dallas Logan on a mission.

"That's all right. Let her in," Austin said, sounding more tired than worried. If he couldn't see Ronny in the room, neither could she.

Dallas might be hell on wheels, but compared to his nightmares she was a walk in the park. "How can I help you, Mrs. Logan? Your car stuck in the mud again?"

She marched over to his bed and glared at him. "What's wrong with you? You haven't got anything catching, have you?"

"Nope. A pig shot me."

Without missing a beat, Dallas continued at full speed. "I have it as a fact that my daughter was here with you last night. My friend said she was dressed like a homeless person and begging money at the emergency room door. She's obviously lost her mind, and I'm here to do my duty and take her home. The girl obviously needs someone taking charge of her care."

Austin shifted, trying to ease the pain in his leg. After settling, he pulled back up the sheet that had slipped down a few inches. He'd need all his strength to deal with Dallas. It would have helped if he'd been dressed and could stand over the lady, or better yet have twin Colts strapped to his waist.

"Your daughter was in her right mind when I saw her last. She's an adult. If she needs your help, she'll ask for it."

"Oh, you know more than a mother does, do you? No one in town even knows who you are, living out on the lake with the squirrels and frogs. Folks say all the way back to your grandfather that Hawks have never been friendly. Sounds like to me there may be a whole nest of crazies out on that little lake, and my daughter has fallen into hard times if she's out there with you and those wild Delaney girls."

Austin opened his mouth to argue, but he wasn't sure where to start.

When he raised his finger and pointed at her, Dallas took a step backward. "What are you wearing?" she asked.

Her eyes rounded and he guessed the sheet must have slipped a few inches again.

Austin looked down. Maybe he should have let the nurse last night dress him in a hospital gown. The sheet did little to hide the outline of his body. "A bandage," he said calmly. "All I'm wearing is a bandage."

"You're not even decent, sir. I've half a mind to turn you in as a pervert. Who knows how many people you've exposed yourself to besides my daughter."

The cavalry arrived: the nurse, the doctor, and a chubby security guard who looked like his nap had just been interrupted.

"Arrest this man!" Dallas demanded. "He's a pervert who exposed himself to my little girl! He almost showed his privates to me, and I'm sure he was about to hit me. Who knows what would have happened to my dignity if a naked man knocked me senseless?"

For a moment, Austin started to explain, and then he

realized everyone was moving around, protecting him, not Dallas.

She tried to shove past them to confront him, but the nurse blocked her path.

Austin fought the urge to lean over and look under the bed. Ronny had to still be in the room somewhere. She would have had to pass her mother to get out.

Dr. Addison Turner had had enough. "Mrs. Logan, you are the one who'll be arrested for harassing my patient. This man has just had surgery and this wing of the hospital does not allow visitors."

"Don't you dare look at me that way. I'm not the one almost exposing myself, and I'm not the one who is crazy enough to think a pig shot me. This man needs to be locked up and kept away from my daughter. He's probably on drugs. Looks like the type."

The security guy snaked his arm around Dallas's left arm.

She swung her huge purse like a weapon and hit him once before the nurse circled her other arm and held them both behind her while Dallas wiggled. Dallas was pinned to a moving torture rack, and she let everyone know that they were hurting her, smashing her purse, and embarrassing themselves by picking on a lady old enough to be their mother.

The chubby security man said pleasantly, "Now, Dallas, we can walk you out or we can drag you out. Which would you prefer? Before you decide, I have to tell you that we dragged the last woman out by her feet and her dress slipped all the way to her neck before we got her to the parking lot."

"Well, I never!" she answered, holding her head high as they marched out with arms locked.

Austin could hear her lecturing them, but thankfully her voice was receding as she was guided down the hallway.

The doctor looked down at him. "You all right, Captain?"

"I'm fine. Nice entertainment you got in this place, Doc."

She grinned and headed to the door. "I'll be back with your release papers in an hour. Try not to get in any more trouble."

Suddenly, the room was quiet again. Austin took a long

breath and smiled. Dallas Logan was a woman of conviction who saw herself on a mission. She might be running full speed ahead in the wrong direction, but at least she was moving, which was more than he could say for most people.

"You can come out now," he said.

Ronny circled out of the bundle of extra curtain near the corner of his bed.

"You know you'll have to face her someday." Austin took her hand gently, liking the feel of her skin on his.

"I know. For the first year after I left home she wouldn't even talk to me. Claimed I ran away from home, even if I was in my midtwenties. She made up terrible stories about me going wild. I'm not afraid of her. I just know there is no reasoning with a person who is never wrong in her own mind."

He saw the sadness in Ronny. The beautiful lady had experienced her share of trouble, and he didn't want to add to it. "How about calling Kieran and seeing about getting me back to the lake? Even with the wild hogs, I've got a feeling we'd be safer there."

"I agree. Uh . . . *Captain?*"

"Another time, another life. The doc must have read my records. This wasn't the first tumble I've taken or the first shot a doctor dug out of me."

"Lucky to be alive," she said softly.

"That's what they tell me." He didn't add his thoughts about the jury still being out on that one. Maybe the lucky ones die young in glory.

He guessed she didn't have anything else to say. Truth was, neither of them was much on conversation. He learned more about her from listening to her talk to Dusti and Abby while he dealt cards than he probably would have ever learned on his own.

He wasn't good with people. He'd understood the army, but the outside world didn't make sense to him most of the time.

Austin guessed she was the same. They'd both traveled all over the world but could barely keep a conversation going. He did love watching her move, though. He'd always thought *love* was just a word that people said. Even now, watching her tidy up the room, he figured he felt more lust than anything else. *Love* wasn't a word he'd probably ever use.

Surely that wasn't anything a lady like Ronny Logan would want from anyone, much less him. She seemed to treasure her silent life on the lake.

Yet she'd kissed him.

Chapter 21

TRUMAN FARM

REAGAN WALKED AROUND THE ORCHARD WITH UTAH TUCKED in a carrier that strapped around her. He was asleep, but still she talked to him as she wove among the tables.

"My uncle Jeremiah would be worried about the poker players bothering the roots of the trees. He never liked folks coming onto the farm much. Except, of course, for Miss Pat Matheson. She could come over anytime she liked. He even built steps over the fence between the Matheson ranch and the back of the orchard."

Utah didn't answer. He just kept sleeping.

Reagan smiled. In truth, the orchard looked beautiful with brightly colored tables among the trees. Tomorrow would be a practice run for all dealers and volunteers, and then the next day the games started at seven. It would still be daylight when everyone sat down to play. Phil Gentry, the unofficial expert on poker tournaments, thought that half the games would be over before dark. The winners' tables would be set up in the barn where they could hang enough lights to make it easy to see. Twenty tables of ten would start, then the winners would move to two tables, then finally one. With any luck, the three rounds would be over long before midnight and everyone could clean up and go home.

Reagan looked forward to getting back to normal. Her quiet farm. Her little group of friends. All of it gave her peace, and maybe that would be enough.

Some thought the last games might go on all night when the winners from all the tables joined the last table. By then there would probably be no first-time players or men who were "just lucky." This last table would be the two people who were winners at each of the second-round tables. They'd held the entries to exactly two hundred so all would work out. Dusti Delaney had been the last to buy in.

If by any chance Dusti made it to the final table, that was the game Reagan wanted to see. She knew nothing of poker, but she guessed that the two who made the last table would have bragging rights for years, and she'd love it if one of those was a woman.

"It's almost sunset, Utah, we'd best get to the western chairs," Reagan whispered as she moved back down the trail toward the house. "It's going to be a great one tonight."

In the years since her uncle died she'd thought of removing the lawn chairs he'd set in the yard so he could see the sun rise and set each day, but something had always kept her from doing it. Often Miss Pat Matheson would come over from next door and join her just before sunset. They'd watch the sky turn and talk of the day, and then Pat knew she would be invited in for a piece of pie before her nephew, Hank, came to pick her up.

All the stories of the three families who'd founded Harmony passed from Pat Matheson to Reagan. Pat's health might be going, but her mind was still sharp. She often said it was because she spent thirty-six years of teaching reciting her times tables over and over. She claimed it sharpened her mind.

Reagan wanted to tell her the truth about Utah and how he came to the farm, but she couldn't share the story with anyone before she talked to Noah.

She'd told herself she'd give the facts to Noah calmly and without crying, and then she'd wait and see what he planned to do about it.

Whatever he did wouldn't involve her. Reagan had made up her mind that she couldn't marry a man who lied. No matter how much she loved him. She couldn't. She'd been lied to all her childhood by social workers and counselors. She'd even lied to herself.

But no more.

If Noah kept the baby, he'd raise him alone. If he didn't want Utah, Reagan had decided she'd adopt him. Maybe Noah would visit. Maybe they'd become friends helping raise the baby, but they'd never marry. They'd never be lovers again. If she allowed that to happen she'd always worry, when he was out on the road, if he was getting drunk and sleeping with a nameless woman.

In the darkness between the orchard and her house, Reagan cried. The sounds of the night blanketed her sobs, and the wind wiped her tears. There had been very few times she'd let even one tear fall, but tonight before all the craziness started, she'd cry for the loss of her dream of loving one man all her life.

By the time she reached the yard, she'd shoved her tears aside.

Big Biggs was waiting for her on the porch.

"Howdy, Reagan. I figured you'd be out walking with that baby." Big stood up, looking like a mountain on her gingerbread-trimmed porch. "When's your friend going to come after the boy?"

"A few days," Reagan lied. "You got time for some supper?"

"No, I'm just delivering some supplies the hospital figures they'll need out here if a fight breaks out." He scratched his head. "I don't know why they think anyone would fight. It's just a card game. I'm not even going to drink more than one beer. Ester's signed me up to drive the bus delivering folks from here to their cars parked half a mile away. She thinks they can walk in. It'll still be light when the games start. But when they leave, with all the curves on Lone Oak Road, some of the drunks trying to find their cars would be roadkill."

"Come on in, Big, and have some pie?" Reagan didn't want to be alone. "You can tell me if you talked your brother and Beau Yates into playing out here before the poker starts. That will draw folks early and give the losers something to do after they leave the tables."

"Pie sounds good. A few pieces won't spoil my supper." Big followed her inside. "Beau and Border will be here early while everyone's paying in and getting set up. Harley said no one will be at the bar while the game is going on. He plans to open about eight so all the losers can drown their sorrows. I asked Harley if he planned to come out and he said, 'Why?' like having fun wasn't in his vocabulary."

As they always did, Big sat at the kitchen bar and she stood on the other side. This made them about the same height and they could talk. Big understood her. He'd raised himself, pretty much, along with his little brother. He understood how important it was to have someone who would cover your back. Someone you could trust.

When Utah woke, Big said he had to get back because Ester should be finished burning dinner by now.

He let himself out while Reagan climbed the stairs and gave Utah his bottle in the old rocking chair that Uncle Jeremiah had said rocked him to sleep.

After Utah finished, she put him in the swing she'd bought and let him rock while she cooked her dinner and ate alone.

"Funny," she said to him. "You don't do anything but cry, poop, and eat, but you're a lot of company to have around. If your momma comes back, I'm loading her Chevy up with all the stuff I've collected. I'll tell her you really love the swing."

He smiled at her, and though she knew he was just passing gas, she smiled back.

Logic told her she should start laying out plans, but there were still too many questions. Would the baby stay? Would Noah take him? Would she say good-bye to Noah for good? Would she want to stay in Noah's life as a friend? Could she?

She'd loved Noah from the moment he had befriended her. Even when she was mad at him, she still loved him. How could she turn that kind of love off? And, if she didn't, could she survive the next time he lied to her?

Reagan tossed most of her dinner in the trash and picked up Utah. "I got enough to worry about right now. How about we just decide to worry about it tomorrow."

Utah made a little sound and she added, "You're right. Tomorrow's a busy day. How about we worry about my problems when this poker game is over. I'll have the rest of my life to figure it out."

Armed with a bottle, more diapers, and Utah, she headed upstairs again.

Her cell phone remained on the kitchen table. Even if there was a midnight call, she wouldn't answer it tonight. Noah didn't know it yet, but she was already pushing him away.

Chapter 22

DELANEY FARM

DUSTI MISSED HER POKER LESSON BECAUSE OF AUSTIN HAWK. Everyone had their hands full getting him home and settled into his place.

To her surprise, Austin seemed grateful and thanked them all, though he hated being fussed over. He didn't take offense at Abby's orders, even told her she was doing a good job. She'd taken on the nursing part of his recovery and told Dusti that as long as she gave orders like a general, Austin listened.

Ronny took over the cooking. Kieran set up a bed downstairs and shifted all the furniture around so Austin could move with crutches from his porch to the kitchen. The doctor had told him to stay off his leg for a week, but he showed no sign of having heard her. Within an hour he was hopping around.

Dusti didn't have a job, other than hauling supplies from one side of the lake to the other. While she was in town buying groceries, she dropped by the bookstore and bought two books on how to play poker. Dusti knew the game now, but she kept forgetting the vocabulary. Reading the first chapter of a book seemed easier than looking dumb.

The flop, the turn, and the river all got mixed up in her mind. Why couldn't he just say the first three cards on the table, the next one, and the last one to go down faceup.

Dusti decided Texas Hold'em's vocabulary was made up by men who wanted to convince their wives that the game was hard so they'd never ask to play.

By the time she read the first few chapters, Dusti was convinced Texas Hold'em was made up not by husbands but by fools locked away in an asylum somewhere.

While the others moved Austin Hawk's home around, she studied on the porch. She had to stay focused. This was too important to let a day slip. This was the only way out she'd thought of in two years, and she was going to fight as hard as she could.

When Kieran finally joined her back at her farm, she was shuffling cards.

"You ready to play, lass?" he asked, and the twinkle in his eye made her consider which game he was talking about.

"I'm ready to play cards. Teach me to win."

They began.

She watched the way his hands handled the cards and the chips, but she listened to every word he said. His Scottish accent came out stronger at times, and he'd grin at her as if he knew exactly what she was holding, but he taught her the rules, over and over, almost as if she were learning a foreign alphabet.

"It's a game of strategy, not luck. If you don't get good starting cards in the hole, fold." He was all business as she shuffled for another round. "From the minute you see the flop, start thinking of what someone else has at the table that can beat you. When the flop doesn't help you, fold. Whenever you're not sure, fold. Never pay to see the other players' cards. Never bluff a player with nothing left to lose."

Dusti took it all in. Only a few days left before the game and she planned to be Harmony's winner. The rest of her and Abby's lives depended on it.

Kieran left midafternoon, saying he had to do some things with his grandmother. Dusti wanted to scream that there was no time, but she couldn't. He was giving her all the time he could.

"Come back tonight after you eat supper with your granny," she said as he opened his car door. "We can work a while longer."

"Sure," he said. "But only for an hour or two. No more."

For a moment his smile vanished, and she wondered what he was thinking. She still couldn't read him.

Dusti watched him drive up to the road to Rainbow Lane. He was pulling away from her even though he was trying to teach her all she needed to know. Maybe it was because he knew that there was a chance he'd be playing against her in one of the final rounds. Or maybe it was getting harder and harder for him not to kiss her.

The knowledge that if she played against him, she'd have to beat him, hit her straight between the eyes.

That would make for an awkward date after the game if she beat him. She was so attracted to him. In all their talks she'd told him why she wanted to win. Hell, she'd told him her whole life story, but he hadn't said a word. All she knew about his was that he flew planes for a living and traveled all over. He'd mentioned his past, his parents, but the man seemed to have no present, or future.

Was Kieran down here just to play poker, or did he have an important reason for coming back to Harmony? He'd taken off work to be here. This game had to be important to him. But why?

She'd know soon enough.

Chapter 23

‹❦❧›

WALDEN CABIN

RONNY WALKED THROUGH THE TRAIL BETWEEN THE TREES
that separated her place from Hawk House. Kieran had used
an old lawn mower to cut down a path so she wouldn't have
to circle down by the shore or get lost in the willows. Using
the shortcut, she was surprised how close her cabin was to
Austin's place.

The evening sun seemed to just sit on the western horizon, in no hurry to leave. She'd planned to be at Austin's
house earlier, but the cookies took longer to bake than she'd
thought they would.

One of the few secrets Austin had shared about himself
was his love for cookies. Ronny had been told once by the
Biggs boys, who had lived next door to her before she left to
travel, that she made the best cookies in the world. Now it
was time to test her theory on an expert.

It had taken an army to move Austin home from the hospital. Everyone agreed that by boat would be the least painful. Her ATV would be too bumpy, and walking down from
the road carrying a stretcher would be impossible.

So they loaded supplies in her little blue boat and put Austin in the Delaneys' fishing boat, and Kieran brought up the rear with Austin's rowboat. The Scot handled rowing like an expert, and Ronny couldn't help but wonder what the man couldn't do. He was big, but Kieran handled himself like a man comfortable with himself.

Abby insisted on going as slow as possible, so Ronny went on and had most of the supplies unloaded before Abby pulled up to the dock.

Austin made it, with Kieran's help and one crutch, to the porch, where he rested before hopping his way into the living room, where they'd moved his bed.

The big house seemed to melt down to a three-room apartment where he had everything he needed.

Everyone worked around him while Austin napped. He got so tired of telling them how he felt that he started saying, "I'm fine," if anyone passed within three feet of him.

Ronny had finally left him with Kieran to go home and clean up while a roast cooked. Now, as she walked the path, the roast felt like it weighed twenty pounds inside the picnic basket she carried.

When she stepped into the house with her food, the place was silent. For a moment she thought something must have happened, and then she saw Austin leaning back in a recliner they'd pushed near the windows.

"You all right?" she asked, realizing he'd probably watched her walk up.

"Yeah. I've been moving around a little. Doc said to take it real easy until the stitches heal, so I'm becoming a bum. Until you came along I was thinking about taking up bird watching."

"And after I came along?" she asked.

"I've decided it's far more fun watching you. So I'll be a bum who has only one hobby."

"You're allowed one day of being a bum, so just sit there and you can watch me bring in your supper. While we eat we'll find something to watch on that old TV of yours."

"I don't even know if it works." He didn't sound very interested in finding out.

She hurried into the kitchen and began setting the dishes out. A big salad, potatoes, carrots, rolls, plus the roast smothered in onions and tomatoes. A fine family dinner, she thought. When they were finished, all leftovers would go in the fridge to make at least two or three more meals.

When she looked up, Austin stood three feet behind her. "You shouldn't have gone to so much trouble."

"I didn't mind. I love to cook." She almost said that she hadn't really cooked since Marty died, but tonight she wouldn't think about the past.

Austin slowly closed the distance with the help of the crutch. "I've been waiting all afternoon to be alone with you. There's something we need to finish before we think about eating or even talking."

His hand brushed over her hair and cupped the back of her head as he pulled her mouth to his. The kiss was hard and hungry, but she didn't pull away. He was kissing her the same way she'd kissed him at dawn. All need, no polite tenderness.

When she broke free she tried to push him away, but he leaned against her, pinning her to the counter. "You shouldn't be doing this, Austin. You're supposed to rest."

"I'm fine. I just have to touch you. All day long, I've been thinking about finishing that kiss you started. I can't stop thinking about being this close to you, so stop talking and start kissing me, pretty lady."

She circled his waist and did exactly what he suggested. When his mouth moved to her throat as if starving for a taste of her, she whispered against his hair, "If you fall, we'll both tumble. I don't think I could hold you up."

His one free hand moved over her body, pulling her silk shirt away from her trousers so he could feel her skin. As his tongue invaded her mouth, he circled her middle and lifted her off the ground. He set her on the counter, spread her legs apart, and leaned against her. "Now if I fall, you can watch. Otherwise, I want you so close I can feel you breathing against my chest and smell your hair and taste your skin." His hands moved over her as if starving for the feel of her. "I love touching you."

When his fingers moved along the inside of her leg, he studied her reaction to his boldness. "I need both hands to do this. You wouldn't consider moving to the bed, would you?" "No." She laughed. "I'm here to feed you." Even as she pushed him an inch away, she loved the idea that he couldn't keep his hands off her. A few times over the past year men had gotten too close while dancing at a captain's dinner or hugging good-bye when she left a tour. All seemed to enjoy touching or hugging a woman, but Austin made it very plain that it was her he wanted, not just any woman. Only her.

Ronny thought both the Delaney girls were far prettier than she was. They were easy to talk to and fun to be around, but yesterday when they'd all been together Austin only watched her. Sometimes she wondered if he even saw the others in the room.

"One more kiss, then we'll eat." He cupped her head in his hand and moved her so that her mouth was exactly where he wanted it as he lowered his lips.

She didn't want to argue with his request. She bowed her back slightly and pressed against him as their kiss deepened into something that would not, could not end fast.

The crutch clanked to the floor as he moved his other hand up under her shirt and covered her breast. Her lace bra did nothing to guard against the warm, tender advance.

Ronny moaned in pleasure as he molded his fingers around her flesh.

He swayed slightly as he tightened his grip. "You feel . . . you feel . . ." His words were mumbled between kisses.

She broke the kiss, wanting to see his face as he touched her. All she saw were dark green eyes rolling up in his head.

Austin hit the tile like a falling oak. His whole body seemed to bounce once, and then his head hit for a second time before silence.

Ronny screamed and ran for her phone. She dialed the Delaney place and yelled, "Come quick!" to whoever answered before she dropped the phone and ran to Austin.

Ten minutes later when Abby, Dusti, and Kieran stormed in, Austin was sitting on the kitchen floor holding his head. Ronny had managed to drape a wet towel across his neck and place a pillow under his leg, but she didn't know what else to do.

"What happened?" Abby asked as she knelt and began running her hands up and down Austin as if looking for a switch to turn on the battery.

"I kissed him and I think he fainted." Ronny stepped back, letting the others take charge.

While Abby and the Scot helped Austin to bed, Dusti asked Ronny, "You have that effect on most guys or just the wounded?"

"I don't know. I've never kissed a guy like that."

Dusti moved closer. "Like what?"

"All out. You know, like it's more important to kiss him than it is to breathe."

Dusti took her arm. "Maybe you should sit down, Ronny. You don't look so good yourself."

Ronny nodded. "I feel all messed up inside. My stomach hurts. I didn't know kissing could hurt so much. How could something feel so good and hurt at the same time?"

"You've got to slow down, girl. Kissing is like eating ice cream, you can't do it too fast. At this rate, if the kissing knocks him out, the lovemaking will kill you." Dusti glanced into the living room. "Let me guess. He feels the same way you do. Can't keep his hands off you. Has to kiss you or die kind of thing." She leaned closer and whispered, "How many times have you two kissed?"

"Two, no, three. Then I kissed him in the hospital just because I couldn't think of anything else all night. But that kiss was fast. I just wanted one taste. Only he said he wanted to do it right this time, and it was *really* right." Ronny let out a sob. "Or it was until his eyes rolled back and he hit the floor."

Dusti poured her a glass of tea and stared at all the food on the counter. "Did you two get around to eating first?"

"No." Ronny shoved her tears aside and smiled. "I guess we had other things on our minds."

Abby interrupted with her medical report. "He's got a knot on his head the size of one of our eggs. Probably a mild concussion, so we need to watch him closely. Keep him awake for a few hours and make sure he eats when he takes the medicine." She spotted the bruise on Ronny's face. "When did you get that?"

"Before dawn yesterday, when he had a nightmare," Ronny answered as she moved her hair back over the bruise. She didn't miss Dusti's frown.

"Were you kissing him at the time?"

"No. Just spending the night."

Dusti shook her head. "I never would have thought it of the two of you, but maybe you should think about not seeing one another. This attraction you two have could turn deadly."

Abby looked from Ronny to Austin and then back at her sister with that my-sister's-gone-nuts look. Austin looked like death warmed over and Ronny wasn't the passionate type at all.

Ronny almost laughed aloud. Austin with his unfriendly ways didn't seem to want to be around anyone, and she knew they all saw her as a lonely lady who wouldn't know how to handle a man's attentions. She and Austin were an unlikely pair, but maybe Dusti was right. At this rate, they might kill each other. Even knowing that he was hurt, she couldn't stop thinking about the way his mouth tasted and how good his hand felt moving across her body.

In fact, if he had a free hand right now and was interested, she had a body waiting to be touched.

Giggling, Ronny realized she'd gone mad.

He was forceful and demanding about wanting her, and gentle, too, like he was afraid he'd hurt her. Strange as it might sound, she wouldn't have had him any other way. If he'd just lasted a few more minutes there was no telling where they might have gone with one hand on her breast and and the other moving up her leg to—

Austin's yelling interrupted her hot daydream.

"I'm fine," he complained. "You guys can go back and finish your game. I promise I'll stay right here and eat my supper, take my pills, and probably attack Ronny if she comes near again." He stared at her as if he'd just read her mind.

Ronny laughed but didn't miss the Delaney girls' glare.

They had no idea Austin was kidding. Or maybe he wasn't. She could always hope.

Kieran, who'd been standing in the archway between the rooms, looked at the food spread out on the counter. "We're not leaving you, fella. You're weak from loss of blood and there is no telling what this neighbor would do to you in your weak state. You need protecting." The Scot grinned. "In fact, we're staying for supper. You got any cards around this place? I could finish the lessons while we eat and watch over you so Ronny won't try having her way with you again." He didn't seem the least worried about Ronny, only about the food getting cold.

While Austin complained, Kieran pulled plates out of the cabinet and began to fill one. Ronny giggled when he winked at her. There was nothing else to do but pull the bread from the oven and find napkins. Austin was having company for supper whether he liked it or not.

Halfway through the meal Dusti seemed to notice that Austin hadn't said a word. She leaned back in her chair and patted his knee. "You know, Austin, you should get out more and let the people of Harmony get to know you. Then they'd have reasons not to like you."

"Quit teasing him," Abby snapped. "He must have a terrible headache."

"It's what he deserves, attacking sweet Ronny while she was bringing him food. If you ask me, he's lived out here too long. Gone feral like the wild hogs."

Ronny's voice was almost lost in the laughing. "He didn't attack me," she said. "I attacked him first. He was just returning the favor." She moved closer to the couch as if planning to protect him.

He watched her, then captured her hand when she meant to pat his shoulder. "You're arguing with chickens," he whispered, "and you can attack me any time."

Ronny giggled. "Ditto." It didn't matter that no one understood what was between them. It was simply between them.

The group calmed as they began another lesson in playing poker. Austin pouted and glared at them, but no one noticed. They ate and talked and laughed like old friends.

Austin might as well have been a picture on the wall. He sat on the couch, his leg stretched out on a box.

When Ronny brought the dessert, she sat on the couch beside his good leg and fed him cookies while she pretended to be interested in the poker lesson.

Austin would have complained that he didn't need help, but every time she reached across for another cookie, her breast brushed against his arm.

No one noticed or paid any attention to his not-so-subtle comments that they should all call it a night. She just kept feeding him cookies and letting her breast move a little slower over his arm with each passing.

For the first time in a long time, Ronny was having fun and getting turned on at the same time. It felt grand to be alive.

At this rate he'd grow fat from eating cookies, or faint again. He looked like he didn't much care which as long as she stayed close.

Chapter 24

THURSDAY, TEN P.M.
DELANEY FARM

DUSTI WAS SITTING OUT ON THE DOCK WHEN KIERAN DROVE down Rainbow Lane and turned into their drive. By the time she noticed him it was too late to slip her jeans back on, so she did her best to act like she wasn't sitting in her underwear and hoped he wouldn't notice.

He grinned, reading her mind. "Looks like a grand way to cool off, lass." He lifted a bag. "I figure I've eaten enough of your food, so I brought by ice cream hoping you'd still be awake."

She started to stand, then remembered that she wasn't dressed. "Turn around."

"Not a chance," he answered.

She stared at him as she stood and tugged on her jeans. To his credit, his eyes never dropped lower than her smile.

"We're here to play poker," she said, walking past him. "So as soon as I eat half that ice cream, we're playing one last time."

"That's the plan."

And surprisingly, that was exactly what they did. He dealt the hands faster, making her think quicker. "It's got to be almost instinct," he'd say over and over again. "You have to take it all in and compute what your move is. The longer you think, the more time you're giving the other players to think."

Dusti played every hand, barely noticing when he tried to distract her, or bluff her, or force her to respond with emotion and not logic.

Two hours later, when Dusti said good night to Kieran, she knew she might as well have said good-bye. Tomorrow was the big game and both would be playing to win. Neither had mentioned the other half of their bet. He'd said he would teach her to play, and she'd agreed to a date. If she lost, she wasn't sure she'd want to go, and if he lost, he might be the one to call it off.

For a man who wanted to go out with her and claimed she'd turned him down three times, he didn't seem all that interested in her now. Most of the times she'd cuddled up to him, he'd reminded her they had work to do if she planned to learn to play in time.

The next afternoon, when Dusti made her twenty-dollar donation to play, she found herself searching the mob for a tall Scot. It seemed everyone in town either wanted to support the library, so they were out on the Truman farm helping out, or had come to play.

While Dusti got her number and rack of chips, Abby whispered, "Where did some of these guys come from?" Men in business suits, cowboys, oil field workers, all ages came to play. Of the two hundred, only ten were women.

Dusti smiled as she and Abby backed to the edge of the crowd. "Remember what Kieran told us. There are all types who play. Assume everyone is already playing you even before you sit down at the table. Like that woman, who looks like she came to pole dance, may be a real pro, and the man in dark glasses may have made millions."

"Or," Abby added, "she just woke up from a bender last night and forgot to change clothes, and he is cross-eyed and doesn't want to confuse people."

Half an hour later they'd met all types. The flirt. The once-high roller. Mr. Lucky who bragged about all the big games he'd played. The bully who seemed determined to bother as many people as possible.

Then Dusti's number was called. She ran to her table. She'd decided she wanted to play across from the dealer, and as the second one there she got her pick of chairs.

She was so glad Bill Ottoson from the gun range was the dealer. He seemed levelheaded and not too talky. Dusti had watched a few of the tables that had already started and the dealers weren't the best. Mrs. McNabb, for one, wanted to know before she started if everyone had washed their hands. George Hatcher, owner of the bookstore, spilled his coffee as he sat down to deal, so his game started late. Most of the people drafted to deal would only have to do the job for the first hour or so. Then the two hundred players would drop down to twenty. Only the winners moved on.

Dusti did what Kieran had told her; she studied every person at the table. Two were already half drunk. Three looked barely old enough to play. One had brought her knitting. Another lady giggled with excitement when she sat down, saying she was happy to be playing with other ladies.

One older man in a battered Stetson took the seat next to the dealer. Dusti had seen him in town but didn't know his name. He shuffled a stack of chips like they were cards, and she knew he was the man she'd have to beat.

The last man who sat down asked how much each color chip was worth. Dusti didn't bother to look his way again.

All over the grounds people were sitting down to play. Some were talking, or cutting up. A few were bragging about other games or complaining about the heat, but they'd all come to win. One of the two hundred would go to Las Vegas, expenses and buy-in paid, to a game that would pay out millions.

Music drifted from a wagon-bed stage by the barn. Volunteers rushed to fill drinks and set up the buffet. By seven thirty, a line of those already out of the game was forming for the barbecue.

By eight, several of the poker tables had been converted to dining tables. Volunteers and those who'd already lost were dancing to the music of Beau Yates. Three people remained at Bill Ottoson's table: Dusti, the guy in the Stetson, and the little woman who knitted.

Kieran's words came back to her loud and clear. Never underestimate a player. She'd been right about the cowboy, but the knitter was a complete surprise. The woman broke most of the rules Kieran had told her. She counted her chips. She took her time thinking about each hand, and she even asked for advice now and then.

More tables were emptied, yet they played on. The urge to bet big and get the game over climbed along Dusti's spine, but Kieran's words in her head kept her on task.

Two tables were roped off near the barn for the next round.

"All in," the cowboy said, shoving his multicolored chips to the center.

Bill smiled as he waited and said the first general comment he'd made in more than an hour of play. "When I was in the navy, we used to call that 'betting the rainbow.' All chips. All colors. I've always thought some folks live their lives that way. Playing every day all-out, win or lose it all."

"Call." The knitter looked interested for once.

Before Dusti could react, the cowboy stood and walked away, cussing his luck. When she glanced at the cards on the table, she saw he'd been beaten by the knitter.

"Well, I never," the knitter said. "On the Internet no one ever does that."

Three hands later the lady folded her knitting and walked away, seemingly in shock that she'd lost.

Dusti thanked Bill and ran to the food. With very few tables still playing the first round, she'd have to eat fast. Soon, she'd be called to the next round.

Two bites later, someone stepped in front of her and said, "Want to dance, lass?"

She forgot the food and jumped off the bench. "I won," she said, hugging him. "I won the first round."

"Good." He laughed. "I'm a great teacher."

"Or, I'm a good player." She moved with him to the music. "How'd you do?"

"I won half an hour ago. I've had two plates of barbecue already, and one of the Red Hat ladies has tried to pick me up twice. If they don't start the next round soon, I'll be too fat to sit in the folding chair and probably married to a woman three times my age."

Dusti wanted to tell him all about the game she'd played. The way she'd watched every player and read them right. How she'd almost yelped when she won her first big pot.

Only she couldn't tell him. Kieran was in this as well. Somehow, they weren't on the same team anymore.

As they two-stepped, she looked around at all the people laughing and talking. "If I had a camera, I'd shoot some shots. This whole night seems magic."

He leaned down, pushing his chin against her hair. "I got one in the car. It's an old one my dad had. Still uses film, but I love the pictures I get with it. I always travel with it just in case one day I discover an ounce of talent for photography. My dad had quite an eye for seeing things others don't notice."

"Could I borrow it?"

"Sure," he answered, smiling down at her.

Five minutes later Dusti was shooting pictures. Couples dancing, Beau Yates lost in a song, the Red Hat ladies line dancing. The lanterns in the apple trees. Reagan holding someone's baby up close to her cheek.

Dusti almost missed the call for the next round.

As she sat down, Dusti set the camera where she could see it and remember what she was playing for. It felt so good in her hands, reminding her of her dream. She had to win. Abby had to finish school, and then it would be her turn. Someday she might just make her living taking pictures. Her mother used to say Dusti could see things through the lens of a camera that most folks go all their lives without seeing.

Kieran sat down at the other table. The second round was starting. He looked calm, but she knew he was already sizing up every other player.

When the dealer called him by name, the cowboy across from Kieran made fun of it.

"Sounds like a girl's name."

"It's not," Kieran said simply. "It's a fairly common name in Scotland. Pronounced like 'Care-an' with a roll on the *R*."

"Oh, you're a foreigner."

"No, I'm not. I live in New York."

The cowboy grinned. "Then you're a damn Yankee."

"Let's play cards," the dealer interrupted.

Dusti grinned, knowing exactly what the cowboy had been trying to do and also knowing Kieran wouldn't take the bait. His words drifted in her mind. *Play your hand. Never get emotional. Never let another player affect you. Never be out to get someone.*

As the dealer at her table started, she was now playing with only men. The game went faster this time. Everyone at the table knew how to play. No one knitted.

To her surprise, she won the second round easily.

After running to the bathroom in Reagan's house, then grabbing a sandwich, she stood on the edges of the circle and watched Kieran play. He was ice, never looking at the crowd, never looking at his cards more than once. He played hand after hand. Now and then she held her breath when the pot was big or the cowboy across from him kept calling him Kieran without the Scottish accent that made his name sound so different.

By the time Kieran won, Dusti was seriously considering bopping the cowboy on the head, but Kieran simply stood and offered his hand to the man.

The cowboy mumbled something and turned away without shaking. No one seemed to notice but Dusti. Even Kieran dropped his hand and walked toward the table of iced tea without a backward glance.

"I won," she whispered behind him a few minutes later.

He turned and smiled. "We're down to two, lass. It's just me and you now."

The evening had drifted into night without her noticing. One more round and the game would be over. She took pictures for a while during the thirty-minute break, then found him for a dance beneath the stars.

He placed his hand on her arm as a slow song seemed to melt the tension in the night. "We've got a few minutes before the next round. How about we don't talk and just dance. I like having my arms around you."

Dusti wished she could ask him a few more questions, but she knew it was too late. So she slid her hand around his waist and moved her body close against his.

And they danced. For a few minutes neither focused on manipulation or analyzing their competitors. Both wanted there to be no one but the two of them and the music.

Chapter 25

HAWK HOUSE

THE EVENING OF THE BIG POKER GAME AT THE TRUMAN FARM, Ronny waited until Abby's boat left Austin's dock before she brought dinner. She didn't feel like sharing him with anyone. The Delaneys had taken turns keeping him company since he fell, but tonight they would all be at the poker tournament. Ronny would be alone with Austin, exactly the way she wanted it.

Last night she'd left with the others because she saw the dark circles under Austin's eyes. He'd endured the pain silently, but she knew he was tired and hurting. He was a man used to pushing his body to the limit, and it appeared he planned to do the same now. Most of the time he ignored the pain pills and forced himself to stand or walk more than was necessary. Maybe, if it were just the two of them, he'd let his guard down and relax.

When she entered Hawk House without knocking, she was surprised to find Austin dressed in clean clothes, his hair still wet from the shower. He sat on the corner of his bed that faced the kitchen.

"You took a shower?" Ronny said her thoughts. "What about the bandage?"

He smiled up at her, and she thought he looked younger. Maybe a few years younger than she was. His actions had always made him seem older, but now, smiling, she saw the boy who had once been inside the man.

"About time you got here. I'm starving." The look in his eyes left no doubt that food wasn't all he wanted. "I thought since everyone left, we might have a date. Of course, we can't go anywhere and you'd have to cook, but still, we could pretend. You're a lady I'd like to take out on a date. I'd show you off to the whole town if I could."

"I like that idea. Who knows, maybe someday we can walk the town square together, but right now, I'm worried about how you took a shower." She set the basket on the counter and began unloading dinner into the refrigerator.

"Abby took the bandage off and stood at the door while I showered. Then she rewrapped the wound. She dresses a wound better than most medics I've seen."

"Oh." A new feeling battled in her mind. She was a bit jealous. Something she'd never expected. "Did you kiss her?"

He didn't answer for a while, just watched her. "Come over here, Ronny."

The frown she knew so well returned, creasing his face. She slowly walked to him, thinking her question made her sound like a teenager with her first boyfriend.

He took both her hands in his. "We need to talk. I'm not in the habit of kissing women, any women. Up until a few months ago I was in the army, and any woman I met was usually in a bar near the fort. I sometimes went home with one for the night, but we skipped the kissing part. I stayed away from women like you because I didn't want any ties. I didn't plan on leaving a widow or worrying about a girl double-timing me back home. Some of my buddies went half nuts about things like that."

"Forget I asked about Abby. I was just being funny." She could feel him moving away from her even though he remained on the corner of the bed.

"It's not about Abby. This is about me and you." He swore and mumbled, "I'm no good at this. Maybe we should forget talking."

"Say what you need to say, Austin." She braced for good-bye.

His green eyes fired a moment as if he were preparing to fight, then he took a deep breath as if organizing his thoughts. "I'm saying I don't think I can walk away from you, Ronny." He smiled suddenly. "And it has nothing to do with me being shot in the leg. What's between us can be no one-night stand. You've probably had a lot of lovers, but for me this will be my first try at anything besides sex. I want to do it right."

She knelt down beside him, knowing how hard his words came. "We'll have to talk about things. I'll need to know how you feel. You're not an easy man to read."

"I know," he said.

"I want to know what you're thinking about things . . . about me. I want to know all about you, good and bad."

His fingers moved into her hair and she rose to meet his lips. The kiss was gentle and soft, like a first kiss. As he kissed her lightly, he whispered against her cheek, "I can't stop watching you move. I love the way you smell and how you come to me hungry for the feel of me. I'd like to make love to you all day and all night long." He held her face in his hands. "Is that a good start? Is that enough about what is on my mind?"

Pulling away, she sat back on her feet. "It's a good start, I think," she whispered without looking at him.

He waited, and then his words came, more hurt than angry. "I'm moving too fast. You're probably used to lovers taking their time. I'm sorry. I didn't mean to frighten you. Hell, I went from asking for a first date to talking about making love. There was supposed to be a middle part there somewhere."

She studied his face, knowing she had to start this with the truth between them. "I've never made love."

Doubt flashed in his eyes.

"I've loved one man. He was in a wheelchair. He died."

She'd just boiled her entire life down to three short sentences.

Austin pulled her up as he stood. Without a word, he lay back on the bed, taking her with him. Then he just held her close as if he needed to think about what she'd just told him.

For no reason at all, Ronny felt tears running down her cheeks. She didn't know if she was crying because a chapter in her life was ending or out of fear over the chapter that was beginning. All she did know was that Austin would be there to hold her through the changes.

Brushing her hair away, he kissed each tear. "We're going to take this slow. We'll figure it out together. Ronny, you're too important to me for me to get this wrong. I need to do this right."

His hands moved gently over her body. "And when we make love, we're both going to know that is exactly what we're doing. No one-night stand. No games."

"Just promise me one thing." She fought back tears. "Promise me we will make love."

"You can bet on it, pretty lady."

Chapter 26

TRUMAN FARM

REAGAN FELT SHE WAS IN THE MIDDLE OF A MERRY-GO-ROUND. For two days people had been at her farm offering to help. It seemed everyone who didn't want to play poker wanted to watch. With all the money going to support the library, except first prize, even people who didn't approve of gambling saw this night as a good cause.

Women's groups delivered desserts, and half the businesses in town pitched in with paper goods, bottled water, and decorations. The library committee couldn't agree on a theme for the night, so they simply went with *Summertime.*

Maria, Joe's wife, had brought her two youngest children over about noon on the day of the game and said she'd keep Utah for the rest of the evening.

Reagan was surprised at how hard it was to let him go. The little fellow mattered to her more than she wanted to admit. Even though she'd only had him a short time, if his mother came back, it would be hard to turn him over to a woman who seemed to care so little. She'd smoked with him in the car, called him "it," as if he were a thing, and driven away without glancing back. Just thinking about how little his mother had cared about him made Reagan want to run upstairs and hug Utah one more time today.

Only by the time people started coming in to pay their money to play, Reagan was lost in preparations. The Friends of the Library had set up offices in her kitchen and were running everything as if the room were a command post. Players were taking their seats, food was moving into ovens, drink table were being set up.

When Reagan had heard her front door bang open, she'd been the only one who even seemed to notice.

"Rea." Noah's voice sounded loud and clear above the hum of worker bees. "Rea, are you in here?"

For a second she almost jumped up and ran to him like she always did. The need to feel him lift her in his arms ran all the way back to their high school days when they'd said they would always be best friends.

"Rea," he said more calmly as he stepped into the kitchen and spotted her working with several others. "There's my girl." His smile was wide and open.

Reagan thought she heard her heart breaking over the noise around her. She turned and watched the tall, lean cowboy move toward her. He'd become exactly what he said he'd be the first time they'd talked in high school. He'd said he would be one hunk of a good-looking man when his body filled out and his face cleared up. His laughing brown eyes now reflected his sharp mind and his warm brown hair was a bit too long, silently marking him as a rebel.

Three of the women at the table jumped up to hug him. McAllens were related to half the people in town, and everyone kept up with Harmony's favorite son, the great bull rider Noah McAllen.

Everyone wanted to know how he'd been and how the rides were going. One said she watched him on TV last week. Another gray-haired woman said she had to have a kiss. Then they all joined the line forming. They all loved him, and he loved playing to the crowd.

Reagan just watched. She'd realized a long time ago that part of him belonged to the town.

Noah was the hometown hero. He'd gone higher than even his father had with the rodeo, and folks still talked about Adam McAllen.

Looking over the gray hair, Noah winked at Reagan as if to say he was sorry, but he had to play the role.

Ten minutes later he grabbed her hand and pulled her out the back door, with all the ladies giggling.

Reagan shoved away from him as soon as they were out of sight of everyone.

He just smiled that killer smile of his. "Hey, Rea, I know I've been gone a long time, but it's me, remember, the guy who loves you and has since he first saw you in high school. Dear God, I've missed you and that wild hair of yours. Even when you were more kid than woman I spent hours thinking about what that hair would feel like in my hands."

When she didn't move toward him, he grinned and held out his arms. "I'm sorry, Rea. You know I'd rather be here with you, so get over being mad at me and come closer. I'm home now."

"I don't want to hug you, Noah, until you answer a few questions." Her words cut their way along the inside of her throat. She didn't want to say what had to be said.

He almost pulled off looking serious. "Go ahead, play hard to get, Rea. We both know where this is going to end up. I busted my butt getting home in time to help with this little party you're throwing. I know you haven't got time for me right now. I'm here to help. But tonight when everyone finally leaves, it'll be just you and me."

She folded her arms to keep from touching him. "You were due three weeks ago."

"I know, but I had a chance to ride up north and I couldn't turn it down. If I'm ever going to walk away with enough money to fix up my old place, I've got to keep going."

She wasn't even sure if the ranch was his dream anymore. It was more likely just something that he said when he was home. They'd had the same conversation for three years and he was no closer to coming back to Harmony to stay than he was then.

"Noah, you don't have to 'bust your butt' coming back to Harmony any more, or to me. You can stay on the road as long as you want. I'm finished waiting for you."

He opened his mouth to say something, then stopped. Her words finally registered in his mind. "Rea, don't kid me. I haven't had any sleep in two days. You almost sound as if you're breaking up with me, and we both know that'll never happen." His gaze narrowed on her face and for a blink she saw the flash of doubt across his handsome face.

"Noah, I *am* breaking up with you. 'Never' *has happened*."

"No." He shook his head. "You can't, not like this. Not because I didn't make it in as soon as I said I would. If it's that important, I'll promise I'll be in next time I say I'm coming."

She wanted to run as far away as she could from him, from them. The hurt in his eyes shattered her heart, but she'd made up her mind. "You'd promise that the way you promised not to sleep with anyone else while you were on the road."

"I haven't . . ." he started, but she saw the lie in his hesitation.

Reagan knew she had to get it all out. If they were going to have even a polite friendship left when this was over, she had to be honest now.

"A woman came by several days ago. She left something for you. She said she'd had sex with you like 'sleeping with a bull rider' had been on her bucket list. She handed me one of the wooden boxes I ship apples in. Said it was what you store your gear in on the road. Inside was a three-week-old baby. Your baby."

Noah was shaking his head, but she didn't give him time to talk.

"She said you were drunk and you called her by my name." Almost in a whisper she added, "You called her my name, Noah. How could you do that?"

Noah closed his eyes.

"She named the baby Utah. Said you'd know why."

The name had been the last blow. Noah looked like he'd been stomped on by a herd of bulls. It took him a few minutes to find words.

Reagan waited as if silently facing a firing squad.

"I was drunk that night in Salt Lake. I swear, Rea, I don't even know how she got in my room. She was just there. I knew it was wrong from the start, but I was so lonely that night. I thought that it wouldn't matter. It meant nothing to me."

Reagan raised her head. "Thank you for being honest. The baby has your eyes. I see you in him every time I look at him."

He took each word like a silent blow.

Reagan stood, a soldier determined to deliver the entire report no matter how much it hurt. "I couldn't believe she just left him here. She said she had other kids at home and a husband who wouldn't be happy about her bringing home a bastard. She said she wouldn't claim him even if you found her."

"Where is he now?"

"He's upstairs with Maria."

Noah tossed his hat aside and dug his fingers through his hair. "I don't know if I can handle this, Rea. A baby. I don't even remember what the woman looked like, or her name." He faced Reagan. "I don't guess there's a chance in hell of you believing me when I say that was the only time it happened. Sure, women hang on me all the time, but I never took any to bed. Not before or after that one. That night I was so drunk when I woke up I wasn't sure if it happened or I dreamed it."

"It doesn't matter. Utah is here now. You can have a test to make sure, but the woman didn't have any reason to lie. If she'd been after money, I wouldn't have believed her. She seemed to want this kept quiet as much as you probably do. She said she'd never, ever come back."

He sat down on the back step. The great bull rider had just taken the tumble of his life, and Reagan had no idea how he'd handle it. Because this time she wouldn't be there by his side.

She knew she had to get back to the preparations, but things had to be said between them. "One thing, Noah. If you decide you can't keep the baby, I can. I'll not keep him for you. If I take him he'll be mine legally, but you can still see him. Whether you tell him you're his father is up to you. But from now on there is no us."

She walked back into the house trying her best not to shatter into a million pieces. Before she could think about what had just happened, people began calling her, first from one direction, then another. They needed help. The biggest fund-raiser of the year was under way and Reagan had to turn her mind to all that had to be done and close away her breaking heart.

An hour passed before she had time to glance out the back door.

Noah was gone.

Reagan climbed the stairs and took a sleeping Utah into her arms. For a while she just rocked him, wishing she could talk to him. Silently promising him that if she had her way he'd never be tossed around from home to home.

A child no one wanted.

A kid like she'd been.

Closing her eyes, she could still see the hurt in Noah's face. Her words had crushed him far more than any bull ever would or could.

Reagan let tears fall as she remembered all the loving, kind, funny things he'd done to make her laugh and love. Could she really give him up? Could she live without her Noah in her life?

Could she live with a liar . . . or a man who could walk away from his own son?

Maria found her and the baby asleep in the rocker half an hour later. She'd been drifting, wishing today were a dream and she'd wake up. The only problem was that today had been the nightmare she had to wake up to.

Reagan handed Utah to her gently.

"You go," Maria said. "Many are looking for you."

Reagan nodded and stood. "I'll be back as soon as I can. Once the second round of games start, maybe I can give him his bottle."

"You come, but don't send that cowboy. He made so much noise coming up the stairs he woke up the baby." She huffed. "Then he said he had to hold Utah, but I don't know why. I swear that man never held a newborn before in his life."

Reagan walked out of the room realizing Noah must have climbed the stairs to see his son. An eight-pound baby had devastated both their worlds, and Reagan had no idea where the next step in her life would lead.

All she knew was that she wouldn't be holding Noah's hand for the rest of the journey.

Chapter 27

BUFFALO'S BAR

NOAH POUNDED ON THE DOOR OF BUFFALO'S BAR FOR FIVE minutes before Harley, the owner, finally opened up.

"What you doing here?" he grumbled. "I thought you'd be at the poker game if you were in town."

Noah didn't want to talk. He didn't want to think. He only wanted to drink. He walked to the bar and leaned against it as if the wood would somehow give him comfort.

It didn't.

Half an hour later the place was starting to fill up with people who didn't care about the poker game going on over at the Truman farm and losers who were out in the first round.

Everyone who knew Noah offered to buy him a drink, and Noah didn't turn down a one of them.

By dark he stumbled out on the deck and stared in the direction of Reagan's farm. Though miles away, he swore he could see the glow of lights from the orchard. She was there, all alone in a crowd of people. He knew her so well. He knew why she'd agreed to have the fund-raiser. Harmony was her town, her home. She cared about the town and the people.

He also knew why she said she'd keep the baby. Reagan had spent the first fifteen years of her life being tossed around.

He called himself every name he could think of, but *damn fool* seemed to be his favorite. A hundred *what-if*s danced with the *maybe*s in his mind. What if he'd come home and told her the night after it happened ten months ago? Would she have forgiven him then? Maybe he should have come back five months ago when he had downtime. She would have married him then, and maybe they'd have worked this out together.

Reagan had always been the one he loved. Even before he figured his life out and ran around with wild women on the circuit, he knew that someday he'd come home to her. She was the one he wanted to grow old with. She was the one he made love to in his dreams.

She didn't understand how hard it was on the road. All the world gets mixed up when your whole life revolves around eight seconds. Bad food and hotel rooms that all look the same. Bars that smell the same. Women who act the same, always coming on to him. Always wanting him to be their one wild moment.

Reagan was his base. The only place where he could step away from all the noise and smoke and crowds. The one person who understood him.

Noah tossed the empty beer bottle he'd downed into a trash can that looked like it had served as a bumper pad for the steps for years. Damn it, he understood her too. He knew what it had taken for her to tell him good-bye. He felt her hurt as much as he felt his own. When they'd met, he'd always been the one to make her feel like she belonged. Folks were nice to her from the first because they knew she was his friend. She needed him as dearly as he needed her. They fit together.

Only she'd said she didn't want to see him again. Never! He was no longer a part of her life.

Noah remembered all the times she'd been afraid and down. He'd always been the one who pulled her up and made her laugh.

He wasn't drunk enough to see the answer, but he was sober enough to know he had to try. He had to go back and convince her that this was something they could handle together. If she wanted the baby, she'd have to take him too. In the years they'd been friends and lovers, there had never been a problem they couldn't work out.

Noah started to his pickup and realized he couldn't drive. His big sister, Alex Matheson, was the sheriff, and if she caught him one point over the limit she'd lecture him all the way to jail.

A guy he used to know from high school walked out and waved at him.

"Where you headed?" Noah asked, guessing where he'd be going tonight.

"Thought I'd go back to the tournament. It shouldn't be long until the last round will be played, and I want to see who made the final table."

"Mind if I ride along with you?"

"No, come on. I've still got two beer tickets to use."

Ten minutes later Noah was in the crowd. He didn't care anything about the few tables still playing the second round of cards. All he wanted to do was find Reagan and reason with her.

It took a while, but finally he saw her standing near the stage listening to Beau Yates play. The sadness in the way she held herself, her arms folded across her, as if she believed no one would ever hold her, tore at his heart. The knowledge that all this was his fault stabbed at him.

For a moment, on that night more than ten months ago, he'd known what he was doing was wrong. The woman hadn't felt right in his arms. She was tall and her hair blond, not curly red like Reagan's. He should have stopped and ordered her out, but instead he'd closed his eyes and pretended Reagan was with him.

It hadn't worked. Even when he was having sex, it didn't feel right. Reagan wasn't in his arms. He'd rolled away and fallen asleep, wishing he'd stopped and calling himself a fool for going all the way with a woman he didn't even know.

He had to convince Reagan the woman meant nothing. Reagan was his world and it took this to know it.

"Reagan," he said from a few feet behind her. "Rea, you got to talk to me."

She twirled around and faced him. "No, I don't. Not here. Not now. Maybe not ever. Go away, Noah."

He grabbed her arm. "We're going to work this out. We have to. It hurts too badly."

She jerked out of his grip. "You're drunk, Noah. Go away."

"No. I'm not going away. Not until you talk to me. Not until I make you understand—"

Before he could clear his head enough to think of what to say to make her stay, huge arms locked around him from behind and lifted him off the ground.

Noah was kicking and fighting, but the human forklift who had him didn't loosen his grip. They were moving away from the crowd. Away from Reagan. Away from the one person who made his life worth living.

"The lady says she doesn't want to talk to you, cowboy, so maybe you should go away."

"Biggs!" Noah stopped fighting. "Put me down, Big. You're not part of this. This is between Rea and me, no one else."

They were still on the edge of the crowd, but Big set him down hard.

Noah stumbled, trying not to fall. "Stay out of this, Big. This is not your problem. I came to talk to Rea."

"You've always been my problem, McAllen. I'd have to be a blind man not to see that you've hurt Reagan again. And this time if she says she doesn't want to see you, I plan to make sure you stay away."

Noah swung wildly and Big ducked. The huge construction worker shoved Noah hard, sending him flying into a huddle of men who'd decided this show was part of the entertainment. A few guys seemed to catch Noah and toss him back toward Big.

Swinging again, Noah hit his mark on the second try, and Big's head jerked from the blow.

"I don't want to fight you, Noah." Big swore and shook

his head as if clearing away the pain. "I only want you gone. So leave."

"Well, I'm fighting you, Big. It's been a long time coming, but it's time you stepped out from between me and my girl. You've been the third wheel for long enough."

"I've been her friend," Big corrected. "And she ain't your girl anymore. From what I saw she wants no part of you. Whatever you did this time, Preacher, you hurt her bad."

Noah didn't react to the nickname folks used to call him years ago when he rode. "What makes you think I did anything? There's always two sides. Maybe she's the one who is being stubborn for not even listening to my side."

"You don't have a side. Not the way I see it." Big widened his stance. "It's always your fault, to my way of thinking. So get off her farm and leave her alone."

Noah knew Big had a serious girlfriend. He also knew the grown-up thug loved Reagan.

"I'm not leaving." He swung again, plowing a fist into Big's middle. "Maybe *you* should go."

The giant didn't move. "I'm not fighting you. Wouldn't want to mess up that pretty face, Preacher. Since you've already knocked out all your brains riding, way I see it, all you got left is your looks."

A crowd gathered, offering advice about the battle they'd all seen coming for years. Suddenly their argument was drawing more fans than the poker game.

Noah swung again. "You're fighting me, because I'm not leaving until you do."

"I don't want to hurt you, Preacher." Big almost sounded like he was trying to reason while Noah continued to swing.

"What makes you think you'll hurt me? I ride thousand-pound bulls for a living."

Big ducked again before he answered, "Yeah, and I move mountains for a living. So don't push me and stop swinging. You're about as bothersome as a giant horsefly. I don't want to put a dent in that pretty face, Noah."

Cowboys were lining up behind Noah. Men in steel-toed

boots were backing up Big. If a brawl started, twenty or more men were ready to jump into the battle, and none seemed interested in why the two men were fighting.

Suddenly, a huge Dodge Ram, with a rack of bright lights mounted on top, dug its way through the crowd.

Before Noah could move, his sister, the sheriff, and her husband climbed out, pushing back the crowd. Hank Matheson wasn't as tall as Big, but his bulk could have taken Big on if need be. Only he ignored Big and turned to Noah.

"This is stopping right now!" Alex yelled in her official voice. "Noah, get in the truck. Big, back down or I'm taking you both to jail. We're not having a fight here tonight. Do you both hear me?"

"Good, put us in the same cell and we'll settle this." Noah took a step toward Big, and his brother-in-law shoved him back into place.

Big didn't budge an inch. He might as well have been planted in one spot.

Noah watched his sister scan the crowd. He knew she was dealing with a mob, and once again tonight it was all his fault. If a fight broke out this close to the house, Reagan would have damage to her place. One more thing to blame him for.

Hank climbed onto the bed of his truck. "Noah, Big, this isn't happening here. You two are not ruining this night for everyone else."

"We're fighting this out tonight, Hank. Here or in jail, I plan on teaching this idiot to stop butting into my life." Noah was still yelling, but an ounce of the fight was gone. No matter how old he got, one look from his big sister could always remind him of the fool he was making of himself.

"Not here." Hank's words were almost calm.

"Then where?" Big demanded.

"Up past the orchard is a pass-over to my land. You can trade blows out there but not on Truman land."

Everyone started moving toward the trees except Noah.

His sister stood in front of him, blocking any way out. "Don't do this, Noah. Whatever this is about, don't fight Big."

"I have to," Noah said as he stepped around her and headed toward the trees. "You'll have to arrest me to stop me."

He saw her glance at her husband.

Noah heard Hank's words as he headed up the trail to the orchard. "It'll be a fair fight on plowed ground. That's all I can promise. You can't stop this, Alex. It's been a long time coming."

Noah didn't know if his sister replied. She'd been protecting him since their big brother, Warren, was killed eleven years ago, but she couldn't protect him from the hurting now. Nothing Big could do to him would be nearly as painful as the last look Reagan had given him.

The fight was nothing. Noah wanted it. He needed it. Maybe it would beat some sense into him.

Hank made the men who came to watch stay at the fence line between the Truman and Matheson properties. Noah and Big walked twenty feet out into a field bumpy with dirt clods.

"Anyone want to tell me what this trouble is about?" Hank asked as he stood between them.

"No," both said at once.

Noah wanted Biggs mad. If the big guy was going to hit him, he welcomed the blows. Hell, he deserved them. "I'm going to teach a lesson to this brain-dead fool who thinks he can come between Rea and me."

Big puffed up just like Noah knew he would. "I'm tired of listening to you, cowboy. You think you're hot stuff just because you can stay on a bull for eight seconds, but you can't even stay home long enough to make someone who loves you happy."

"That's right, Big, she loves me. Not you, me."

"I've had enough. This ain't going to be much of a fight, but it's about time I knocked some sense into you. You're fixing to get religion real fast, Preacher, and the blood you're going to be washed in is gonna be your own."

Noah rushed forward swinging.

Biggs took a blow to the nose and another to the middle before he shoved Noah off him.

Landing in the dirt, Noah jumped up and ran at Big again.

Blood flew from Big's nose as he dodged.

Noah caught him on the chin and Big fell backward.

Finally, Big threw a punch hard and fast. His massive fist landed one hit against Noah's chin, ending the fight and knocking Noah out cold.

Chapter 28

TRUMAN FARM

As the music that flowed around the orchard at the Truman farm ended, Dusti Delaney tried to smile, but Kieran's gray eyes looked as tired as she felt. The red in his hair was almost brown in the lantern light and she thought he looked like exactly what he was, an adventurer. He'd come back to Harmony to play cards yet he'd taken her on the adventure with him. She knew then that it wasn't the prize but the journey that mattered to him.

Nervous that she'd discovered such a truth about him, she studied the orchard, the barn, anywhere but his eyes. "Where did everyone go?" she asked, more for something to say than out of interest.

Kieran shrugged. "Some went over to the Matheson land to see a fight between two drunks, I think. Most went home. The last round doesn't start until eleven. When you're not playing, the fun of watching doesn't last long."

He took her hand. "We've got thirty minutes to relax. The last game is set up in the barn, where the light will be a little more dependable."

"I'll be playing you." Dusti closed her fingers around his.

"That's right, and I'll know if you're not playing your best, so let's rest while we can. You need to relax, but don't let the game go yet. You've got one more challenge."

He was still helping her, teaching her. Or, at least she thought he was. For all she knew, he might be playing her now. Kieran O'Toole wasn't an easy man to read.

They walked to where the grass grew tall near the orchard. He sat back, leaning against a tree, and she spread out beside him. Neither touched. It wouldn't be fair. Not now. They didn't need distractions.

"What can we talk about?" she asked, knowing it couldn't be the game.

"I don't know. How about the pictures you took?"

She told him about all the moments she'd captured. She'd gotten some really good shots, and the old darkroom back at the farm was still waiting for her. Dusti knew it would take her most of the night, but she'd develop the film before dawn.

He talked a little about how his dad had taken pictures everywhere he went for as long as he could remember. Every time they moved, the "boxes of memories" had to come with them.

"I've tried, but I didn't inherit his talent. I carry the camera, but I rarely remember to snap a picture." Kieran laughed to himself. "Most of the memories I'd pack along in a box if I could would be of here. When I'm in Paris or Rome I often think of Harmony. There's a peace here. Austin and I talked about it once when we had dinner in New York. We think the people who live here don't even see it. They don't know what they have."

"Dust storms, grass fires, and wild pigs," Dusti reminded him.

"Oh course, lass, but Harmony also has the prettiest girls in the world, and clear air, and long sunsets, and . . ."

"I get your point. Maybe I should spend a few days capturing all this beauty you see. I could probably get the chickens to pose for a few shots."

"I'd like that," he said as he closed his eyes and folded his arms across his chest.

Dusti watched him for a while. He was relaxed here. Even waiting for the biggest game in the county to begin, he was relaxed. She couldn't help but wonder if he was the same in all those big cities he passed through.

Finally, when someone blinked the yard lights, he moved. When he opened his eyes, she saw no sign that he'd been sleeping. "Win or lose," he whispered, "will you send me the pictures? I'd like to cover a wall of my apartment with them. Then when I come home, I'll be feeling like I'm coming back to Harmony."

"Sure. If you'll send me postcards of the cities you visit. I think it must be fascinating to travel the world for a living. Every time you fly somewhere new, you have to mail me a card."

"Fair trade. You can dream of traveling and I'll dream of Harmony. Sometimes I think it would be heaven to look out the same window every morning until the seasons make a full circle, or walk into a room and know what's in every drawer without looking." He was silent for a while, then added, "When I'm all alone in a city, I think about how great it would be to walk down a street and say hello or wave at all the people. I'd know where I was, not just the name of the place, or a street number, but I'd know where I was even blindfolded."

"Sounds pretty boring to me." She stared up at the stars.

"You wouldn't think so if you ran into a wall and door frames in the dark once a month because you forgot the layout of the room or thought you were home. I once fell off a balcony thinking I was headed to the bathroom. Luckily I was on the first-floor balcony. Unluckily, I was sleeping nude that night."

She laughed. "I'd pay to see that."

"Which one? Me falling off, or me naked?"

"Both."

"You might get your chance one day, lass."

"Which one?" she asked, as if serious.

"Both, probably," he answered. "I'm a heavy sleeper who

tends to walk in my sleep, and I've always considered paja-
mas extra weight in my luggage, except of course when I'm
traveling to Granny's house."

"You still take the long flannel footies to your grandmother's?"

"No, she always buys them for me every Christmas.
They're there waiting for me on the twin bed in her sewing
room."

She giggled at the thought of Kieran hanging off both
ends of a twin bed.

He reached over and held her hand as if they'd been lovers for years. His easy conversation had done the job; she'd
relaxed.

Finally, she asked, "When will you be leaving?"

"Tomorrow morning. I really did just come to play and
check on my grandmother."

"Tomorrow," she said, and before she thought, she added,
"I'll miss you." She wanted to add that she'd miss all the
*could have been*s too. For the first time she hadn't acted on
an attraction, and she had a feeling she'd always regret not
having more time with him.

"You won't have time to miss me much. Remember your
promise. We have a date."

"You still want that?" The thought of spending an entire
evening alone with him and nothing happening between
them sounded like pure torture.

"You bet. I've got it all planned out in my mind."

"Wanna tell me?"

"No, lass, ye'll have to wait until the time is right. You
made me wait long enough before saying yes to this date, so
it won't hurt you to wonder for a while." He winked. "I used
to wonder what you looked like in your underwear, but now
I know. Fires up my daydreams, I can tell you that."

"Okay, a real date, but don't make it too long or I'll be
married with three kids before the invitation arrives."

He laughed and brought her hand to his lips. The kiss was
light, almost casual, but it made her want more.

A chime sounded from the front porch. The last round was about to start.

Time to play for her future.

Win or lose.

With or without Kieran by her side.

Chapter 29

TRUMAN FARM
LAST ROUND OF TEXAS HOLD'EM

DUSTI WALKED AHEAD OF KIERAN INTO THE OLD BARN THAT now served as office and packing space for Truman Apples. With the aged wood and the empty boxes lining the walls, the place smelled of apple cider. The kind folks drink hot with a touch of cinnamon, not on warm nights like this one.

Bill stood as she neared the small square table. "I'll be the dealer, this last round," he said simply. "One of you will walk away the winner tonight. Good luck to you both."

Dusti nodded at him. He'd been the best dealer. It was only fair he deal the final round.

She took the seat to Bill's left. Kieran took the one to his right. The tall Scot had taken off his shirt and now wore only a T-shirt that molded to his perfect body.

"V-neck trick, I'm guessing," she whispered, knowing he'd be the only one to understand. He'd warned her about wearing something low cut. Said it wasn't playing fair.

He shook his head. "There's just no breeze in here to cool off." Then, she swore he blushed.

"I'd never pull that trick." She fought down a laugh. There was something about a redheaded man blushing that was so hot.

Gray eyes met hers. "You don't have to, lass. I could look at you in jeans and a flannel shirt and forget what planet I'm on."

Now it was her turn. She felt her cheeks warm.

"Let's play poker," Bill said. "I'm starting to feel like more of a chaperone than a dealer."

As the cards were shuffled, Dusti stared at Kieran, wanting him to look at her again, but he kept his head down. Even when the first two cards were dealt, he didn't look up. It was almost as if she now sat alone.

She thought of all the ways he'd been able to read her. In the earlier games of the tournament, she'd tried hard not to widen her eyes when she got a good hand or lick her lips when she was nervous bluffing. Only this time it wouldn't matter, because he wasn't watching her.

It occurred to her that he didn't want the advantage. Even though he'd told her he'd be playing to win, he planned to simply play the cards dealt this time. It bothered her that he'd thought to be so considerate, almost as much as it irritated her that she wouldn't even have considered returning the favor. Kieran O'Toole was a better person than she was, but then she'd always be near the back of that line.

Her mother's favorite saying was, "Why can't you be good like Abby?" But the way Dusti saw it, the angel-in-the-family part was already taken, so she contented herself in trying out all the other roles.

Dusti forced the images of being bad, really bad, with Kieran from her mind. She had a game to play first. There would be time with Kieran later, even if she had to track him down.

Round after round flowed in the evening air. A dozen men stood watching. The music had stopped, but Dusti could hear the muffled voices of people cleaning up the food and drinks. The fund-raiser had been a great success. The library would have its remodel, and one ticket to Vegas waited for the winner.

One ticket into the biggest pot around. One chance to change her life.

Dusti concentrated, weighing every fold, every call, every bet. She could almost hear him in her head. *Don't fidget. Don't play with your chips. Don't give your opponent any advantage.*

Only now she was playing with Kieran. Only Kieran. He probably knew a dozen signs that he hadn't even mentioned to her, and she didn't really know him at all. For all she knew he'd been bluffing from the moment he'd walked up to her in Buffalo's Bar.

Play the game, she reminded herself. *Play to win.*

She knew Kieran was doing the same thing because he was giving away nothing. He never looked at his cards more than once. His raises were steady and planned. No wild bets or plays to make her nervous or try to corner her into doing something she might regret. Straight poker.

Half an hour passed. Bill asked both if they needed a break. Dusti shook her head and looked up at Kieran. He did the same without looking back at her. She might as well be playing with a total stranger. He seemed all focused on the game. If he had one thought in his head besides poker, she couldn't read a thing.

Bill passed her a pocket pair. Two cards face down. Two aces.

Dusti fought not to smile. The best two cards she could have. Her effort to remain totally still didn't matter, he wasn't looking at her anyway. Yet, she fought to keep from dancing in the chair.

She had more chips than he did. She'd been winning more hands lately. Her luck had just gone from good to great. This could be the last hand if she played it right.

Bill turned the flop. A four of hearts, a seven of clubs, and an ace of diamonds. Excitement shot through her, almost making her jump up and hug Bill. She had three aces.

The first round of betting began. He raised her. She hesitated as if thinking about folding, then met his bet. There was no way she'd fold, but he didn't need to know just how good her pocket cards were.

Bill turned another card and lined it up with the others. A seven, giving her a full house. Three aces and two sevens. Even if he had a seven or four in the pocket, he couldn't win.

Kieran didn't move. She raised, tripling the bet. To her surprise, he stayed in.

The last card, called the "river," flipped on the table. Another four.

Now two pair were showing on the table. Even if he had another seven or a third four, he couldn't beat her.

She tripled the bet again, knowing this would put him very low on chips.

"All in," he said. "Call."

Dusti smiled and turned over her aces. For the first time in the game, he looked straight into her eyes, but he wasn't smiling, he was staring as if memorizing her face.

"Very nice, lass," a tired Scottish voice said. "You got me beat." He tossed his two cards toward Bill.

She knew she should be a good sport and shake hands, but she squealed and jumped up to hug him.

He pulled her close and whispered, "I must be one great teacher. I just didn't plan on you beating me." His words were stilted, almost rehearsed. "Beginner's luck. We'll have to play again sometime."

As he turned her loose, folks watching surrounded her. Hugging, patting her on the back. Telling her dumb things like they couldn't believe a woman won.

Dusti's eyes filled with tears as Abby broke through the crowd and held on to her. "You did it, little sister. I'm so proud of you."

"We're almost there," Dusti added. Tonight had been the easy part. Vegas would be ten times harder. Anyone who could afford a thousand-dollar buy-in would know how to play. The hard poker was yet to come.

Just stay in the game to make one of the paying spots, she reminded herself. In a month they'd have the tuition for nursing school. By fall, Abby would be in school again.

Abby cried, which only made Dusti cry harder.

No one but Kieran saw the dealer pick up the cards he had tossed on the table. Bill turned them face up as he put them on top of the deck.

Two fours.

Bill glanced up, a question in his stare.

Kieran shook his head.

Bill's nod was so slight, no one but an expert poker player would have noticed it. The old man slipped the deck back into the box.

Two fours. The only hand in the deck that could have beaten three aces and two sevens.

Bill grinned. "Over four-thousand-to-one odds of making that four of a kind."

Kieran answered in a whisper, "I guess it just wasn't my night."

He moved into the crowd, smiling as if he'd been the winner tonight and not the one who'd lost.

Chapter 30

⟨❦⟩

TRUMAN FARM

NOAH WOKE UP ON THE COUCH IN REAGAN'S OLD PARLOR.
She'd updated some of the furniture and lightened the room
with beautiful antiques, but the pictures of all the dead Truman relatives were still hanging on the walls, spruced up in
new frames. That was his Reagan. She liked the feeling of
having family close, no matter how ugly they were.

His Reagan. His Reagan?

He closed his eyes and listened to voices coming from the
direction of the dining room. The fight. Reagan's hurt look.
The stupid things he'd done. All drifted back into his brain
like smoke from a dying fire. If wishing he were dead short-
ened life, Noah figured he had a matter of minutes before he
stopped breathing.

The voices kept interrupting his self-hatred.

"Why'd you bring him here?" Rea snapped in anger.

"I don't know." Big's deep voice sounded almost whiny.
"My nose was bleeding. It's hard to think when you've
turned into a human faucet. I knew Ester was still here and
she'd fix me up, so I just headed your direction. I wasn't

thinking about Noah folded over my shoulder. I just wanted to get to her."

Reagan sounded frustrated. "But why'd you bring Noah back *here*? Couldn't someone else take him somewhere else? Couldn't you have just left him in the dirt? Hank would have taken him home."

"Hank said I knocked him out, he was my problem. He wouldn't even let us in his truck. Said we'd bleed all over it. He drove off without even waving good-bye. Downright unfriendly, if you ask me."

"Oh, forget it, Big. When he wakes up I'll have someone drop him off at a McAllen's door. One of his cousins will have to take him in, because he's NOT staying here."

Noah decided he'd be wise to stay unconscious for a while. It might be his only way to survive on Truman land.

"How's your nose?" Rea asked more softly.

"I think it's about stopped bleeding. I can't believe he busted my nose. I always thought my nose was my best feature and now it'll probably point toward my left ear," Big whined. "I swear if he hadn't pushed me, I planned to let him hit me till he got tired. But, hell, Rea, he sure knows how to get on a man's bad side."

"I think he's about on everyone's bad side."

"I don't care. My nose hurts."

"Well, how do you think Noah's going to feel when he wakes up and finds out you knocked him out? Half the population of Harmony saw you carry him in here. The town hero just went down with one punch."

Big laughed. "I told him I didn't want to fight, but he kept calling me names. If he wakes up mad, you want me to knock him out again?"

"No. It probably wouldn't do any good, but I'm not nursing him. I think Hank was right. You knocked him out. You got to take him with you when you leave."

Noah cringed when he thought he heard the smack of a kiss.

"Don't look so unhappy about it. I love you, Big," Reagan said. "Take him home with you, would you? Or, drop him at

Angel De La Cruz's place. They used to rodeo together, maybe he'll take him in."

"Might be a good idea. The only difference in Angel and Noah is Angel was smart enough to get out while he had some brains left. Course, he does get that funny look in his eyes now and then like he's thinking of running with the bulls or something crazy like that."

Noah heard another smack.

"Thanks, Big," she said.

"I know, I love you too," Big answered. "But I got to tell you, it ain't easy being your friend. Noah's not good enough for you and I wouldn't mind seeing him gone, but I hate seeing you look so sad. Want to tell me what he did this time?"

"Nope. You'll find out soon enough. In this town secrets are like morning glories, they come out with the dawn. When you find out, you'll probably go looking for him to hit him a few more times."

Big's answer came fast. "If you say so, I might as well go pound on him a few times before he wakes up. I plan on sleeping late in the morning with my Ester cuddled up close. I figure that's about as near to heaven as I'll ever get." He laughed. "She's a great cuddler, Rea."

"I know, Big, you've told me before. She's one lucky woman to have you. Maybe you should go on home. If you beat on Noah, much as he deserves it, you might make your nose start bleeding again, and that would cut into cuddling time."

"You're right."

Noah only heard parts of the conversation from then on because they moved to the kitchen. He knew they were probably eating pie. Reagan made the best pies in Texas. He wished he could join them, but he doubted he'd be welcome.

He wasn't sure how it happened, but in the few hours he'd been home, he'd managed to mess up every relationship in his life. Rea hated him, Big wanted to beat on him, and his sister and Hank probably wouldn't answer their door if he knocked. Hell, even Harley at the bar wasn't speaking to him. With his luck the Red Hat ladies would clobber him with their purses if he stepped on the porch.

Slowly, he stood and picked up his hat. Without a sound, he walked out of Reagan's house. In the night he slipped away from all the people still milling around and caught a ride back to town. He could think of nowhere he wanted to be, so he crawled into his pickup and went to sleep thinking tomorrow had to be a better day, because this one was running on being the worst he'd ever had.

At dawn he had a headache, with bruises running along his left jaw, and his ears were still ringing. Noah figured he'd have to get better to have the energy to die.

After drinking a cup of coffee with friendly Harley, who didn't say anything but "That'll be a buck," Noah drove over to his parents' house and picked up all the camping equipment he could find. Of course, they were gone. They were always gone. Since they got back together, life had been one long honeymoon for them. Half the time Noah swore they forgot they even had kids.

By noon, he'd set up camp next to the falling-down remains of what had once been his great-grandfather's house. The land should have gone to his brother, Warren, but after Warren was shot in the line of duty as a highway patrolman, Noah's father lost all interest in the small ranch. He deeded it to Noah when Noah turned eighteen.

For a few years Noah tried to keep it up, even ran a few head of cattle on it, but he wasn't home enough and soon the place went to ruin. The north wall of the main house had fallen in and Noah guessed wild animals were living in what had once been his bedroom. If his family found out, they'd probably adopt the hogs and saw him off the family tree.

The ranch, which had been meant to be passed down to every generation, was no more than mesquite trees and tumbleweeds now. Fences were down, the roads were barely passable, and he had no idea if the well still functioned. When he was in high school, Noah had dreamed of raising horses here, but sometime over the years he'd given up on that dream.

He set up the old tent he'd used in Boy Scouts and unfolded a chair. It was too hot to even think about building a fire. He decided that when he got hungry, he'd drive into town and bring back takeout. Living real cowboy style, he thought.

Not exactly roughing it like his great-grandfather did, but evidently, Noah wasn't made of hardy stuff. Last night one woman had stomped on his heart and one blow had knocked him out. With his luck his great-grandfather would rise from the grave and drop by to kick his ass as well.

Wallowing in self-pity seemed to be his only plan for the day.

"Home," he said aloud as he leaned back in his folding chair. He had enough money in the bank to live in the best hotel around or even buy a house in town, but right now he didn't feel fit for civilization. Maybe he needed to live off the land for a while. Civilization didn't seem to want him. If the Texas panhandle had had a few trees, he'd have considered becoming a mountain man for the rest of his life.

"Speaking of living." Noah grinned at a jackrabbit hopping across the field. "Here comes breakfast. All I have to do is catch it, kill it, skin it, and cook it." On second thought, he might be dead of starvation before he could do all that.

The rabbit disappeared over the shoulder of the dirt road as a pickup plowed toward Noah.

Noah didn't move. He just watched as Hank climbed out of his truck. His only brother-in-law was still frowning.

"You didn't happen to bring breakfast?" Noah yelled.

Hank shook his head. "It's past lunchtime. Most folks have worked half the day by now."

Noah nodded, as if that made any sense to his stomach. "What are you doing out here, Hank? Did my sister tell you to drive over here to lecture me?"

"Yep," Hank answered, as he pulled another folding chair up in the dirt and sat down. "Noah, it's about time you grew up."

Noah waited for the rest. About how he should stop drinking, give up the rodeo, and become a family man. Take responsibility for his life, love Reagan like everyone in town thought he should. Hell, Hank would probably throw in "join the volunteer fire department" for good measure.

But Hank didn't say another word. He just sat there, staring at Noah like he was watching a chipped fender rust.

"That's all?" Noah finally broke the silence. "That's the worst lecture I've ever had."

"That's all," Hank said. "You grow up and man up, and we'll all be happy."

"What about me?"

Hank shrugged. "You happy now, Noah?"

"No," Noah admitted. He hadn't been happy for a long time. Not even the wins made him happy. When he was home, all he thought about was getting back on the road, and when he was on the road, all he thought about was getting back home.

Hank finally stood. "Don't make me drive all the way out here to have this talk again." He walked to his truck and drove off.

Noah stared at the dust, deciding Hank Matheson might be the smartest man he'd ever met. Some men have to climb a mountain in Tibet to get that kind of advice.

He stood and walked over to what was left of the house he grew up in. Noah knew little about building, but he decided before he could build anything he'd need to haul off the trash, so he spent the rest of the day moving truckloads of broken windows, boards, and a few thousand tumbleweeds to a trash fire in a clearing.

Then, with a dozen tacos from the drive-through in Harmony, he sat on the hood of his truck and watched all the trash burn. Tumbleweeds lit up like Christmas trees while dead branches popped in the fire. He had the feeling his whole life was ablaze and he had no idea how to put out the fire.

As the smoke blended with the night clouds, Noah realized he'd have to fix himself first before he could even try to go back and fix what was wrong with his relationship with everyone in town. Right now he guessed he could win an election as the most hated man in town.

He tossed an unopened bottle of beer in the fire and reached for the water in his truck. Leaning back, he stared up at the stars.

His drinking days were over. That would be his first step.

Chapter 31

⁂

DELANEY FARM

DUSTI AND ABBY WENT BACK TO THE HOUSE MAKING PLANS. With her ticket came three nights in a hotel and forty dollars a day for food. If she took crackers and stole food off the breakfast buffet, she could live on one meal a day and save the extra for cab fare to and from the airport.

Abby kept crying and saying how she couldn't believe her dream of finishing school might really be about to happen. "You can make the top ten, Dusti. You're good, really good. Just think, you beat Kieran."

Dusti caught herself brushing her fingers over Kieran's old camera and thinking that the "beating Kieran" part didn't make her as happy as she'd thought it might. She wished he were with them to celebrate, but now wasn't the time.

A little after one in the morning Abby went to bed, but Dusti stayed up, working in her darkroom. It felt so good to be doing something she loved again. The smell of the chemicals, the shadows dancing in the darkroom's one light, the feel of wet paper against her fingers. When they'd had to sell her cameras she'd thought she'd never use this room again, only over the years she couldn't bring herself to even rip the paper off the one window. It was like this was her one love and as long as she had this little darkroom in the corner of the basement, she had hope of her dream coming true.

She wanted to be able to give Kieran one finished picture to take back. He'd taught her to play. She owed her one chance to him, and maybe a picture would let him know how grateful she was.

He'd said he was having breakfast with his grandmother at the Blue Moon Diner before driving to the airport. Dusti guessed if she could be at the diner by eight, she'd catch them. Even if they came in at opening time, Cass would never get them served and paid out before eight.

As she worked, the last hand she and Kieran had played turned over and over in her mind. Kieran had started the third round out strong, winning more hands than he lost. About the time Dusti was thinking she'd have to go all in sometime soon, she'd finally started winning.

And she'd kept winning.

It occurred to her that she hadn't even seen his last two pocket cards. Not that it mattered. He couldn't have had two aces with another showing on the table. That would make five aces in the deck.

He'd looked more tired than unhappy when he lost, she thought. Maybe because this was something he did often. Maybe losing at the very end was something that had happened before. Despite all the chips on the table, each man who walked away lost only twenty dollars and a long-shot chance of more. So Kieran had really only lost the buy-in.

Dusti closed her eyes and swore. She wished he'd at least kissed her before he left, but he'd walked out with some of the others. He wasn't likely to kiss her at the diner in the morning with half the town watching. Just her luck, the first guy she'd thrown herself at in two years and he'd slipped like egg yolk from her grasp.

If she didn't keep her mind on something else, she'd wear out her imagination thinking of what making love to him would be like.

The sun was coming up when she finished the picture she wanted to give him. An enchanting shot of Kieran leaning against the side of the barn with the orchard reflecting off the metal sides as the sun went down. She'd played with it until the shot looked like it could have been taken last night or a hundred years ago. Timeless, she thought, and beautiful. The strong profile of an adventurer resting for a moment.

She hoped he'd like it. In an odd way the Scot looked totally at home next to the barn. He was watching the dancers with a slight smile on his lips.

Lips she'd probably never taste, Dusti reminded herself as she hung the picture to dry and ran upstairs to take a shower and get dressed.

In the shower she decided he might be a bad kisser. That might be why he didn't even try.

No, that was impossible. Not with lips like that.

Maybe he didn't know how? If he traveled he might not have had much opportunity.

If that was his problem, she'd teach him to kiss. After all, it would be only fair. He'd taught her to play poker.

Stepping out of the shower, she decided getting her mouth on Kieran's would be her next goal in life. Some might think that shallow, but Dusti could do shallow.

As soon as she reached her gambling goal, she had the next project lined up. If he didn't call for the date, she planned to start delivering eggs to his grandmother and pumping the old lady for information.

Even taking extra time with makeup and her hair, she still got to the diner before seven thirty. She waited a while, then went in, deciding she needed coffee to stay awake.

At nine, Kieran and his grandmother still hadn't come. He'd said he had a morning flight. With the drive, he'd have to start before ten to make any morning flight.

Dusti paid her bill and walked out of the diner. Five minutes later when she drove up to Kieran's grandmother's house, his rental car wasn't there.

Worry filled her more than anger. Something must have happened. Maybe his grandmother got sick or fell? The old lady had been living in the same house all Dusti's life. Years ago, when their mother delivered eggs in town, Kieran's grandmother was one of their sweetest customers.

Dusti knocked on the door, thinking of a dozen things that might have happened. He might have had a friend take the rental car in or planned to get Derwood to fly him over to catch his flight. Or maybe Kieran had flown himself to Harmony. He was a pilot, after all. She'd never even thought to ask if he had his own plane.

When Kieran's grandmother answered the door, Dusti let out a sigh of relief.

Mrs. Mills's hair had turned completely white and she'd rounded, but she still looked healthy and she was upright.

"Morning, dear," she said, as if it had only been days and not years since she'd seen Dusti. "How may I help you today?"

"Hello, Mrs. Mills, I'm looking for Kieran. I brought him a gift and wanted to give it to him before he left."

"Oh, he's gone, dear, but he said if I saw you to tell you to keep the camera. His father had others."

"All right. I'll take care of it until he comes back."

Mrs. Mills shook her head. "He won't be back until Christmastime, dear." She smiled. "He says he has to come in for my cooking, but I know it's more likely he doesn't want to spend time with either of his parents and their new spouses. I sometimes think when they left the marriage neither one remembered to take him. Maybe that's why he never seems to land anywhere for more than a week."

"He seems happy, though." Dusti wasn't sure what to say. She felt she'd just learned more about Kieran than he'd told her all week.

Mrs. Mills nodded. "I guess he is, but it seems to me he's waiting to land somewhere he can belong. Until then, he's just drifting, not getting attached to anyplace or anyone."

Dusti walked away thinking about what Mrs. Mills had said. Maybe the old girl was right. It somehow fit. Maybe he wanted the pictures to make his place seem like home. But if that was true, even with all the world to pick from, Harmony must be the closest thing to home he had.

She fought down tears. The man she'd thought had it all figured out had nowhere to land.

She'd send him all the pictures of the farm last night and a hundred more of Harmony. If he wanted to feel at home, she could give him that, if only in pictures.

Chapter 32

HAWK HOUSE

RONNY WOKE WITH THE SUN BLINKING THROUGH THE CURtains of an open window. She'd slept the night away next to Austin Hawk and he hadn't killed her . . . or made love to her, for that matter.

Looking over at him, she thought he seemed peaceful. His arm lay across her middle, loosely holding her near. When she wiggled, he didn't move. Didn't even seem to be breathing.

He's dead! she thought, sitting up in bed as his arm lifelessly fell away. *I've been sleeping with a dead man. No wonder he didn't have nightmares or make love to me. He's dead!*

She poked him with a stab of her finger as if testing roadkill for signs of life.

Austin opened one eye and said, "No, I'm not dead."

"You read my mind." Ronny considered the possibility that *mind reader* might be worse than *dead guy.*

"It wasn't that hard. You still look about to have a heart attack. Let me guess. This is the first time you've woken up with a man?" He laughed. "You're so adorable, Ronny. You're always on edge waiting for the worst-case scenario to tumble on top of you."

"I spent my childhood living with Dallas Logan. She wouldn't let me go to school because there were too many germs at school. I was ten before I realized other children weren't called germs. Every time I left the house, she quoted facts about the numbers of stolen and murdered women each year. Based on what she said, I thought my first job would be in human trafficking, and if I lived through that I'd move right into unidentified victim."

"That explains it." He pulled her back down. "You're safe. My fangs only come out at night."

"I slept here with you all night." Ronny needed to state an obvious fact. "Right here, with you."

"I know, honey, I was right here too. Remember me? I'm the guy on the other side of the bed." He raised one eyebrow. "Am I going to have to introduce myself every morning to you? If so, that could get rather boring because I'd really like last night to become more of a routine than a shock to you every morning."

She giggled, something she couldn't remember doing for a very long time. "You didn't have a nightmare. You didn't fight in your sleep."

He rolled to his back and stared at the ceiling. "That hasn't happened since the fire. I fight sleep every night because I know what's coming, but you're right. Last night I don't think I dreamed at all. I do remember waking up a few times and patting on you, hope you didn't mind. The feel of you in the darkness is like returning to a memory logged into every cell of my body. It feels so right."

"I touched you too, hoping to calm you so the nightmares wouldn't get in. And they didn't. What do you think that means?"

She leaned against his shoulder. He'd dressed last night, saying they'd have a date, and they hadn't even left the bedroom.

"It can only mean one thing. You've got to sleep with me from now on. It's the only polite thing to do."

"Is that an invitation or an order, Hawk?"

"An order," he snapped.

"I don't take orders." She smiled and waited.

He reconsidered his order. "A standing invitation. Any night, just come on over. I'll share the bed with you."

"That I'll consider." She climbed out and tried to straighten her once-starched shirt. "What time is it, anyway?"

"Ten, I'm guessing." He stretched, silently telling her he didn't care, because watching her was his only plan for the day. "My leg feels pretty good this morning. I guess the doc was right. I've been totally off it since you walked in last night. Maybe we should stay in bed all day to finish the healing."

"We forgot supper last night and you took a shower and got all dressed up so we could have a date." She glanced over at Austin. In jeans and a knit shirt, he looked pretty much the same except for morning stubble, but she looked like she'd slept in her clothes. Which she had. "Want some dinner now? I set it in the fridge before I came to check on you. Supper sounds good about now."

He reached for his crutch. "I'll race you to the kitchen. I'm starving." He used the crutch one step, then carried it the rest of the way.

Fifteen minutes later they were on the porch eating cold fried chicken and potato salad out of storage containers when Mr. Carleon walked up from the direction of her cabin.

Ronny stood and introduced the two men, feeling as if she'd been caught cheating.

Mr. Carleon was formal, as always, and polite. "I'm sorry to interrupt your brunch, but I need to talk to Miss Logan about a matter that won't wait. If you will excuse us, Captain Hawk."

Austin nodded but didn't look happy.

Ronny set down her plate and followed Mr. Carleon back to her cabin. She'd lost her appetite. It had to be terrible news or he wouldn't have hiked down from the main road. Someone had died or had an accident.

Maybe her mother had been arrested again. No, he wouldn't come down for that. Everyone in town knew no matter what

Dallas Logan did, she'd be out within an hour. Last time the deputies took up a collection for her bail.

"I've e-mailed and called several times but couldn't reach you," Mr. Carleon began. "I wasn't aware you were helping care for Captain Hawk until I stopped by the Delaney place."

"We're all pitching in," Ronny said, not wanting him to think that she'd adopted Austin. "Why do you call him Captain?"

"That's his rank. I don't believe he's retired yet, just on medical leave."

She wasn't surprised Mr. Carleon knew all the facts about Austin. "What brings you out here?"

"I have news that won't wait much longer. Also, I said I'd come if I was unable to reach you by phone."

"I've been busy since Austin was shot." Ronny knew she didn't have to tell him everything going on in her life, but she felt she owed him an explanation. "I'm sorry to have put you out. I planned to call you this morning." She didn't add that she hadn't because she'd left her phone in her cabin last night.

"No trouble. I enjoyed the walk. I thought you might be busy helping. I heard about the accident from Dr. Addison when she and her husband, Tinch, came to breakfast this morning, and from your mother an hour later when she came by to see if Martha Q had heard about Hawk. The accounts were radically different."

"I can imagine, but, Mr. Carleon, you don't have to worry about me. Austin killed the hogs and Kieran told me the farmer set up traps to catch any more who come near. After hunting with guns, he said his sons will be checking traps from now on."

"I wasn't worried about you, dear. Any more than I always do, that is. I came out to tell you that Ivan, Marty's hiking buddy, is getting married next weekend. Ross, remember him, the pilot who came up to help when we moved Marty from the hospital in Oklahoma to your little duplex?"

"I remember."

"Well, Ross called me and said he'd stop by and pick up the two of us and we'd all fly down to the wedding. It's going to be a real Texas shindig. Boots, hats, and two-stepping. I thought you might like to go. It'd only be for a few nights, then we'd fly back."

"I think I would. I remember the three men. All adventurous like Marty must have been before the accident. They were with him when he fell. They got him off the mountain. Right?"

Mr. Carleon nodded. "From what I hear, Doc has traded his wild ways for volunteering with one of those organizations that goes into places where people never get to see a doctor. Ross still flies, but he spends most of his time writing books about where to find the adventure in life. Last I heard he was a consultant for some TV show called *Try Not to Be Eaten Alive before Dawn*. Of course, Ivan will settle down once he's married. Ross told me when he called that the bride said she wasn't going anywhere that didn't have an indoor pool for her honeymoon."

Ronny laughed. "It will be worth the flight to see what kind of woman would marry any one of them. Marty used to tell me all about the wild places they went to. He said they hiked the Pecos Wilderness once for a week without bathing. When they finished, they drove to the nearest town and not a single restaurant would let them in until they rented a room and showered."

They talked like old friends as the morning turned into afternoon. If he noticed her wrinkled clothes, he didn't see it as important enough to mention. Mr. Carleon was like that. He saw only the good in people he liked. People he didn't like, he didn't see at all.

Ronny told him she'd like to stay longer at the little cabin she called Walden, and he said he'd take the New York apartment off hold.

"I'd like to go back to work. Not at the post office, of course, but maybe open my own accounting business or even a bakery. I think it's time I stepped back into life." The words came out far easier than she thought they might.

He smiled, spreading wrinkles across his lean face. "I think that's wonderful, but you know, miss, you don't have to work. You have enough to—"

"Mr. Carleon, I think you've done a wonderful job of taking care of me, but I'd like to work before the money Marty willed me runs out."

"It won't," he said simply. "You have over a million in accounts that pay you roughly eight thousand a month without touching the principal. You also have a stock account that's been building. Your current draw on your bank account, per month, including rent, is about two thousand. At that rate, you'll never run out."

She leaned back and thought about what he'd just said. "Does anyone know about the money?"

"No one in Harmony. I set it up through a bank in Dallas. You can take over running it any day you like, miss, or I'll manage it for you until you're ready."

"You like doing it?"

"I do. It gives me something to do. Life wouldn't be near as pleasant if I didn't get to walk to my office every morning and keep all accounts up to date. Makes me feel useful."

Ronny grinned. "Then please continue, Mr. Carleon. And, please understand that I want to feel useful too. I just don't know how, yet. As for the money, I'd like you to donate a hundred thousand to the fire department. Marty always worried about Harmony not having the best equipment."

"I'll do that. And don't worry, miss, you'll find your way. Maybe that wounded captain next door will help you out."

Smiling, she asked, "You don't mind that I'm seeing him?"

"I'm happy for you both. I ran a check on him before I rented the cabin. He's a good man fighting his way back from terrible times, I think. Marty used to tell me that just looking at you made him feel better, and I didn't miss the way Captain Hawk stared at you. I think he feels the same."

"We're not . . ." She had no idea how to finish the sentence.

"I'm not asking," Mr. Carleon added. "One question before you get the ATV out and drive me back up to my car. Do you want me to buy this place for you?"

"It's for sale?"

"I can get it for a good price if you want to live out here.

We could have a real road put in and rebuild the dock. Even enlarge the cabin fairly easily."

Ronny hugged her knees. "Leave the road as it is, but rebuild the dock. I think I've found my first real home. As for adding on, I think it's just about perfect just the size it is." She almost added that she wouldn't be sleeping there, but that seemed too big a step to tell anyone yet, even herself.

"I'll get to work on it as soon as we get back from the wedding." Mr. Carleon stood. "Oh, I almost forgot, congratulate Dusti Delaney for me."

"For what?"

He smiled. "She won the poker game last night. I would have thought you'd have heard the party from here."

Ronny shrugged. "I guess I was asleep." Turning away, she smiled to herself and rushed down the steps, suddenly in a hurry to get back and tell Austin the news from the poker game.

Mr. Carleon talked as they drove toward Rainbow Lane. He was settling into Harmony as well, even thinking about buying the house next to the bed-and-breakfast. "Mrs. Biggs, Martha Q's cook, assures me I can still come over for meals. If I had a house I could finally get my things out of storage. They've been there so long I'm afraid they'll all have to be insured as antiques."

When he said good-bye he gave her one of his rare, polite hugs and hurried off to his car. She had no doubt he was already making his next to-do list in his head.

Ronny also planned all she'd do to fix the place up as she drove back down to the lake. Her own place. Her own home. It sounded like a dream come true. She'd enlarge the kitchen and maybe build an office space by the front window so she could work and look out on the lake. As long as she could get reliable Internet she could work from the cabin and only go into town when she wanted to.

When she walked back over to Hawk House, Austin wasn't on the porch where she'd left him a few hours before. Their half-eaten lunch was still there. He wasn't in his three rooms, but his jacket rested on the railing at the bottom of the stairs.

Ronny began to climb. The second floor. No one. All the bedrooms were empty, almost as though no one had ever lived in them. The third floor had only one room. If he'd gone up another flight, it had to have been torture on one leg.

When she stepped into the third floor's only room, she saw what must be his space. Equipment sat around. Special backpacks designed with oxygen masks. Books and manuals were also scattered on the floor, some with pages blowing in the breeze. When he'd said he lived in only a few rooms of the house, she hadn't thought that they would be the kitchen and third floor.

Only this room didn't look like a home, even a vacation one. It looked more like a barracks, or a lair for a warrior about to leave again to fight. Nothing about the room reminded her of the man, or even the boy who'd stayed here once. She got the feeling that if Austin never returned, nothing personal would need to be boxed and sent to him.

A shadow moved past the window. Someone had to be walking around outside on the widow's walk, and no one was here but Austin.

Ronny stepped out one of the long windows and saw him standing, looking out toward the lake. It wasn't safe here. The railing was little more than knee high. If he tripped, he'd fall two floors.

"Austin," she said softly. "You all right?"

"You left." He didn't look at her. "That man came up and you walked off without saying a word to me."

She moved a few feet toward him. "I've mentioned Mr. Carleon. He wouldn't have come if he hadn't needed to talk to me." She wasn't sure she liked this Austin. He was right, she hadn't said good-bye. She hadn't thought she'd be gone more than a few minutes, but still it didn't seem something to get angry about.

The man before her seemed angry and brooding.

"Are you mad at me?" If he was, over something so small, logic told her to run. This man who put down no roots, who left his mark on nowhere he'd been, would probably never be what she needed.

Deep down inside, Ronny admitted exactly what she needed and never had. She needed a forever man. Not a man who set her blood on fire, but a man who'd be there when she needed him. Who'd sleep with her every night. Who'd hold her when she was happy and sad. Who would never, ever yell at her.

Austin might not be that kind of man. He might never be. People change, but could he change that much?

He touched his leg as if rubbing away pain. "Of course I'm not mad. I was worried when I heard an engine fire up. Thought you might be taking the old guy back across the lake. I thought I could see you if I came up here, but it must have been the ATV you started because your boat never moved out on the water."

"You were worried about me?" Worry she could accept. Anger she couldn't.

"No. I'm sure you can take care of yourself. I just . . . Hell, can we drop this whole conversation?" He moved toward her, balancing every other step with his hand on the roofline.

"Sure, I don't understand it anyway." She guessed between the two of them they barely had the skills to communicate with guppies, much less another human.

"If you hear another engine, it's me. This Thursday I'm flying off to attend a wedding and I don't think I'll be back for three or four days."

"Have a good time." He didn't sound like he cared one way or the other. "I'll be fine here. I don't really need any watching after, and you've left enough food for months in my refrigerator."

Suddenly Austin was back to being a stranger. After he'd held her so tenderly last night and kissed her so passionately a few times before, now she felt like she didn't even know him.

In silence he moved slowly back down the stairs. He didn't seem to know what to say any more than she did.

Ronny cleaned up the picnic they'd had on the porch. When she came back in, he was reading.

"You want to play some cards?"

"No," he answered.

"TV?"

"No. Thanks for bringing the food. I'll be fine."

She could walk away. She didn't need moody. They were both people who liked solitude; wishing something more had happened between them was crazy. She should just walk away and drop off food tonight on the doorstep.

But something that Mr. Carleon had said stopped her. Austin Hawk was a good man fighting his way back from terrible times. His words had made him an easy man to walk away from, but he'd be a hard man to forget.

Somewhere inside this hard man was the man who'd held her close all night. The man who worried about her. The man who cared.

Ronny walked to his chair and sat down on the arm. "Then there is only one thing to do," she said as she leaned over and kissed him hard on the mouth. When he didn't move, she cupped his face and kissed him again.

For a second, he didn't react, and then he pulled her onto his good leg and crushed her against him.

She'd found the one thing he wanted to do. His kiss was full-out, no-holds-barred passion.

Exactly what she wanted. If what they had together was going to end, she wanted to end with a memory she could carry always.

They needed to concentrate on communicating in other ways besides talking. She dug her fingers into his hair and held on tight as his hands slid over her back and hips, pressing her to him as he leaned back in the recliner with her on top of him.

Several minutes passed before he broke the kiss and smiled at her. "You finally figured out what I wanted."

She leaned against his shoulder. "What was that?"

"You attacking me. No matter how I fight to keep from touching you, I always surrender when you come to me."

"Why didn't you just tell me you wanted to kiss me?"

He shook his head. "I guess I didn't know how. To tell you the truth, I'm surprised you even like me enough to speak to me." He kissed the top of her head. "When you press against me, it blows my mind, but I want you to know, you're welcome any time."

"Again," she said, straightening as she lowered her mouth to his. With her mouth brushing his, she whispered, "Why don't we put off talking until we get tired of doing this."

"That's not happening, pretty lady."

As evening cooled the air, they learned that as long as they were touching they had no problem communicating.

Chapter 33

TRUMAN FARM

REAGAN SPENT THE DAYS AFTER THE POKER GAME GETTING her orchard back in order. She moved between the apple trees and back and forth from the house to the barn with Utah strapped in front of her. As always, she found her peace in the orchard. Trumans held to their land, Uncle Jeremiah had always told her.

With Noah gone, she felt the land was all she had left to hold on to. The apple business had been good to her over the past few years. With planning, she'd always have the farm and the trees. As long as she had a home, she could weather any storm and she could take care of Utah if she needed to.

Thanks to the Internet, she'd bought everything for him. In only a few weeks he'd grown to the point that nothing Maria had brought that first day fit. He needed clothes and furniture, swings and bouncy chairs, toys. She needed books and bottles and special soap. The list seemed endless.

Maria called often and dropped by to help, but Reagan rarely left the baby with her. She set up a crib for his naps in her office and worked around his schedule.

Everyone said she was getting thin, working too hard. She couldn't tell those who cared about her that the baby and the work were saving her. Helping her to be too busy to realize that her heart had broken. Several times a day she thought of Noah, and just the knowledge that she couldn't call him stabbed at her heart.

Now and then someone would mention that Noah was still in town. He was living out at his run-down ranch, cleaning up the place. It wasn't far from her farm. She could have easily driven over to see what work he'd done. But there was no reason to go past his ranch. Noah was out of her life. This was the way she wanted it. The way it had to be for her to survive.

Reagan told herself she didn't care, but some nights she'd look in his direction and think she could almost see a light shining from his old place. The McAllen ranch had the best sunsets, her uncle said once. She couldn't help but wonder if she'd ever see it again from his ranch.

On the second Sunday after he'd left, the old pickup he'd driven when they were in high school turned off Lone Oak Road and headed in her direction.

Reagan watched him coming from the second-story window, and for a moment she felt like she'd stepped back in time. He was a skinny kid again and she was a runaway trying to fit in. Noah was coming over to pick her up so they could drive over to some little rodeo, eat dinner from a taco truck parked out by the arena, and hope he won enough money to buy malts for the ride home.

Only that was years ago and nothing was the same now except the old truck kicking up dust on her drive.

The cowboy who stepped out was Harmony's Noah, her Noah. Not the rodeo star with a spotless white hat and hand-tooled leather boots. Not the man living life high and wild. But just Noah in jeans and a shirt that looked well worn. She couldn't help but think he still looked like a western hero stepping out of an old dime novel.

He stood by his truck for a while, as if expecting shots to be fired from her porch. He'd told her once that he'd grow up to be good looking, and he had. Tall and lean with a smile that used to light up her world.

Finally, she walked out on the porch and waited to see what he planned to say.

He sauntered up slowly, like a man unsure of his direction. He was tanned darker by the sun than she'd seen him in a long time. His hair was a bit too long. His boots scuffed and worn. Noah, the guy who'd done ninety percent of the talking since they'd met, didn't say a word. He just stood there in front of her as if waiting for another blow to knock him down.

"Your spark plugs need changing," she said calmly. "I could hear the engine missing even when you turned off Lone Oak Road."

He offered a sad smile. "Your uncle told me that one of the first times I came by. He thought you were too young to go with me."

"I was." She remembered how frightened she'd been that he might turn into a monster after dark. "But he didn't try to stop me, just fixed your truck so we'd be able to make it home."

Memories drifted around her. Her uncle complained about Noah for a year, but he never failed to tell her to "feed the boy" or "tell the kid to make sure he gets you back on time."

"I miss you, Rea." Noah finally broke the silence.

She couldn't speak. She just waited. *Missing* seemed too small a word to hold how lonely she felt.

"I haven't had a drink since Big knocked me out. I'm not going back to the rodeo circuit. Those days are over." He looked down at his boots as if trying to remember a speech. "I've been fixing up my old place. It still looks like hell, but Tannon Parker said he'd start hauling in the cattle I bought next week. Thought I'd start with a hundred head and work my way up."

"Why are you here, Noah?"

He looked down at his feet again. "I'd like to see the baby. If he's mine, I want to claim him. None of this is his fault."

She nodded. "Wait out here. I'll go get him."

When she returned, Noah was sitting in the west-facing chairs. She put Utah in his arms and stepped away.

It was too hard to watch. Reagan walked back inside and

forced herself not to look out the window. She knew Noah loved kids. He was always telling stories about what one of his cousin's kids did. Or at least he used to love children. Reagan felt like she barely knew the man sitting in her front yard.

When she heard Utah cry, Reagan rushed toward the door. Noah was standing there looking helpless. "I think he's wet or hungry. I don't know. He's just not happy. I even tried singing to him."

"That probably made him mad. You can't sing," she said as she took the baby.

"I can't? Wish someone had told me. I've been singing for years."

"Believe me, Noah, we've all tried."

He looked like he was in deep thought. "That may explain why nobody ever passed me a hymnal in church."

She wasn't falling for his charm. "I think the baby may be wet. I usually change him and then feed him a bottle as we watch the sunset."

Reagan held the fussy baby, but she didn't invite Noah in.

"Do you think I could come back some sunset and feed him?"

"All right." Reagan closed the door without saying good-bye.

Noah stood on the porch staring at a door he'd felt comfortable just walking through for years. But not now.

He'd worked till he dropped every day and he still couldn't sleep. Now Rea wouldn't even talk to him.

Walking back to his truck, he had no idea how to fix what he'd broken, but he wasn't sure he could live without her.

No matter how long it took, he'd keep trying.

Chapter 34

❧

Delaney Farm

Dusti drove into town to mail another set of photos to Kieran O'Toole. This would be the fourth and last install-ment of what she called her Living in Harmony series. She'd had great fun with the old camera he'd said belonged to his dad. Something about looking at the world with a camera in her hands made everything seem different, far more interest-ing, a wonder in her everyday world.

She hadn't known how much she missed it until now.

In every packet she mailed to New York City, she included a letter thanking him for all his help and telling him she was counting down the days until the trip to Vegas. She and Abby had repacked her suitcase half a dozen times trying to decide just what she should take. This tournament was rela-tively small compared to all the others in Las Vegas, but the money was great; all she had to do was place in the money. Even the lowest money win would be enough to send Abby back to school.

In truth, she'd been so busy taking the pictures she hadn't thought much about the game. Her win was all that the folks in town talked about, and if possible that made her more nervous than anything else. Everyone was counting down the days with her.

Mrs. Mills, Kieran's granny, even answered the door for her weekly egg delivery by saying, "Five more days, Dusti. Five more days. Are you excited?"

"Of course," Dusti answered, feeling more fear than excitement. "I just dropped some eggs by and wondered if Kieran had called to tell you he got my pictures. Our phones at the farm aren't dependable."

"No, dear, he hasn't called, but I'm sure he will. Do you have time to come in for a glass of tea?"

Dusti wanted to dart back to her truck now that she'd found out what she needed to know, but the old lady was too sweet to disappoint, so she nodded and followed her to a kitchen that hadn't been remodeled in fifty years.

As they drank sweet tea, Dusti searched for something to say. "I guess you know your grandson taught me to play poker. That's why I won the other night."

"I know, dear. He's pretty good at the game. Never could beat me, though."

Dusti's eyes widened. "You taught him to play?"

"Sure. I had to do something with him every summer, and I'm not one for baseball. Back years ago, my husband always played on Friday nights. I decided if I wanted to keep up with my man's night out with the boys, the easiest way was to become the dealer. So I set up a table in the backyard and made sweets. Even when my husband suggested changing locations, none of the other men would hear of it." She grinned. "They liked my sweets."

Dusti laughed. "Mrs. Mills, you're brilliant."

"I am, dear." She laughed. "Want me to get out the cards and show you a few secrets? I didn't watch men play for twenty years without learning a few tricks, along with the recipes, of course."

Dusti almost jumped out of her chair and hugged the woman. No one at the game had been as good as Kieran, and she'd just found his master.

Mrs. Mills stood and pulled her phone from her apron pocket. "Mind if I call my friend? She always plays. Didn't win as often as I did, but picked up two husbands at the poker table."

"Of course. I'd love to meet her."

When Mrs. Mills produced the deck from her hutch drawer, she added, "These lessons don't come free. I'll expect pecans with those eggs every week come fall. One week's delivery for each lesson. Fair enough?"

"You got yourself a deal."

The doorbell rang. Dusti waited in the kitchen, but she could hear the laughter.

"When you called, I dropped everything and came right over. The girls are riding again," the newcomer announced.

Both women laughed as they moved into the kitchen.

Dusti stood and turned to face Martha Q Patterson, the owner of the town's bed-and-breakfast.

"Morning, Mrs. Patterson," Dusti said, thinking of all the wild stories she'd heard about Martha Q and her seven husbands.

"Call me Martha Q. If you're sitting down to play poker with us, you're sitting down as an equal. We'll try not to take advantage of you."

Mrs. Mills nodded. "If either of us had decided to play in that game at the Truman farm, you wouldn't be packing your bag." She winked as if she were teasing, but Martha Q added "amen" like it was the gospel truth.

Dusti found it hard to believe that Kieran's sweet little granny was friends with a woman who folks used to claim had slept with every man in town. And that there were card-sharps in a town of goldfish.

Mrs. Mills patted Martha Q's hand. "Now, we're not playing for money today. We're here to help this girl learn to play in Las Vegas. She's not going into a friendly kitchen game, she's going into the lion's den, and no one, including my grandson, can prepare her for that game but you and me."

"Does anyone in Harmony know that you two have played

in Vegas?" Dusti found it almost impossible to believe they'd kept such a secret for so many years.

"No one alive." Martha Q winked.

"You killed them?"

Both women laughed. "No, dear," Mrs. Mills said. "We outlived them."

"Before I play with you, Dusti Delaney, you have to swear you'll never tell anyone about this game. You'll go to your grave with our secret." Martha Q shrugged. "I don't much care about it myself. I start half the rumors about me, but Mrs. Mills is a lady. A very proper Methodist to boot. I wouldn't want people talking about my friend."

"How long have you two been friends?"

Both shrugged. Finally, Martha Q answered, "More years than I admit to being alive."

Dusti raised her hand, loving that she'd stumbled onto such a secret. "I swear." Even if she thought about telling somebody, no one would believe her.

"Then let's play some poker."

Three hours later Dusti left with a loaf of Mrs. Mills's banana bread and a few secrets of the game. She might not be able to reach Kieran, but at least she was still learning. A few more lessons and she just might have a chance at getting into the finals.

On the drive home she laughed about all the stories she'd heard. The two had once run off to Vegas when they were in their fifties. Mrs. Mills was newly widowed and Martha Q was between husbands.

They'd slipped away, both telling lies as to where they were going. Mrs. Mills had won so much cash they'd been afraid to leave the casino. Martha Q had stuffed the cash in her bra while Mrs. Mills ran to get the car. Every man in the place tried to pick Martha Q up on her way out.

Martha Q claimed secret friends are far better than secret lovers, and Dusti had no doubt it was true. They'd stood beside each other through marriages, deaths, and rumors.

When all this was over and Abby had gone off to school,

Dusti planned to spend her one night a month out at Mrs. Mills's house. Playing cards with her and Martha Q was far more fun than playing games at Buffalo's Bar and taking a chance at going home with a crazy cowboy who didn't stay till dawn.

She laughed as she turned onto Rainbow Lane, remembering how she'd asked Martha Q if she'd ever waited for the right man to come along.

Martha Q had answered, "Yes, and he did, several times."

Chapter 35

NOAH MCALLEN'S RANCH

NOAH WATCHED CATTLE BEING UNLOADED ONTO HIS LAND. It felt good. It felt right. A hundred head was just a start on what he needed, but that was all he could handle right now. Between working on the house and mending fences, every muscle in his body hurt, but it was a good kind of ache.

Working for a living was much harder than rodeoing. The heroes are the men who get up and work every day, all day long. Somehow the world got it mixed up. Sitting on a bull for eight seconds is nothing compared to sitting on a horse from sunup to sundown.

Noah loved it, though. The fresh air. The solid sleep from being too tired to think once the lights went out. The cool mornings. The stars. He hadn't known he'd missed it so until he returned.

Tannon Parker, who owned the trucking company in town, had ridden out with the last shipment to make sure all was running smooth. He and Noah's father were both in the same business, but they'd always been friendly, even lending each other trucks when a huge job came in.

Tannon jumped down from the truck. "Your dad's going to be proud of you, Noah. He used to talk about how you wanted this place as soon as you turned eighteen. He said you had big dreams."

Noah shrugged. "I want to get it up and running before he finds out about what I'm doing. He never cared much about the ranch; it was always the rodeo he loved."

Tannon nodded. "And you, is it the ranch or the rodeo?"

"It's the ranch. It always has been. I just lost my way for a while. I love the rodeo, but like Dad finally found out, you can't build your life on arena dirt."

Tannon glanced over at the house. "Looks like you're rebuilding the old place."

"I'm turning it into a bunkhouse." Noah didn't want to tell anyone that he couldn't stand the thought of living in a home alone. The bunkhouse made more sense. "There's another house in the north pasture I can stay at for now. It's small, but it'll work. All I need is a bed and shower."

"Someone said you were living in a tent." Tannon glanced over at the remains of a campsite.

"Yeah, that lasted until it rained." He guessed everyone in town knew he and Reagan had been dating. Hell, they probably knew she'd kicked him out. It wouldn't take many brain cells to figure out what the fight had been about the night of the poker game. Half the town was there.

Noah needed to change the subject fast. "I guess Dusti Delaney is getting ready for her big trip. She loved to party in Harmony. No telling what she'll find to do in Vegas."

Tannon nodded. He wasn't a man who gossiped, but he would state the facts now and then. "Everyone is throwing her a farewell party next week. You're welcome to come. Just bring a six-pack or something you baked and I bet they'll let you in."

"I don't cook," Noah answered, "and the six-pack will be root beer. I've given up drinking."

Tannon looked serious. "I'm glad to hear that, Noah." He stepped back on the truck. "Hope to see you there."

As he drove off, Noah wondered how many people in

town thought he had a drinking problem. He hadn't really noticed it before, but there were a lot of people, like Tannon Parker and Tinch Turner, who'd never offered to buy him a drink. They shook his hand. Told him they were proud for his wins. Tinch had come over to help him get ready for horses, and Tannon probably had more important things to do besides ride out with cows. Yet both men had stopped by. It was like they were welcoming him home, this time for good.

He'd never thought he had a drinking problem, and he wouldn't blame his troubles now on the bottle. Someone was always waiting at Buffalo's Bar to buy him a drink. For the first time he thought there might be just as many outside the bar wishing he'd quit. His sister was always threatening him. Hank had told him to grow up. Big Biggs had cussed him out more than once when he carried him out on nights Noah couldn't walk straight.

The world was a lot more complicated sober. But there was a world out there that he hadn't paid much attention to until now. A world of neighbors helping each other. A world where a man's worth was measured by something other than the size of the buckle he won.

By the time he'd taken care of the cattle and paid the men who'd helped, Noah decided working for a living wasn't as easy as it looked, but he planned to give it his best shot.

After he cooled down and fed his horse, he rode out to the little house that had been built for a foreman's family forty years ago. It was decorated in abandoned-furniture décor, but livable. The water and fans worked; that was good enough for now. Noah thought he'd probably live at the bunkhouse with the men once it was complete.

Now that the fences were up and cattle coming in, he'd hired out the finishing work on the bunkhouse. Once done, the new part of the building would have an office for him and ten rooms for men upstairs, with kitchen and open area downstairs.

Noah showered and put on clean clothes, then drove over to the Truman place to watch the sunset with his son. At first he'd just used seeing the baby as an excuse to see Reagan, but every time he held Utah, the boy tugged at his heart. As long as she'd let him come over, whether she talked to him or not, he'd keep coming.

When he pulled up, Reagan was already in one of the western chairs, waiting.

He expected her to leave as soon as she handed him Utah, but for the first time she stayed.

Noah didn't want to push his luck, so he talked to Utah. "We got a hundred head on the old place today," Noah started. "Tomorrow we'll brand them and give them their shots. I wish you could see the herd of half-grown cows. Branding is lots of fun and it don't hurt them. Sure tosses around the cowboys, though. One got hit so hard today that he flipped over like a pancake."

Noah glanced over to see if Reagan was listening. Dear God, how he missed talking to her. She'd always been the one he could talk to. The one who cared about him.

"Hank says as soon as I get the corrals back in place, he'll sell me twenty horses. Right now the hands coming in are bringing their own mounts, but a good cowboy needs more than one horse some days. I figure I'll have at least a dozen good mares that will foal by next spring."

Reagan finally looked at him. "You know, Noah, he doesn't understand a word you say."

"I know, but if you can talk to him about growing apple trees, I can talk about ranching. He'll need to know ranching someday."

"What makes you think I talk to him about trees?"

"Joe's cousin told me. Said Joe and Maria say the last Truman walks around talking to the baby like he needs to know all there is to know about orchards."

"Joe doesn't understand half of what I say."

Noah smiled. "He doesn't have to understand English to recognize crazy."

She rolled her eyes, but he thought he saw the hint of a smile.

"Utah's asleep," Noah said. "You want me to carry him in?"

He expected her to say no. Every night he'd come, she'd

made him hand her the baby at the door. Only this time she just nodded and walked ahead of him so she could hold the screen door open.

Noah carried the baby slowly up the stairs and into her room. He knew, without asking, that the crib would be next to her bed.

Just before he laid Utah down, he kissed him on the forehead. At first he'd come to see the baby because he knew it was the right thing to do, but now, Noah realized it was more than that.

For a long while he just stared down at Utah. In this little baby lay his future. Reagan had been right to say she'd take the baby if Noah couldn't. She'd understood, even before he did, that they were the kid's only chance.

When he stepped back, she moved forward to straighten Utah's blanket and noticed the red stain on the blanket's blue corner.

"Blood!" She whispered the word, but her voice shook with panic.

Noah looked down at his hands. "Rea, it's not the baby. Don't worry. It's me. It's not the baby."

She looked back as he raised his palm. "I lost one of my gloves this afternoon. The work was rough and I got a few nicks. I thought the bleeding had stopped. I wouldn't have held the baby if I thought I'd get it on him."

Rea frowned. "The baby is fine. Go wash up in the bathroom before you bleed all over the rug."

He nodded and headed to the bathroom. He'd stayed with her enough to know where everything was. As he washed his hands, he thought about how little time she'd spent worrying about him. If he cut off his own head she'd probably just complain about having to clean up the mess.

At least she'd worried about Utah. Rea would be good for the baby. She'd love him even if she no longer loved Noah.

When he got back downstairs, Reagan was in the kitchen. She didn't even look up when he walked to the doorway.

"Thank you," he said simply.

"For what?"

"For loving him first. If you hadn't taken him in that day, he might have been dropped off somewhere and I might not have ever found him. Or worse, gone home with a mother who didn't want him and a stepfather who hated him."

"You're welcome, but I didn't do it for you."

"I know." He turned to leave.

"You want some soup?" Her voice was barely a whisper.

"You offering to feed me?"

"I might as well. You're getting thinner by the day. If you don't have Band-Aids at your place, you probably don't have food."

"You got that right. If I kept any around, the field mice, who sublet my place, would eat it while I'm working. If you got plenty, I wouldn't turn down a bowl."

"Fine, but we're not together. I'm just offering supper."

He understood. Moving around her was like walking on a glass memory. All the old feelings were there, but they were covered by thin glass that might shatter with one wrong word.

They ate at the bar in the kitchen. Soup and cornbread. She didn't offer dessert. He didn't ask.

He thanked her and offered to help with the dishes.

She said, "No thanks," as she walked him to the door.

Noah drove off smiling. Hope, he thought. For the first time since he'd come home, he had hope. She wasn't friendly, but apparently she was over wishing him dead. That seemed a step up.

The next night, he stopped by and brought malts when he came to watch the sunset.

She wasn't much more friendly, but she did look at him. The hurt was still in her eyes. He wanted to tell her how sorry he was again, and again and again, but he knew it wouldn't matter. Sorry wasn't enough.

He wanted to touch her. Just hold her and whisper how she was his world, but she wouldn't listen.

They sat in the yard chairs long after sunset with a sleeping Utah on Noah's shoulder. Neither seemed to want this time to end.

When he finally went upstairs to put the baby down, Reagan was waiting at the door when he returned. She didn't offer supper.

He stepped out on the porch and turned toward her. Before she could close the door, he said what he had to say, "I still love you, Rea, more than ever. If you want it like this between us, then that's the way it will be, but I'm never lying to you again."

The door closing was her only answer. She'd pushed it shut softly, but it might as well have been made of iron.

As he walked away, he could hear her crying. The sound twisted his heart. She was still hurting. His Rea was crumbling and he couldn't reach her. He knew she was only on the other side of the door but it might as well have been a hundred miles away.

Ten minutes later Noah was in the parking lot of Buffalo's Bar and Grill. Only a few cars were there, probably folks having supper, not customers coming to drink.

For a long time he just sat in his pickup and stared. He'd medicated his pain, both physical and mental, for so long with alcohol, he wasn't sure how to stop. All he knew was that he wanted to stop the hurting between them and he couldn't. He had no idea how to fix what he'd broken.

Half an hour passed before he saw Big Biggs walk out of the bar. He had his arm around a very tall woman and they were laughing. Rea had told Noah all about Ester, Big's girl. She was even prettier and taller than he thought. Crazy thing was, she seemed to like the bull of a man beside her.

Noah climbed out of the truck. "Biggs!" he yelled.

The big guy turned, bracing for a fight. "What do you want, Preacher?"

Noah advanced a few feet. "I want to say I'm sorry about the other night. You had every right doing what you did. I'm a damned idiot."

"You'll get no argument from me. You've been an idiot pretty much since you went pro. It must come with the buckles you win. They're so heavy they cut off the oxygen to your brain."

Noah didn't laugh. "I just wanted you to know. I'm sorry."

"Okay, you're sorry, now good night. I got better things to do than talk to idiots in parking lots." Big turned to leave.

"I come to ask a favor," Noah shouted.

Big huffed. "I'm not interested in doing you any favors. Go back to your friends on the road."

"You'll like this one." Noah moved within striking distance. "I want you to hit me again. Real hard."

Big smiled like he'd just found out it was half-price night at the steakhouse. "That I can do."

Big swung just as Ester yelled, "No!"

Noah braced for the punch, but it still knocked him off his feet.

Lying in the dirt, he smiled up at Big. "Thanks, I needed that," he managed to say.

Big offered a hand up. "Anytime, cowboy."

With his left eye swelling closed, Noah climbed back in his truck completely sober and headed back to his ranch.

The next night Reagan didn't ask about his black eye, but she did invite him in for supper, and once he caught her smiling.

"What?" he asked.

"Does it hurt?" She pointed at his eye. "Because it looks terrible."

"Hurts like hell," he answered, knowing that Big had probably told her all about the favor he'd asked for.

"Want to tell me why you did it?"

"No, and before you ask, I might have to do it again. I seem to be into pain these days. Fell off my horse before lunch. My backside is black and blue. Wanna see? I'm guessing you'll think that's real funny too."

"No, thanks."

Her giggle was almost worth the pain.

When he left, he thought about telling her that he loved her again, but he didn't want to hear her crying behind the door again, so he just tipped his hat and said good night.

On the way home he thought about telling her he hated potato soup and hoped she wasn't planning on serving it every night. But he'd eaten two bowls tonight. If that wasn't true love, he didn't know what would convince her.

Chapter 36

HAWK HOUSE

AUSTIN WANTED NOTHING MORE THAN TO BE ALONE WITH Ronny at the lake, but the Delaney sisters wouldn't listen to his complaining when they called. They were planning a party and claimed they needed Ronny's help. So he had no choice but to pass her the phone.

"Of course we'll come," she'd said, and hung up.

He glared at her. "You must have a mouse in your pocket or think you're a queen, because I'm not going over there for a party. You may know everyone in town, but I don't." He wanted to tell her he hadn't gotten over the four days she was gone to some guy's wedding in Austin, but he'd just sound desperate. Austin loved having her near, but he promised himself he wouldn't get too attached. When it came time to say good-bye, he'd leave. Maybe, if he was lucky, he'd leave before she left him. Since they'd met he'd been counting down the days on a blank calendar without numbers. He didn't know when she'd go, but he knew each day with her was one day less.

This morning, Ronny, after getting him all heated up by

attacking him, calmly pulled away when she handed him back the phone. She had some kind of secret weapon she used against him. No amount of growling frightened her and she only obeyed the orders she liked. If an enemy ever got hold of her secret, the army would be in big trouble.

Austin frowned as he watched her running around looking for her shoes.

She didn't have to say a word.

He knew he was going to give in. "All right. We're going to a party, but don't expect me to be any help. I didn't learn party planning in boot camp." He moved to the window. "I don't know if I've ever been to a party that wasn't at a bar, but I'll bet you I'll hate it." She looked too cute just waiting for him to finish his rant. "All right, tell me all about it on the way across the lake. The Delaney sisters are probably already waiting for you on the dock."

After two rounds of what-do-you-think questioning centered on party themes, Austin gave up listening and moved to the porch. The whole scene sounded like somewhere he didn't want to be, and who cares what colors balloons should be? He'd suggested pink and they'd all three screamed at him, so he guessed they were off the list along with pork rinds as an appetizer.

He could see Ronny inside searching on the Internet and looking like she was having a great time. He decided to let her have all the fun. He'd take the leftover choice, a nap.

Ten minutes later when he was daydreaming about her, Ronny came out of the house explaining that she had to stay at the Delaney house and cook. She offered to take him back to his place, but he could do nothing here as well as there.

He wasn't sure when, or even if, he agreed to stay. His leg was only a dull ache now and then, but the girls seemed to think him still helpless, They offered him pillows and more tea than he'd ever drink. One of them was always passing him saying, "Sit, Austin," like he was the family dog.

Finally out of frustration, he sat down at the kitchen table and watched the women cook. Well, mostly he just watched Ronny. The two Delaney girls kept getting in his line of vision. He decided that he'd write a book one day on the joy of watching Ronny Logan move. He found it hard to believe that no one else noticed how beautiful she was. Every man in Harmony had to be blind, and he had no plans of enlightening a single one of them.

How could she have lived here all her life and only one man loved her? Couldn't the others see the beauty of her? The good in her? The shy humor and honest answers?

Whenever he moved for a better view of Ronny, they all three yelled, "Sit."

So Austin took over Tippie's job of guard duty.

Before dark the yard was full of pickup trucks and people hugging each other. They all seemed happy for Dusti and all wanted to wish her luck. Only a few days until she left.

Everyone walking in the door brought something. Drinks, beer, chips and hot sauce, hot wings. Within an hour the tables and counter were loaded down with food. Every time he stood up, someone brought him a plate of food and wanted to hear about how he killed three pigs heading straight toward him.

Austin gave the abridged version, leaving out the boys. When he finished two minutes later, whoever had asked usually stayed around to tell him every story about wild hogs they'd ever heard. Austin listened for two minutes, then ate his plate of food.

He moved outside to the porch finally, in self-preservation. In the dark corner he could watch and be unnoticed. One more hog story or plate of food just might be the death of him.

After a while, he decided he should try out to play the invisible man for the sequel. No one noticed his six-foot frame. He might as well have been an early Halloween decoration in the rocking chair. Now if they'd all be quiet, he'd enjoy the night.

The one man he called a friend in town was missing from the party. Kieran O'Toole. Austin knew he wasn't the kind of guy to miss the party just because he'd lost, but it took him almost an hour to catch Dusti long enough to ask her if Kieran had been invited. Knowing Kieran, he'd fly in just to wish Dusti good luck.

"Where's the Scot?" he yelled as she passed.

"He flew back home after the game," she answered with a smile, but he saw the hurt in her eyes. "Said he had to get back to work." Pausing, she finally added, "I haven't heard from him since. I guess life in a small town can only be interesting for a short time."

"Don't you owe him a date?" Austin had heard them mention that that was Kieran's price for teaching her to play.

"He said he'd pick the time and place and give me a call. I told him I wouldn't wait long. Next week I'll be in Vegas, and after that, who knows."

Dusti Delaney was as easy to read as ever. Kieran had always had a crush on her, even when they were kids, and she'd never seen it. Every time, over the years, that they'd talked about their days on Rainbow Lane, Kieran would always say, "Wonder what Dusti is doing now?"

Austin could tell she didn't want to take the time to talk about his friend. She mattered to Kieran, but Kieran was just someone she once knew, nothing more.

Austin watched Dusti pull Hank Matheson toward him and guessed she didn't want him asking her any more questions about Kieran.

Hank followed Dusti to the porch, seemingly happy to find Austin in the shadows.

As before, the two men had plenty to say to one another. Since they'd last visited, Austin had taken the time to read up on some new equipment coming into the fire station. The army had been using something like it for five years. He agreed with Hank that the training would be essential if it was going to be used properly.

Austin finally relaxed. Though he and Hank didn't talk about the same kind of fires, he felt comfortable with the volunteer chief of Harmony's fire station. He might be ten or fifteen years older, but there was a calmness about the man. Austin could see why a woman like the sheriff would find peace being around him. Hank Matheson had exactly what Austin wanted in his life: balance.

They talked of the shooting and the hog problem, and then

the conversation shifted to town matters. Hank told him about changes coming up in how he trained the men signing up, and Austin volunteered to come down and help him set up a new routine for volunteers coming in to train.

"Most are just kids," Hank said. "I've got to make sure they hear every word I say."

"I can help with that. It was most of what I did in the army. They don't realize, one mistake can get them killed."

Hank agreed. "I could sure use some help if you've got the time."

"I've got nothing but time right now."

They talked on making plans, both excited about what had to be done.

As Hank walked away, Austin realized that for the first time he felt like a part of Harmony and its people. What he'd offered to do would not only keep the firefighters under Hank safer, it would keep the town safer.

Austin leaned back in the old ladderback rocking chair and watched the people circling in small groups, laughing, kidding, talking. They came in all ages and sizes, but he felt so much older than most. Maybe it was what he had gone through, living day by day in danger.

Now, watching them having a good time, he wondered if maybe even as a boy, it had been more that he didn't want to know the town than that the people didn't want to know him. He and Kieran had plenty in common as kids. They'd both been moved around and passed off from one person to another. Neither of them particularly wanted to make friends here in the summers. If they had, it would simply be more people to leave behind.

Only now, things had changed here in Harmony. Kieran, in his shy way, had probably simply smiled, waved, and run, as he always did. But Austin was wounded and could no longer run. Now, for the first time in his life, he wanted to stay in Harmony . . . and the reason for it was headed right toward him. His long-legged, well-rounded-in-all-the-right-places, beautiful neighbor.

Ronny handed him a glass of sweet tea. "Nice party," she

said, looking quite the country girl in her bare feet and short shorts that one of the Delaney girls had loaned her.

He smiled. She was, like him, invisible to most. Several people said hello to her, even complimented her cooking, but none stayed to visit.

"Come over here," he said so only she could hear. "Please."

She smiled and moved in front of him. When she sat on the porch railing, she placed her bare feet on one of the chair's rungs between his legs.

"Talk to me, pretty lady." His hand circled her ankle. "Tell me about what you're planning." He'd seen her talking with an older woman who was dressed like she'd retired from the circus, and the conversation looked like a serious one.

Her words were soft, meant just for him. "I was talking to Martha Q. She says if I decide to do accounting, she'd be my first client." Ronny's eyes danced with excitement. "I want to settle down here and maybe start a business. I thought accounting, but it might be more fun to open a bakery. Everyone loved my salads and pies tonight. Only the bakery would have to be in town, and I could do accounting from the cabin."

He moved his fingers along her leg slowly as she told him of her dream. It wasn't big, really, not get-rich-quick, no mansion in town or big ranch, but it sounded good. She could work her own hours and take off during the slow times.

"I'm buying the cabin," she said about the time his fingers reached her knee.

"What?" He stopped, pulling his interest away from where the hem of her shorts ended just below her hips. "Did you say you bought that old cabin?"

She nodded. "I thought I'd live there for a while. Eventually, if my business grows, I might just use it as my getaway place, but for now it is my first real home."

"Ronny, you've got all the world to pick from and you pick a lake in the middle of nowhere?"

She grinned. "I like it here."

"It's not that simple."

She studied him. "It *is* that simple, Austin. I don't want complicated. Don't act so upset about having me as a permanent neighbor. I'm sure you'll get used to it in time."

"Oh, I'm very happy about that. Trust me." He could think of no one he'd rather have within walking distance of him.

He slid his hand over the back of her calf. Maybe it *was* that simple. "Ronny," he said, knowing he might get shot out of the water, but he had to try, "any chance you'd come over again tonight? We didn't finish what we'd started when the Delaneys called. I was dreaming earlier that we might do a little more than cuddling. My leg feels fine."

"I'll let you know when we're heading back. Dusti says you're a man who's not quite housebroken. The kind that will run off if the door's left open."

He thought about saying that Dusti should know; she'd been hanging around such a man lately. Kieran had left so fast he hadn't even dropped by to wave, but Austin figured he'd probably get a text when his friend finally landed somewhere.

He'd also bet Kieran's first question would be about Dusti.

He looked directly at Ronny. "I just want you next to me. I want to be able to touch you all night. There is something about having you near that rests my soul. Just you being near is all that has to happen. I'm not pushing." He wanted to add that he'd been going nuts for weeks waiting for her to want to go further. Didn't she know that paradise was just around the corner?

She raised an eyebrow. "I'm not making any such promise, Captain. I might just decide to attack you and not stop until I've had my way with you."

"I'm betting on it." Austin grinned. She'd just described his favorite fantasy.

It took every ounce of his strength to stay in his chair. All he wanted to do was pull her down to the boat and head home. No woman had ever turned him inside out like Ronny. He had a feeling no woman ever would again.

She walked away with promise in her eyes, and he knew that for the first time he was in love. Head-over-heels, madly in love with a shy lady who could change the orbit of his world with one look.

Thoughts of heaven didn't have long to live in Austin's mind. They were smothered when a chubby woman dressed in a bright purple jogging suit sat down in the chair next to him. She was out of breath and hanging off both sides of the wicker chair. The lady from the circus, he remembered, who'd talked to Ronny earlier.

He knew nothing about fashion, but surely that amount of jewelry didn't go with a jogging suit. If she ever did manage a run, she'd beat herself to death with all those beads.

"It gets any hotter out here, I'm calling the fire department." She pulled out a half dozen tissues from her bra and started patting every inch of exposed flesh.

"How are you, Miss Martha Q?" He smiled, guessing who she was from what Ronny said about making Martha Q her first client if she opened an accounting business. He'd heard about her for years. Kieran said she thought the woman had killed several husbands and a few lovers but no one ever saw her do it.

The woman glared at him. "How do you know my name? I don't believe we've ever met. I may be getting older, but I wouldn't forget a well-built man like you, especially with those scars."

In his short-sleeve shirt she had no problem seeing the scars on one arm and those that ran up his throat almost to his chin.

He grinned. "I always like people who look at others straight on. If you look carefully you notice we're all scarred one way or another."

Martha Q nodded. "You're a wise man, whoever you are."

"I'm Austin Hawk. I own the place across the lake. I think the locals call it Hawk House."

Martha Q seemed to relax a bit. "I knew your father."

He didn't respond. If rumors were true, she knew the fathers of half the people here. "How well did you know him?" She'd either laugh or leave. Austin didn't much care which.

She laughed. "Not that well. He bought me a drink once at a dance over in Bailee. Said he was in town to settle an estate for a house out by Rainbow Lane. I'd just lost a husband and he'd lost a father. We talked about grief. I remember he said the strangest thing. He said he hated the house his dad owned, but he wouldn't sell it because his son loved it."

Austin stared at her. He had no reason to believe the lady was lying, but all he remembered was that his dad hated the house and never stayed around. It never occurred to him that his father had kept Hawk House because of him.

"Thanks," he finally said. "I'm glad you told me that."

"No charge for the truth," she added. "And while I'm talking, I might as well tell you to stay away from Ronny Logan. I saw the way you looked at her. She's a sweet, good girl and she don't need to be your layover love."

"What are you talking about?"

She huffed and wiggled as if settling into a padded chair. "I know you're in the army. Dallas Logan told me. You're just laying over here in Harmony. You'll be gone when the ship sails and leave her pining away. Dallas may not be speaking to her daughter but she worries about Ronny."

"You learn that from experience during World War One or Two, did you?"

"Don't try to insult me. I know what you're doing. Traveling men like you always looks for the shy innocent ones. There are probably broken hearts all over the world waiting for you to come back to them."

Austin decided he was too much of a gentleman to mention that it was Ronny who usually attacked him or that what Martha Q was talking about was none of her business. If Dallas Logan wasn't speaking to Ronny, she likely wouldn't know what was going on at the lake.

When facing an enemy head-on, diversion might be the only option. "Forget Ronny, Martha Q. Any chance *you'd* go out with me?"

She laughed until she choked and had to down half of his tea. "If you were twice the man and twice the age, you still wouldn't be man enough for me."

Austin had no doubt she was speaking the truth. Apparently no one man ever had been if stories were true.

"I might give it a try if I weren't wounded." He winked at her, deciding he liked this lady.

"I know, I heard. You got shot by a pig."

Just as he'd suspected, she'd known who he was when she sat down. This woman should have been a general. She knew exactly what she was doing apparently, and he had no idea where the next attack would be coming from. "You've been talking to Ronny's mother too much."

She shook her head, but her sprayed hair didn't move. "Nope. I've been listening to her too much. She's convinced you're the devil living out here with her daughter. Says if you don't leave the poor child crying, you'll take her off to live somewhere else."

"I'm not leaving her. I'm crazy about Ronny." He couldn't believe he was telling something so personal to Martha Q, but he figured she had her own vault of secrets. "I'd spend the rest of my life hating myself if I hurt her."

"I know. I saw it in your face when she walked away just now. Be careful, son of Travis Hawk, because I got a feeling you'll be the one who falls hard if it doesn't work out between you two."

"You *did* know my dad."

"I said I did." Martha Q picked up his tea and finished the glass. "I ain't got enough life left in me to repeat myself, so listen up the first time."

"Yes, ma'am, but your warning may have come a bit late."

"Then be good to her."

"That I can promise." He leaned over. "Don't worry about her."

Martha Q patted his arm and wiggled out of the chair. "I'll be seeing you around. Next time you're in town, stop by the inn for a meal."

"I'll do that," he said, surprised to realize that he meant it. Austin leaned back as she waddled off into the crowd. How was it possible that he'd ever thought the people of Harmony wouldn't be worth getting to know?

Chapter 37

TRUMAN FARM

REAGAN WATCHED NOAH CLIMB OUT OF HIS TRUCK AND head toward her. When she'd said he could come over to see the baby, she hadn't expected that he would make it a nightly trip. He was as regular as the sunset around the place.

As usual, he sat down and she passed him Utah.

"You wash your hands?"

"Yes," he snapped. "I took a shower. Don't want his first memory of me to be the smell of cow shit."

She grinned as Noah smiled down at his son and began telling him every detail of what had happened at the ranch.

When he finally took a breath, Reagan asked, "I thought you'd be at the party at the Delaney place tonight."

"I'd rather be here with you," he said, looking straight at her. "Rea, there's nowhere else I want to be. Whether we're together or not, I want to be part of your world. I'm hoping, if I don't screw this up, you'll let me keep coming."

She could hear her heart pounding. Over the past few weeks she'd stopped hating him, but she wasn't sure she could open her heart again. Loving Noah hurt too much . . . but not seeing him again might hurt even more.

She changed the subject and they talked about what he was doing on the ranch until the sun went down. When they'd been kids he'd called the place "his," then later when he talked about it he called it "the" ranch. She'd noticed the past week he was back to calling it "his."

When he lifted Utah to his shoulder and stood, they went inside. Somehow they'd reached the point where he didn't have to wait for an invitation to step inside. He'd become comfortable with the baby in his arms and she couldn't forget a time when she'd been comfortable there too.

He was standing beside her now and she was still missing him. She wondered if any other woman in the world hated and loved the same man at the same time. She was circling in a tornado and there didn't seemed to be any hint of where she might land.

Utah was fussy and didn't want to go to sleep, so Noah put him in the swing and tried singing to him again.

When the baby cried louder, Reagan laughed, truly laughed.

Noah, with his black eye, grinned and kept singing.

"You picking on me again, Rea? I've been practicing singing to the cows and they don't seem to mind."

"Keep practicing." She smiled. He'd always known how to make her laugh. "Your eye is looking better. Want to tell me why you asked Big to hit you the other night?"

"No. He didn't really hit me. I kind of walked into his fist. I'd do it again if it'd make you smile, Rea."

"I don't want to see you hurt, Noah."

"I don't want to see you hurting, Rea." He looked up at her and she saw just how much she meant to him in his gaze. Since the morning after the fight at the poker game he'd been doing all he could to prove he'd changed. He'd been her man before he even knew he was a man and now he was trying his best to be the man she needed him to be, but she wasn't sure it was enough, not this time, maybe not ever again.

When he looked back down at the baby she knew that this

time, this one last time, she had to find a way to at least try. Too much of her heart already belonged to Noah. If she pulled the rest away, she wasn't sure she'd have enough of the muscle left to pump blood.

Utah finally drifted to sleep in the swing and they sat down to dinner. She'd cooked a roast in the oven with vegetables piled on top. Noah ate three helpings and was reaching for another when she told him she had pie.

When she passed him a slice, he said, "Thanks," like she'd given him a great gift.

They talked of safe topics, and then Noah casually mentioned that one of his friends had called and said there was big money coming up at a rodeo in Houston this weekend.

"I could make enough to double my herd with a win," he said between bites. "That, and the money I've got saved, will set the ranch up for years. It'd be something, not having to scrape by."

Reagan listened to words she'd heard a hundred times before. She could hear the excitement in his voice. Like a racehorse dying to run. Noah's drug of choice had never been alcohol, it had always been the rodeo, and he couldn't turn down one more chance to ride. One more chance to win or die.

This time she didn't bring up the argument of what if he was hurt or crippled. What if the bull killed him? Some said for bull riders, it isn't if they get hurt, it's when. This time she just listened and added one more reason she'd never let Noah back into her life. In his mind he was already riding in the Houston lights, already flying through the eight seconds, already winning. He wouldn't, or maybe couldn't, see that the fall was coming.

When he left, she kissed him on the cheek and he smiled, happy for once.

She didn't say a word about his going. There was nothing left to say. Noah wasn't hers. He never would be.

"Good-bye, Noah," she whispered as she closed the door.

Chapter 38

Walden Cabin

Ronny had spent the night of the party with Austin, but at dawn she'd gone back to her cabin. Though they'd cuddled and touched, she'd never pushed further and to her surprise, he seemed to be letting her take the lead.

It was almost as if they were passing through their teenage years, moving into passion slowly, one step at a time. She knew he wanted her, and his hesitation made the nights so much sweeter because she knew he didn't want to rush her. The tough man was being kind, and his tenderness touched her deeply.

She'd told herself a hundred times that she didn't want to fall in love again. She wanted a fling. She wanted to be able to walk away without getting her heart involved. The last time she'd loved a man in her mind, but not with her body. This time she wanted it to be the other way around.

Only problem was, she wasn't listening to herself. Austin mattered to her. When he'd gone into town a little after noon, she'd missed him more than she thought she would. He hadn't stopped by to talk, he'd just waved from the dock.

In an odd way, she missed taking care of him. The wound in his leg hadn't slowed him down long, and now he seemed to be pushing himself. He'd stopped using the crutch completely and told Abby he really didn't need her checking on him. Some mornings he put on what looked like a thirty-pound pack and walked along the beach. Once she'd caught him trying to run up the stairs. It wouldn't be long before he'd take the two flights with the pack without even breathing heavy.

He seemed a man driven, but she wasn't sure in what direction.

Ronny planned her day, deciding she'd stop when he got back. Only he didn't come back. She worked through lunch organizing, planning her remodel, getting used to the new computer Mr. Carleon had left with her a week before. It had all kinds of new accounting programs. Figuring them out was almost like working a crossword puzzle, and she loved it.

By late afternoon, she decided she missed Austin far too much to pay attention to her work. So she dressed as if for a date and walked over to his place. She could wait there as easily as at the cabin. She might even climb to the widow's walk and watch him turn off Rainbow Lane at the Delaneys' place, then row over.

As she reached his house, she noticed none of the lights were on and it was almost dark. He hadn't said he'd be late. If he'd thought he'd be coming after dark, surely he would have left a light burning. He hadn't said anything to her. Not even where he was going or what business he had to do. Maybe they should think about talking more? This late, she was starting to worry.

Neither of them was used to telling anyone where they were going. If they stayed together, maybe they should develop that as a habit. "If," she whispered aloud. Her whole life was full of *if*s.

A lantern at the dock blinked on. For a moment, Ronny thought he might be there, then realized it was only a timer clicking on.

The house was unlocked as always. Ronny wandered

through the rooms. The place had the feeling of never having been truly lived in. All the rooms were there with furniture scattered about, but nothing seemed to belong. No Hawk had ever left his signature on any corner. No personal pictures, no books, no keepsakes, nothing that said a woman had ever lived in the house.

She couldn't help but wonder if everything in Austin's life was the same way. When he'd talked about traveling he'd never mentioned a place he returned to for leave or a relative he visited. Maybe there were none.

The only house he came back to year after year was this house, and he hadn't bothered to truly settle in here. The place looked like it hadn't even been painted in thirty years. No memories of past times whispered in the hallways like they do in most old houses.

She began walking slowly through the rooms, touching the walls, saying hello to the place. Sadness moved over her as she realized no one had ever really lived in this fine house, with its strong bones built to withstand any storm. No one had ever cared for it. Even the furnishings were cheap and shabby, as if bought years ago in lots. Ten pieces, including lamps and pictures, at one price.

Ronny brushed one of the faded seascape scenes framed in plastic.

The frame slipped, showing the true color the wall had once been painted. Blue, not gray, she thought as she lifted the picture.

Behind the painting were rough scratches on the wall.

For a moment she thought they were scars, and then she made out letters and numbers cut into the plaster with little skill.

AUSTIN HAWK WAS HERE 1996

She brushed her fingers over the carving, tears drifting down her face unnoticed. Seventeen years ago a little boy must have wanted to belong so badly he'd carved his name.

Now she knew why he'd returned. Here, this place, was as

close to a home as he had. This part of Texas, where few knew his name, was his base. When he was broken and hurting, he came here.

She smiled. He was a hard man to figure out, but an easy man to love. He didn't know how to talk to her. She laughed. He didn't even know how to act interested when she talked sometimes.

Ronny walked to the dock and waited. She knew what she had to do.

Chapter 39

THE LAKE

AUSTIN IGNORED THE THROBBING IN HIS LEG AS HE LOADED his boat and headed for home. This morning, when he'd left, he'd thought of taking Ronny's little blue boat. She'd left his place after breakfast saying she wanted to spend the day making plans for her cabin. She'd even shown him pictures she'd cut out from magazines.

He must have not put enough effort into acting interested, because she'd gathered up all her samples of paint, wallpaper, and tile. She'd smiled and promised to be back for dinner.

In a moment of insanity before they crawled out of bed, he'd promised to cook supper. But ten minutes after she left he was missing her too badly to just hang around. He had to do something or go insane. Visiting Martha Q wasn't on his list, but if he didn't think of something before he got to town, he might even do that. Otherwise the day would be endless without Ronny.

Now, with food and books and gear piled high, Austin realized if he'd taken her boat, he'd be relaxing while he rode back across the water. Instead, he had to row. He pulled hard on the oars, wanting to get home as soon as possible. He had lots to tell her, but halfway across he started wondering if she'd take a swing at him if he asked her to put on those short shorts she'd worn to the Delaneys' party. Surely she wouldn't get mad. He wouldn't be upset if she asked him to strip completely.

What he didn't know about women would fill an ocean, and he wasn't sure asking Martha Q for advice had been a good idea. He'd hoped for a few pointers, not a total brain meltdown of all he didn't know about women listed in categories.

When he looked up and saw Ronny's silhouette waiting for him on the dock, he couldn't stop smiling like some fool falling in love for the first time.

Which, he knew, was exactly what had happened. He was in love for the first and probably the only time in his life. It had taken all these years for one girl like Ronny to speak to him and come close enough to see who he really was. The tough-guy mask didn't fool her at all. She saw right through it. He'd better hang on to her, for he guessed he had about as much chance of finding love again as lightning striking the same spot twice.

Also, if he was dumb enough to screw this up with Ronny, he'd never find another woman so perfect. He'd measure every woman he met with Ronny and none would come close to her.

He didn't notice her arms were folded until he was tying up. That meant something, he was pretty sure, but he didn't know what.

When he'd dropped by Martha Q's for a lecture a few hours ago, she'd mentioned something about folded arms, but as usual, he was only half listening. The old woman had a habit of repeating everything two or three times. By the time he'd finished his tea and coffee cake, Austin was thinking of asking her if he could have the abridged version on how to make a woman happy. Her lecture had gone on too long, causing him to barely make it home before dark.

"You shouldn't be rowing." She pointed her finger at him. "You should have taken my boat."

He didn't know what to say. Telling her to stop pestering him never worked, and yelling at her would be like kicking a kitten. Silence seemed his only defense. In truth he liked the idea that someone cared enough to worry.

"Austin, if you pull those stitches out . . ."

"They're out." He finally got a word in. "I went by the doc and she pulled them out. Told me not to come back unless another pig shot me." He knew he was abbreviating the doc's orders, but he didn't want Ronny and the Delaney girls thinking they had to watch over him any longer.

Ronny shook her head and fisted her hands on her hips. "I love you, Austin Hawk, but I'm not putting up with your lies. What did the doctor say, and don't even think about not telling me everything or I'll call and check on you."

He felt like he'd just been hit with a solid gold shovel. He didn't know whether to be happy about the gold or mad about the hit. She'd said she loved him in the same sentence she'd called him a liar. No wonder married men walk around confused all the time.

"I brought dinner." He reached into the boat for the bag, hoping food would provide some distraction. "Burgers from the diner." He couldn't look at her. He needed a moment to think. He'd heard women say they loved him because they thought that was what they should say when the hotel light went out, but he had a feeling that when Ronny used the word, she meant it.

He lifted out the two bags and stepped onto the dock, careful not to flinch when pain shot up his leg. "I'm fine, Ronny. I swear. You don't have to take care of me." His words came out sharper than he'd meant them to be.

She straightened as if at attention. "All right. I guess I'll go back to the cabin. I'm obviously not needed or wanted here."

She'd made it two steps before he dropped the hamburgers and grabbed her hand. "Just a minute. We're not finished."

He half expected her to run, but Ronny never did what he expected.

She pulled her hand free and pointed to the water. "Our dinner is floating away."

He turned and watched the bags bob a few times in the water before sinking. When he looked back, she was smiling, so he thought he'd start over. "Any chance you'd go back to town with me? I've been smelling those burgers all the way home, and my stomach's waiting for a taste."

She nodded. "Only if we take my boat."

"Fair enough." He didn't want to admit how much his leg hurt.

As he tied his boat up and covered the other bags he'd brought with a tarp, she ran home to get her purse. That was another thing he couldn't figure out. Why women take purses with them everywhere but don't offer to pay. If he didn't figure it out fast he'd have to go back for more coffee cake and lectures.

Now his head hurt along with his leg. He needed to stop worrying and simply enjoy being exactly where he'd wanted to be all day. With Ronny.

Austin tried to think of everyday things they could talk about, like who he'd seen in town and all he'd done besides go to the doctor, but her first words kept coming back to him. *I love you, Austin Hawk.* He should have said something right then. Something simple like *I love you too.* Only he hadn't and the moment was gone. Besides, those three words shouldn't be something you have to think about before saying them.

When she returned to the dock, he decided to clear the air. "I wasn't lying to you, Ronny, I'm fine."

She nodded. "Just promise you won't hide things from me. If you're hurting, tell me. I don't want to mother you, but I need to know the truth."

"All right, pretty lady, the truth." He started the engine and they began moving across the lake. "The doc says it will take me maybe another two or three months to be up to speed again. My leg is coming along fine. She's also been checking on my progress from the last injury I took six months ago. The fire scarred inside my lungs as well as outside. Nothing that will affect me living a long life, but when I go back to my job next month I'll be at a desk, not in the field."

"How do you feel about that?"

"I didn't sign up to do paperwork." He cut the engine and they drifted on the lake. "I'm thinking it may be time for me to get out."

For a while, they didn't talk. They just sat, side by side, and let the night move over them. It felt so good having someone near while he just thought over his options. Somehow it didn't seem near as frightening as it did when he was alone.

Finally, he whispered, "Did you mean it earlier?"

"Mean what?"

"That you love me?" When she didn't answer, he added, "It's all right if you didn't. I know people say it all the time and don't mean anything by it. I just wanted to know if—"

"I meant it."

"Oh," he answered. "It's just that we've only known each other such a short time and you really don't know what a hardass I am. My team used to complain that I never smiled or stopped cussing. I'm not what you—"

"I know who and what you are, Austin." She interrupted him again. "I know you. You're the man who stands in the rain because you were worried about me. You're the one who missed me all day and now doesn't know how to tell me how much. You don't want to care about anyone, but somehow I got past your guard and that one fact terrifies you."

He took her hand, wishing he could find the right words to tell her. Just saying that she was right about everything didn't seem to be enough.

She leaned closer and kissed his cheek. "I know the man you are, and the man you want to be, and I love them both."

He kissed her. "I don't know what I ever did to deserve you, but I'd go through it all again a hundred times knowing that you're on the other side, waiting."

They held each other close for a while. He found it hard to believe that she saw through him so easily, and he loved that she didn't put up with any of his manipulating or bullying.

Finally, he started the motor again and they continued across the lake.

THE DINER WAS EMPTY, BUT SHE TALKED HIM INTO TAKING the worst table, a tiny spot by the door. He thought of complaining, but when she sat across from him, her knees slid between his beneath the little table, and he decided he didn't mind her choice at all. The feel of her legs rubbing against the inside of his made it impossible to focus enough to read the menu, so he just ordered a burger.

The cook she called Cass got the food out way too fast, Austin thought, but he was too lost in brushing against Ronny's leg to notice.

As they ate, he told her of the people he'd seen in town. He'd stopped by the fire station and ended up spending the afternoon showing all the men how to handle new equipment. As he described each one of the guys, Ronny filled in the details of their lives. She knew them all. Ronny might not like to talk in crowds, but she'd listened all her life.

She told him about her plans to open an office on the lake. It would be so hard to get to, she'd have to go to her clients. Though she loved people, she also loved her quiet time. She knew of one big ranch run by Cord McDowell that needed a bookkeeper, and she could do most of the work from the cabin. She'd always loved making details fit together, and she thought she'd give bookkeeping a try. She'd be helping people's lives run smoother and she'd like that.

On the drive home she curled up against his arm, and he realized he hadn't thought of the pain in his leg for a long while.

"I liked this, it was almost a date." She yawned.

He patted her knee. "This was a date. Or at least I think it was. I've had so few, I'm not sure."

She laughed, that soft little laugh he loved to hear. "You're right. It was a date. We should have another one just to make sure."

"Sounds like a plan. We'll go out every third night for the rest of our lives. Only we'll run out of restaurants and have to drive into Amarillo at some point."

In the dash lights he watched her straighten. "I guess this means we're dating?"

He laughed. "We're far beyond that."

She made a little sound of agreement and leaned against his shoulder as they drove back to the lake.

SHE HELPED HIM CARRY HIS BAGS OF BOOKS TO HIS PORCH. "Stay with me tonight," he said without turning on a light.

She hesitated, then started down the steps. "It's been a long day. You'll be all right. We both need sleep."

"Stay with me forever," he said, hating that it sounded more like an order than a request.

"Why?" she asked, and she took another step down.

One more step and she'd be out of his reach. "Because I can't watch the one woman I've ever loved walk away. Not tonight, or any night."

She turned slowly and looked up at him, reading him as clearly as she always had.

Suddenly she cried out and ran up the stairs and into his arms.

On this night there would be no holding back.

Chapter 40

Dusti Delaney sat in the Amarillo International Airport waiting for her flight to Vegas. Of course she'd have to go through Dallas first, but in five hours she'd be there. She was so excited she half thought she might just jump out of her skin. She'd found a way out. With this one chance, this one game, she and Abby might find a future. Abby could be the nurse she was born to be, and she could really study photography. The farm on Rainbow Lane would always be home, but it wouldn't have to be their lives. One more bridge to cross before their dreams would come true.

Abby had dropped her off at the airport, but couldn't stay with her once she crossed security, so she'd headed back home. For a few days Abby would run the farm alone, and there was too much to do to waste time.

They'd hugged good-bye at the drop-off, both too excited to talk about what might happen in the next few days while Dusti was in Vegas. Since the party they'd packed and repacked Dusti's bag. They'd talked about all Abby needed to do and how Dusti must be safe in the wild town. They'd talked about everything except what would happen if she won. This close to the end of their plan, they could no longer give words to their dreams.

Both knew if she won it would change their lives forever.

"Win or lose, I love you, kid," Abby yelled as she left.

"Win or lose," Dusti echoed, holding the old camera Kieran had given her to keep for him. She told herself if Abby could have her dream, she'd settle for just a fraction of hers. Unless he asked for it back, she'd keep the old camera. It felt so right in her hands.

She planned to log her trip in pictures. Step by step. Maybe no one would care, but she'd have the trip and her memories so she could never forget.

When she walked over to the coffee shop to buy bottled water, she saw Noah McAllen sitting in the corner, his feet propped up on the empty chair across from him. As always, he looked like a model off the cover of a western novel. Stetson low. Leather vest. Pearl snaps on his pressed white shirt with his initials on the cuff. Handmade boots she'd bet had his name at the top. The man was Harmony's own Brad Pitt and he didn't even know it.

"Hi, Noah," she said. They weren't really close friends, but since he'd been beat up at the same place she'd won the poker game, maybe they should talk.

He raised his hat. His left eye was shadowed in gray from an aging bruise, though it still looked too new to have been from the night of the poker game. "Morning, Dusti. You heading for the big poker game?"

"Yes." She couldn't stop smiling. "I'm about to make my dream come true. If I win in the money, the Delaney girls' lives are about to change. I'm so excited I can't sleep or eat. All I think about is winning."

"Great," he said, tipping his hat slightly with a bandaged hand.

"What about you, Noah? Where are you headed?" At the party someone had said that Noah and Reagan had broken up, but no one believed it. Noah, if he ever remembered to come home, belonged to Reagan Truman. Everyone had known that since high school. He flirted with the girls everywhere he went, but when he walked out he always took Reagan's hand. Maybe bright lights had finally won out over a simple country girl.

Noah didn't look too excited when he finally answered, "I'm headed to a rodeo in Houston. Riding for the money, you know, just like you."

"What happened to your hand?" She had an hour to kill; talking to him seemed better than doing nothing.

"Which one?"

She almost felt sorry for Mr. Good-looking. "Both, I guess."

He held up his left. "Forgot to wear gloves while fixing barbed-wire fence." He held up his right. "Got bit by a rattler while I was cleaning out brush around the old home place. He barely got his teeth in me, but Reagan made me go to the doc."

So much for the rumors that he and Reagan had split, she thought.

"And the eye?" Dusti decided not to notice the bruises that had faded to gray along his jawline.

"Biggs," was his only reply.

Dusti should have let his comment before the medical report drop, but she'd never been one to keep her mouth shut. "You know, Noah, we're not the same, you and I. Even beat up, you still got it all back in Harmony. All the luck and big pots. All the winner's circle you could ask for." Speaking her mind felt great, even if she'd probably pay for it later. "It looks to me like you got everything a man could dream of. Everyone knows Reagan Truman loves you. And some say your ranch will be the best in the county in five years if you work it. A few scratches and bruises don't change the facts."

Noah didn't look like he wanted to hear what she had to say, but she added, "I'm taking a chance on winning everything I've ever wanted. You're taking a chance on losing everything you've already got."

He looked like he wanted to say, *Who died and left you in charge of my life*, but he didn't. Noah was too much a "good guy" to tell her to get lost. He just stared at her.

"You're right, Dusti," he said, "I was just thinking the same thing. Why am I flying out when all I want is here?"

Dusti's phone sounded. She turned away, not wanting Noah to hear two screaming old women wishing her luck. Martha Q and Mrs. Mills couldn't have been more excited if they'd been going with her. When they finally hung up, Dusti turned back to Noah, but his chair was empty.

She looked around the small coffee shop. He'd disappeared and his boarding pass had been left in the center of the table. She picked up the pass and walked back to the waiting area.

"You're welcome, Noah," she whispered, wondering if she'd been any help at all.

Her phone rang again. She didn't recognize the number but answered it simply because she had an hour of nothing left to do now that she'd talked Noah into walking away.

"Hello, lass," a familiar voice said. "You excited?"

"Where have you been? I thought we had a date, Kieran."

"I've been working straight through so I could have time off. I may be in London but I plan to be on call for you the next few days. Anytime you need a break, call and I'll help you out. We're not playing against each other this time. I'm all on your side."

She smiled and walked to the long wall of glass. Here, she felt almost alone with Kieran even though a hundred people could see her there.

Kieran started going over the rules again and kept talking until she boarded the plane. Hours later when she got to her room at the hotel, she called him back and they talked for another hour about all she had to do.

"Get some sleep, lass, you'll need it tomorrow morning."

She promised, then added, "Wish you were here to kiss me good night."

He hesitated for a moment and added, "So do I."

She fell asleep dreaming of what it would be like. She'd never waited for anything in her life. From the moment of first attraction Dusti was usually running full steam ahead. But Kieran had made her wait, and right now she wanted him more than she'd ever wanted any man. A hundred times more.

The next morning she was still thinking about Kieran when she checked in at the poker registration table and took a few pictures of the lights around her and the interesting people milling around. As she waited to be called up, she did what he said; she watched every person.

For the most part the players were easy to separate from the watchers.

The types were all there. The woman with her dress cut in a deep V. The cowboy smoking his last cigar before the game started. The guy with a hood and glasses who looked like he might rob a convenience store if poker didn't turn out to be his game. The little man who pushed his way around as if he planned to make sure he got his fair share of attention.

When she sat down at the table, Kieran's voice was in her head. *Watch everything. Don't talk more than you have to. Don't get involved in a battle between two other players.*

As they started playing, his voice continued. *Fold if the first two cards aren't good. Fold if the flop doesn't help you. Watch the other players for tells.*

The cowboy whose fingers were stained from smoking shook slightly when his cards were good. The guy bluffing to her right kept checking his cards like he thought they'd change on him. A tall man whose hair had slid to the back of his head kept trying to hurry everyone along as if the game were on a timer.

Two hours later, when she'd won the first round at her table, she stood, stretched, and called Kieran.

"I felt like you were with me all morning. I felt like you had my back." She fought not to scream into the phone. "I won."

"More rounds to go," he said, "and I am with you. Now, during the two-hour break, go get something to eat or take a nap. Don't play any slots around. Today just concentrate on poker."

She bought a candy bar and walked the half mile to her room. An hour later he called to tell her to buy strong coffee and step back into the gaming room. "Don't be friendly, lass. You're not there to make friends. You're there to win."

The next round took longer, and a sweet old man next to her kept telling her, "Go ahead and fold, sweetie, I got this one." Kieran's warning reminded her of the trick. Even when the old man told her he was saving her money with his advice, she didn't fold.

She won.

It was late afternoon when she called Kieran back and wondered if it might be the middle of the night where he was. He sounded sleepy when he answered.

"I won again," she whispered.

"Way to go, lass. Now go to your room, order room service, and relax. Let the other winners go out and celebrate. You've got to be ready for tomorrow. Lights out by eleven."

"Would you kiss me good night?" she asked.

"If I were there, lass, I'd kiss you senseless, but it's a good thing I'm not. You need a clear head. I'd only mix it up. Sleep, eat, get ready to play."

When she hung up, she did exactly what he told her to do even though several of the other players offered to buy her a drink. She was here to win, not party.

One of the other players had put his arm around her as if planning to herd her along to the bar. Dusti stepped free and didn't bother to thank him for the invitation.

Kieran woke her early, telling her to eat a good breakfast. He said today would be intense and she had to be ready for anything. One by one he listed everything she needed in her emergency bag. Cough drops, aspirin, tissues, candy that didn't make noise or melt.

"If you get a break in the play, disappear; don't stand around talking to the others. The less they know about you, the better."

Dusti laughed. He was starting to sound like her nanny. "I love you for doing this, Kieran."

"I love you too, lass. Now get in there and play your best game."

She smiled as she walked into the gaming room. He had

to believe she had a chance or he wouldn't be doing this. She'd worried about being all alone, but she wasn't alone. He was with her, along with Mrs. Mills and her advice about how to play in a mostly man's game and Martha Q with her jokes about always keeping her pants on between rounds.

"Been talking to your boyfriend?" the guy with the dark glasses asked. "Maybe whispering sweet nothings to him?"

Dusti straightened, putting her phone away. "Nope," she answered. "Still afraid of the sun?"

She didn't give him time to answer. If she made it through this round, she'd have a seat at the final table. She'd be in the money.

It seemed like she waited hours before it was her turn to play her round. She was exhausted from pacing. She'd even tried to watch the earlier games but couldn't.

Kieran hadn't called back. He must be in the air flying somewhere. He couldn't just forget his job and coach her on the game. She knew that no matter what happened he'd be the first call she made when she walked away today.

Finally, her name was called and she walked calmly to her seat.

In all her scatterbrained life, Dusti had never concentrated on anything so completely. She played exactly as Kieran had taught her to. One by one the others moved away from the table, busted.

The clock seemed to tick by at half speed, until finally only Dusti and the sunglasses remained. Their stacks were almost equal after three hours, but she finally saw her chance. When he raised her, thinking she'd fold, she saw his tell, a slight huff he made whenever he was bluffing.

"All in," she said. "I'm betting the rainbow." All colors of chips rattled into the center of the table.

If he backed away, he lost big.

She licked her lips, the same thing she'd done the last three times she'd bluffed. She had no idea if he saw her. The glasses made him seem more like a bug than a person.

He smiled and shoved his pile in. "Time to shut up or get up, girl."

The cards seem to float over the table in slow motion. He had a pair of jacks. She had two kings.

She hadn't bluffed this time.

She won.

Chapter 41

TRUMAN FARM

REAGAN HAD SPENT THE DAY FIGHTING TEARS.

She knew Noah had left this morning for the Houston rodeo. Half the people in town knew it. He might as well have posted his travel plans in the paper. He'd left his old pickup parked in front of the sheriff's office. His sister or Hank must have taken him.

That had been his way for five years. If she couldn't take him or the weather was bad, Hank always drove him to Oklahoma City or Amarillo, depending on where he could get a flight out. Reagan loved to be the one to pick him up when he got home. They'd hug while waiting for the bags, and then they'd talk all the way home. Once they became lovers, no matter what time of day it was they'd drive straight to her place and spend a few hours in bed. Then she'd go downstairs in just her shirt and make him breakfast and they'd talk about what their lives would be like after his rodeo days were over. The house on his ranch. The kids they'd have. The fun they'd have chasing each other around the house even when they were old.

Only now, Reagan knew those dreams were only pipe dreams. They were never going to happen. The rodeo would never be over. Noah would never give up the life and come home to stay. At least not whole. At least not just to her.

Abby called to tell her Dusti was on her way to Vegas and that she thought she saw Noah stepping out of a big pickup as she was driving away.

Reagan had told a few people that she and Noah were over, but most of the town didn't believe it. They'd probably grow old like her uncle Jeremiah and his next-door neighbor Pat Matheson, never marrying but folks still thinking they were a couple. Reagan had asked Pat once if she loved her uncle and the old woman said, "Yes, but that don't mean I wanted to live with the man."

Maybe women can't help who they love sometimes, but they're smart enough to know not to marry the fool. She was beginning to think she might be one of those women. Reagan didn't want to worry about him being killed every time he ran off to the rodeo. She couldn't live that way.

Picking up Utah, she whispered, "Your daddy is crazy, but I won't hold that against you."

Utah just stared at her, probably still trying to get her in focus. Only now and then she swore he understood something she said.

"I'd better get your diaper changed. It's almost time we went to the western chairs. The sunset's going to be a good one tonight. Clouds rolling in from the north. With luck the orchard will get rain tonight."

Walking down the stairs, she held tightly to her bundle. It had been a month since Utah's mother had dropped him off. If she was coming back, she would have made it by now. Reagan knew it was time to contact a lawyer and make it all legal, but Noah had never said anything about taking the baby home with him. Maybe he was waiting until he finished building. Maybe he just wanted to come over and hold Utah every night.

Babies and rodeoing didn't go together.

"I'll watch over you," Reagan whispered as she walked

out the front door. "I'll make sure nothing bad ever happens to you."

For a moment the setting sun blinded her as she crossed the lawn, and then she saw him sitting in one of the lawn chairs. His long legs were stretched out in front of him. His hat low over his face. His bandaged hand folded over his stomach.

Moving closer, she realized he was sound asleep.

"Noah?"

He jerked and shoved his hat back. "Reagan. I've been waiting for you forever."

"Why didn't you knock on the door?"

"After that good-bye kiss, I didn't know if you'd answer the door." He straightened. His best starched shirt looked wrinkled, and she didn't miss the bag sitting beside his chair.

"So you figured it out. The kiss, I mean," she said, deciding maybe Utah's dad wasn't as dumb as she thought he was. "I was saying good-bye to you."

"It took me a while. I was at the airport rethinking every word we said last night and finally I figured something out. What I was running after was already behind me, so I turned around.

"It took me hours to get home. I thought I'd take the bus. Didn't know it stopped in every little town in the panhandle. I think I could have walked home faster, or bought a horse and rode."

She sat down, wondering how much of his story to believe.

"I told you once I need you and not the rodeo, and I meant what I said. I was just thinking about the money this time. That was all it was. That's all it's been for a long time, but I couldn't seem to knock myself off the merry-go-round. I figured if I stayed here and didn't go to Houston, you'd start to believe me."

"What about the big money you might make?"

"I can make it here in four or five years. But, Rea, I'll be here with you and Utah. I won't be busted up in some hospital waiting for you to come get me."

"I don't ever want to do that again." She remembered

picking him up and bringing him home once. She'd worried herself sick thinking he might never walk again.

Noah placed his hand over hers. "If it takes telling you every day for the rest of our lives that I love you, I'm going to do it. You're a part of me, Rea, the best part. Cutting you out of my life would be like cutting out my heart. I don't think I can do it."

"You lied to me, Noah."

"Yeah, as much as I talk, it's hard to say only the facts, but I swear I'll never lie to you again. Well, maybe about liking potato soup, but never about the important things between us."

"Where were you the night before you called me? It was the last call you made before you showed up at my door the night of the game. I'd gone to see you, but I couldn't find you. I called the Hampton in Vegas and you weren't there." She stared at him, knowing she'd see the lie coming if he tried.

He lowered his head a minute and said, "The guy whose phone I borrowed the next morning to call you will tell you. We were out drinking till after two. You must have called before we checked in." He dug in his bag. "I've got the receipt here somewhere."

"I don't need to see it. I believe you." She knew this time he was telling her the truth.

He looked doubtful. "You do?"

"Noah, you're the worst liar in Texas."

He looked offended. "Man, this is not my week. First you tell me that I can't sing and now I can't lie." He knelt down in front of her. "Rea, I never lied when I said I loved you or that I'm sorry for what happened. I've hated myself every day since that time I slept with that woman. I wanted to tell you, but then we'd both hate me. I thought if you didn't know, it wouldn't matter, but it's been eating me up inside. You're my best friend and I hated having something I couldn't talk over with you. It seemed easier just to keep delaying coming home."

He looked into her eyes as if he could see all the way to

her heart. "Most of all, I hate how I hurt you. I wish I could take all the pain into me. I never want to see you hurt again. I swear."

"I know." She realized what she said was true. She'd known for months that something was eating away at him. She'd thought it was that he didn't want to come home or he thought he'd get trapped if he did. But he'd come home. This time he'd picked her over the rodeo.

He smiled at her. "The guys used to tell me that I was single and I should have a little fun before settling down, but, Rea, ever since the day I said I loved you, I've felt like we're already tied together. I'm about the most married single man you're likely to meet. I don't care if folks say we're too young to tie the knot. You're all I want. You're all I've ever wanted."

He stood. "Look at me, Rea. If you don't forgive me soon, I'm going to be dead. There's only a few inches on me now that's not bruised or cut or beaten half to death."

She laughed, knowing he was doing what he always did, making her smile. And he was right. Almost every night he showed up with a new injury. The whole world seemed to be picking on Noah.

He smiled down at her. "Forgive me, Rea. Let me spend the next hundred years proving how much I love you. Only you. There will never be another drink in my hand or woman in my bed but you, or I promise I'll buy Big a gun so he can stop beating on me and just shoot me."

He didn't look like he was kidding, but he did look like a man very much in love. He'd never had to fight for her. She'd always been his girl even before she knew it herself. But these last few weeks he'd had to fight for her and the life he wanted. And he'd fought hard.

"How do you feel about staying here?"

"I'm not leaving, Rea. This town is where I belong. I plan on being buried next to you in the Harmony Cemetery. Soon as Tyler Wright's son gets old enough, I'll go over and buy the plots. Little Jonathan Henry will probably be middle-aged before he plants us side by side in the McAllen plots."

"No, I was asking how do you feel about staying here with me tonight?"

Noah froze like a preacher who was only half finished ranting and the congregation was already heading down to the front to repent.

"You mean here, with you?"

She nodded. "If you walk through that door, you're staying, for good. Not till the next rodeo friend calls, but for good."

He smiled back at her. "I'll stay, only if you tell me you love me. I'm not into one-night stands."

She stood, Utah in her arms. "I love you, Noah."

He swung her and the baby up. "Then I'm running through that door, Rea. Eyes wide open with you in my arms."

As he carefully carried his family up the steps, he added, "I'm thinking we should get married right away and start working on giving Utah a few more states as brothers and sisters."

She looked at this man she'd loved for so long. He wasn't perfect. Not even close, but he was the only one for her. There would always be a part of him that was the wild bull rider, but she knew he would come home to her every night and love her dearly.

"I think you are right, Preacher. Raising a family might turn out to be a much tougher ride than bulls."

"I've no doubt, but you'll be with me, Rea. That's all that's important. No matter what, you'll be with me. I never knew how much you meant to me until I almost lost you. I never want to have that feeling again. Never."

"Me either."

That night, after they'd put Utah to bed in his cradle in the corner of her room, Noah made love to Reagan with more tenderness than she'd thought possible. As he had every time they'd made love, he whispered her name.

When they were both exhausted, he held her close and played with her hair. "I love you, Rea. Even if you decided never to forgive me, that wouldn't have changed. I love you more than old Jeremiah loved sunsets. Do you think, just once, you could say you forgive me?"

"I forgive you, Noah." She already had. She knew her Noah. She'd seen him die inside when she'd told him to leave. She'd watched him fight to grow into the man she needed. He'd proved it this morning when he hadn't stepped on that plane. He was proving it to her now.

He rolled close and kissed her cheek. "You'll never regret it, I promise. If I ever break that promise, Hank and Big have both sworn to make you a widow that same day."

"That's comforting," she said, as if serious. "Just promise not to sing to our children."

He fell back on his pillow. "You drive a hard bargain, Rea."

She laughed as he pulled her to him, and she knew this time he planned to never ever let her go.

"By the way," she whispered, "Utah's middle name is Truman."

"Who said?"

"He told me. Said he wants to be the last Truman standing one day."

"Go to sleep, Rea. I'll talk him out of that plan tomorrow."

Chapter 42

As Dusti walked back to her room, she couldn't stop smiling. All she could think about was that she was in the money. Tomorrow she'd be in the last round. The final table of winners played now; the first man out in the next game would walk out with ten thousand dollars.

Her phone vibrated.

"Did you win?" Kieran asked.

"I did. How'd you know the game was over?"

He laughed. "I figured it had to be. They just put your name up on the Internet as one of the players in the last round."

"Want to go celebrate?" she whispered. "I could get champagne delivered to my room."

"No. You've got another round to play in the morning. Get some rest. Eat something. Go for a walk. Keep your head clear."

She walked toward her room. "Talk to me for a while."

"Sure, but only about poker. Call me back when you've taken a shower and settled in." He hung up.

Dusti stared at the phone. The man was driving her mad.

She called her sister, ate two bags of M&Ms, and finally

called him back. When he answered, she asked, "When this is over, will we have anything to talk about?"

"Of course. When this is over we'll do whatever you want. I'll bore you with my life story and you can talk dirty to me all you like, but right now, you're still in the game. I've been saving up conversations to have with you since we were kids and went swimming in the lake naked."

They laughed and settled down to business, discussing anything that might come up in the last round.

He tried his best to keep her mind on the game, but Dusti kept drifting to what she planned to say when this was all over. After he hung up, she'd almost fallen asleep when Abby called.

"Start packing, Abby," Dusti said. "You're going back to school."

Dusti closed her eyes and smiled as her sister rumbled. She'd done what she'd set out to do. Even if she went out first, she'd finished in the money. Abby would have her last few classes of college. She'd become a nurse.

When the game started the next morning she was still smiling. Thirty minutes into the last round a man stepped away from the table, and her take-home went up to fifteen thousand. Ten minutes later, another fell and she knew she'd be taking home twenty. Now she could pay the college and buy camera equipment.

Half an hour passed in slow motion before the next man stood and left the table. Dusti almost giggled. Her take-home at this point just jumped to thirty thousand dollars. Abby could finish school, they could repair a few things around the house, she might even rebuild the darkroom.

Twenty minutes later, while she was thinking about all the money she was making, she lost three hands in a row and had to be the one who stepped away. Only she couldn't stop smiling. She'd done it. She'd showed in the money.

She was winding her way out between people who came to watch with a check for thirty thousand dollars folded in her pocket.

As she patted her pocket one more time, making sure it was there, her phone buzzed.

"Good job, lass," Kieran's wonderful voice sounded in her ear. "I'm proud of you."

"Did you already hear about my losing on the Internet?"

"No," he said, laughter in his tone. "Turn around."

She slowly turned around and there he was, standing near a pillar where rows of chairs had been set up for spectators. She'd paid no attention to them. No one had come to see her play.

Only there he was. Tall, redheaded, adorable Kieran.

Dusti ran and jumped into his arms. She wrapped her arms and legs around him as tight as she could, and she couldn't stop crying. He'd been with her the whole time. He'd been watching over her.

Sunglasses guy walked by and pulled off his glasses. "Figures," he said. "The good-looking girls who play always have a guy waiting in the wings."

Neither of them answered his comment. They were too wrapped up in one another.

Kieran held on to her and walked out of the area. He must have known that she wanted to be with him alone for a few minutes.

Dusti watched the bright lights fly by, but she couldn't stop crying.

She'd won. She'd followed her dream, and best of all Kieran had been there beside her all along.

He finally stepped out into the warm, dry, desert air and sat down on a bench without turning loose of her. People were passing on both sides of them, but she still felt all alone with him.

"I'm so proud of you," he whispered, kissing the top of her head. "I knew you could do it."

He just held her for a few minutes, letting her nerves settle down. While she rested in his lap, he whispered, "You've got lots of people to call before you board the plane in the morning. Everyone you know is sitting at home waiting for the news."

"You're staying with me tonight. Aren't you?"

"I can't. I had to move heaven and earth to get a flight out here this morning. I'm due back in Dallas by midnight for a flight out to Heathrow."

"But . . . don't you want to spend the night with me?"

He laughed. "More than you know, Dusti, but I don't want to be a one-night stand. It's going to take a lot longer to cool the fire I have for you. It's been building for years."

"Then why did you come?"

"Because win or lose, it's about time I give you that kiss you want."

Then, as if he'd done it a hundred times before, Kieran lowered his mouth to hers and kissed her like no one else had ever kissed her. The people passing by were no more than water parting as they drifted in a river of feelings. All the times she'd dreamed of kissing him didn't come close to measuring up to this one moment.

A few times they stopped long enough to laugh and talk, but before her blood had time to cool, he was reaching for her again as if starving for one more touch, one more kiss.

Once they walked inside, he asked if she was hungry, then laughed when he saw the desire in her eyes. She'd tried to pull him to her room, but he wouldn't budge. Both knew they only had a short time, and this kind of passion wouldn't be satisfied in an hour.

He was still kissing her when they got to the airport two hours later.

When he ran for his plane, she turned and walked away, thinking she'd finally been completely kissed. And, touched, she added. The feel of his hands moving over her body warmed her skin. She had no doubt how dearly he wanted her and he'd left a longing in her.

The twenty-minute ride back to the hotel seemed like five. She felt like she'd been diving under deep water and needed time for her breathing to come back to normal.

Once she was in her room, she stripped off her clothes, lay down atop the covers, and turned the air conditioner on freeze. It was going to take her body hours to cool off.

Kieran had been right about one thing: If they'd kissed while she'd been learning to play, she never could have concentrated on learning to play poker.

That evening as she talked to all her friends, she didn't mention that Kieran had watched her win. She couldn't, for if she did, she'd never stop talking about him.

Once, during the kiss, he'd whispered that this was only a first taste of what was to come on the date.

He'd been there for her. Win or lose, he'd been there. And now he was promising to be there again, this time for just her.

Dusti no longer had to look at the check on the dresser; she already knew that today her life had changed. It would never be the same and it had nothing to do with a poker game and everything to do with Kieran O'Toole.

Chapter 43

RONNY WOKE ONE SORE MUSCLE AT A TIME. SUNLIGHT BLINKED in between the curtains across the front window. She thought it was a very good thing that Austin's house was in the middle of nowhere because anyone walking by could have glanced in the window and seen her in her birthday suit.

Laughing, she almost wished her mother would pick this morning to drop by. But that wasn't likely and she couldn't imagine Dallas Logan arriving anywhere quietly.

A bird flew close enough to land on the porch railing. He seemed to look in, hoping for a snack he could steal.

Ronny rolled to grab a blanket. When she did, her body tightened as if she'd just come from a workout.

She'd never dreamed making love would be so physical but every night seemed to be wilder and more wonderful. She'd better start carbing up before bedtime or working out, because loving Austin Hawk would give her a heart attack before she turned forty.

She shoved her hair out of her eyes and looked over at him. He slept on his stomach, the scars along his shoulders showing in the sunlight. She hated that he'd known such pain, but he was right, they were just part of him. He was built strong. No one would ever call him a ladies' man. They wouldn't see the beauty of him like she did. They'd never see how hard he tried to be gentle and loving or how totally he loved her. Austin Hawk was a man who ran full speed into what he believed in, no holding back.

He couldn't seem to understand that she loved him just the way he was, scars and all. His grumpy nature that she saw through. His sharp orders that he snapped when he thought he was just asking. His kindness. His caring.

Poking his arm, she waited.

He didn't move.

The worry that he might be dead wasn't there like it had been those earlier nights when she'd just slept beside him. Maybe because last night and the night before and the night before that he'd proved to her that he was very much alive. Even after they'd made love, he'd hold her so close, as if what they had was so good he feared it might vanish if he didn't hold tight.

She poked him again.

"I'm alive, Ronny," he mumbled. "Stop poking me. That one-second poke only works on roadkill germs."

"I know," she answered remembering how kids in school used to say that if you poked a dead animal longer than one second, dead germs would jump on you. "I just like poking you to make sure. The only time you're completely still is when you're asleep."

He rolled over and grabbed her, rolling her beneath his body. "You still love me this morning? You're not leaving or waking me up to say good-bye?"

"Yes, I still love you, and no, I'm not waking you up to say good-bye." He felt so warm above her. Her very own cuddle blanket made of rock. "But, you've got to go a little slower and easier on me. I'm sore all over this morning."

"Me? You're the one who wouldn't stop last night." He moved his fingers along her side, reminding her of how she'd begged for more and every time he'd been willing to grant her wish.

She smiled, remembering. "Well, that's true, but I've

been waiting a long time, and I think it may take years for me to get enough."

"Good, that settles it. I'm applying for that job in town." His words were muffled against her throat as he kissed his way down her body.

"What job?" She pulled his face up to hers and for a second they both smiled, knowing he'd finish what he'd started as soon as they talked.

"The firehouse has extra funds and is planning to hire a real fire chief. Hank says he's retiring as the volunteer chief, so the job's available as soon as I want to apply and can muster out of the army."

"But Hank loves that job. He's been the chief for as long as I can remember."

"Loved," Austin corrected. "He loved the job. But now he wants out. He told me that Alex is quitting being sheriff to run for county judge, and of course she'll get it since half the voting population of Harmony is either Matheson or McAllen. So, he claims someone will have to stay home with the kids and run the ranch."

"But . . ."

"Four months from now they'll have their first. A boy. Hank says they're naming him Warren after her brother who died." Austin smiled down at her with pride. "Don't tell me I knew something about the people of Harmony that you didn't know."

She shoved him. "Roll off me. I can't think naked. This is too much to think about."

When he let her go, she jumped out of bed and slipped into his shirt. Then she began to pace, feeling like something wasn't right. "I feel like Harmony is changing. Really changing. It doesn't seem natural. Everything is always the same in Harmony. We could put it on the welcome sign. Nothing much ever changes here."

He watched her, looking fascinated as always.

She didn't look at him. She had to piece everything together.

Finally, he said, "I have to go back to the fort for a few

months to muster out. You wouldn't want to come along with me as my wife, would you? We'd have a few dinners to go to, but mostly we could just relax, maybe see Washington, or take the train over to New York for a weekend. It would be a great honeymoon."

She looked up. "I came back to Harmony for some peace, to settle down, to feel at home. Becoming someone's wife wasn't in my plan. Never once in the past year have I thought about getting married, and never have you, I'm guessing."

"But you love me and you attack me on a regular basis. I think that means you should marry me. I'm not sure, though; we could always ask your mother."

She tossed a pillow at him.

As he ducked, he tumbled off the bed.

When he crawled back under the sheet, he said, "I'm calling your mother and talking this over with her. I bet she'll agree with me. You should marry me. You can't just keep on using me like I'm your own private sex toy."

Ronny jumped back in bed. "All right, I'll marry you, Captain, but you can never tell my mother about the attacks." She grinned. "It would give her a heart attack to know what her daughter plans to do every day before she eats breakfast."

"My lips are sealed. No one would believe me anyway. Shy, silent Ronny Logan. The whole town loves and watches over you. They'll never know what you did to me last night and hopefully every night for the rest of our lives." He raised an eyebrow as if her words were just catching up with his brain. "Or what you're planning to do before breakfast? Did you just say that you planned to attack me before breakfast?"

She was back to her shy self, as ladylike as ever. "I'm sorry. I should be careful about your leg, but I forgot about it last night. I wouldn't want to hurt you again this morning."

"I see what you mean. From what I remember about last night, it could have fallen off at some point and I wouldn't have noticed."

She laughed her light little laugh. "If you marry me, it might be like it was last night fairly often, though I'll try to take it easy on you some nights. Maybe only do it once, or twice." She slipped her hand beneath the sheet.

"I'm betting on it, pretty lady."

He pulled her to him and kissed the top of her head. "When we marry, you could use the cabin for your office, but you're staying here with me."

"In the third-floor bedroom." The idea of waking up to a view of the lake sounded like heaven.

"I don't care which bedroom. Just as long as we're in the same one." When she rested her head on his chest, he continued to plan. "I've got quite a bit of money saved up. We could have a grand honeymoon. Go around the world if you like."

"I've done that. I'd like to come back here for the last of our honeymoon." Her hand moved across the hair on his chest as if she were petting a bear. "We could spend our days making this house into a real home and our nights making love."

"Sounds good to me. I've traveled all I want to for a long while. I'd like to watch fall settle over the lake."

"Me too." Her hand moved lower.

He lost interest in the conversation, but she told him about the curtains they'd put over the windows and the new furniture they'd buy and how she wanted to remodel the kitchen.

Finally, she lost her train of thought as he began kissing his way down her body.

"Tell me about it later," he ordered. "I'm busy right now."

She didn't seem to mind the order at all. She knew he was concentrating on loving her.

A few hours later when they were dressed and eating breakfast in the kitchen, they decided to move their bed to another room.

The plan was simple. They'd move the bed to every room in the house and then make love. Once they'd finished, they'd decide which room would work best as their bedroom.

Only they didn't agree. So they had to start all over again with the test.

The next morning when Austin suggested they do the

same test with every piece of furniture they bought, Ronny threatened to move back to the cabin for some rest.

He gave in and they cuddled in for a nap, but even while she slept she knew he never stopped touching her.

If happiness could be measured in a bucket, hers was running over.

As Austin slept, she thought of her first love. If she hadn't loved Marty so much, she might not have been able to love Austin enough.

He hadn't known how to be romantic even in asking her to marry him, but she didn't care. They matched and that was all that mattered.

Chapter 44

DECEMBER
NEW YORK CITY

KIERAN AND DUSTI'S DATE FINALLY HAPPENED WHEN SNOW was falling in Central Park. He took her for a carriage ride around the park with cups of hot chocolate in their hands and a warm rug over their legs. Dusti was so excited to see him she barely saw all the beauty around her. They'd talked almost every day since Vegas and she'd continued to send him pictures of her world in Harmony. Her fears that they'd have nothing to say after he taught her to play were unfounded.

When the carriage finally stopped, they had dinner in a little side-street café where the waiter fussed over them as if they were family.

Kieran looked different in his winter suit and long coat. He looked like he belonged in New York. She thought of how he'd dressed in Vegas and realized he'd looked like he belonged there too. She realized that this man across the table from her was a man of the world and she was simply a girl from Harmony. They shouldn't have worked, but over the months of talking they'd become best friends.

He'd kissed her lightly at the airport, but the time apart had left him shy once more around her.

They talked of the poker game and his grandmother as they ate. They talked of Harmony and all the people he'd met.

"Everyone asks about you when they see me now. They think of you as my man."

"I *am* your man," he said between bites.

She nodded. "I thought you might have forgotten about the date. It's been almost five months and you rarely mentioned it when you called." Her bedroom wall was covered in the postcards he'd mailed from all over. She knew he'd been busy.

"I was waiting for the right time. August and September you were moving Abby into the dorm at Tech and getting used to handling all the work by yourself. It wouldn't have been fair to pull you away then."

"I hired some help with harvesting the pecans. We've had a good year." He was right about the time. With Abby gone she'd worked from dawn to dark most days, taking only a few hours off as the leaves turned so she could capture them with her old camera. She photographed the fall parade downtown and the fair with all its light and winter moving across the lake one morning at dawn. Through his camera she'd seen the beauty of her world.

"I thought you might need help when the pictures kept coming. Some nights I wondered if you slept at all. You were running the farm during the day and living in the darkroom at night.

She nodded. "I had to give up my wild life. Between talking to you and pictures, the only partying I had time for was visiting your grandmother once a week."

"Thanks for doing that. But you didn't have to."

"I wanted to. It made me feel closer to you." She wondered how this man had come to mean so much to her so quickly. He simply understood her.

He winked at her as if reading her thoughts, then changed the subject. "You like your new camera?"

She smiled. "I do, but I still get out the one that belonged to your father now and then and take a few pictures. It seems to capture some great shots."

He talked on about his dad and how he'd loved to take pictures, but Dusti was only half listening. The date was nice—perfect, in fact, as if it had been planned for months. But it wasn't what she'd dreamed it would be.

Kieran had kissed her at the airport, but it had been only a hello kiss, and during the ride around the park he'd kissed her again, but it had been only a light kiss that people do when celebrating. Not the buckle-her-knees kind of kiss she'd wanted. She'd flown all the way to New York, not for a date, but for one more kiss like he'd given her in Vegas.

She told herself she didn't expect him to toss her over his shoulder and run off to the first hotel room, but she'd been waiting for him long enough. She'd done everything short of tripping him and falling on top of him to let the man know she wanted him.

Nothing was working. The food was good. The atmosphere perfect. The night chilly but not too cold. Only Dusti was hot and getting no closer to being satisfied than she was three hours ago when he picked her up.

"I wanted you to see the windows decorated for Christmas. Want to take a walk after we eat?"

"Sure," she said, thinking a dark alley might be nice.

Only when they left the restaurant, he placed his long coat over her shoulders and started walking. And walking.

She was about ready to tell him to take her back to the hotel when they turned a corner and she saw the lights of a gallery.

"I want to stop in here for a moment," he said, pulling her through the door.

Two steps inside, Dusti froze. Suddenly, under bright lights, she was surrounded with Harmony. The barn, the dancers, the tables under the trees.

"I didn't know how to tell you over the phone. I showed your work to a friend of my father's who owns this place and he loved it. The next thing I knew, it was on his walls. He thinks you are a real find."

She walked slowly around, looking at the pictures she'd sent to him. The county fair. The town square. The trees outside her window.

Kieran smiled at her. "They'll go on sale tomorrow if you agree. Five hundred apiece for the little ones. A thousand for the big ones." When she looked at the one of him standing by the barn, he added, "That one is not for sale. That one is mine."

She finally turned to him. "You make me feel like a real photographer."

"You are, lass. As real as they come. The dealer said he'll handle as much of your work as you can send. He was thinking you might do a Winter in Harmony show next month. I showed him what I call Winter on the Lake yesterday and he said it took his breath away."

Suddenly she felt like Cinderella at the ball. She knew it would chime midnight soon, but she wanted to enjoy every second until then.

The gallery owner talked with her. People came in and acted excited to meet her. Kieran stood beside her telling everyone she was his girl. His hand never left the small of her back.

When they finally walked back to her hotel, she couldn't stop smiling. "You pulled it off, you know. You gave me the best date in the world."

"It's not over yet."

When he opened the door for her, he whispered, "But I want you to know this is not one date. The town thinks I'm your man, and that is what I'd like to be. We're only five hours apart. I'd like you to come to New York every time you have a few days off and I'll come to see you. We're not dating. We're together."

"Kieran, I don't belong in New York and you don't belong in Harmony."

He unlocked her hotel door. "I know, but I belong with you and you belong with me. We'll work out the details later. For me home isn't a place, but a person. You're that person, lass. As long as you agree, we can be together anywhere and I'm home."

She stepped into the room. "That sounds like a plan."

"It's all been a plan, lass, since the moment you asked me to teach you to play poker. I thought if I could just get close enough to you for a while, you might just fall for me."

She pulled him into the room. "You're right about the plan, Kieran, but it didn't start when I asked you to teach me. It started when I looked across the bar and saw you standing there watching me. And, it wasn't your plan to get close to me, but my plan to get close to you."

He pulled her against him and slowly removed his coat from her shoulders. "We'll argue about it in the morning."

"Sounds like a plan." She giggled as the very best part of their first date began.